LOVE IN PURGATORY

TIMBER PHILIPS

COPYRIGHT

~

ISBN: 978-1-950222-20-9

Edited by Barbara J. Bailey

Book design by Maggie Kern

Cover art by Dar Albert at Wicket Art Designs

DEDICATION

As always, to my wonderful and understanding fiancé, who has loads of patience when it comes to me writing these things. I love you, through good times and bad and everything in between, just like the title suggests.

To the real Vonfrost, I never forgot you, often think about you, and am still writing for and with you. I am so glad we could reconnect just as this story found its happy ending. We really must stop these long gaps in communication. Seven years is just too long.

CHAPTER ONE

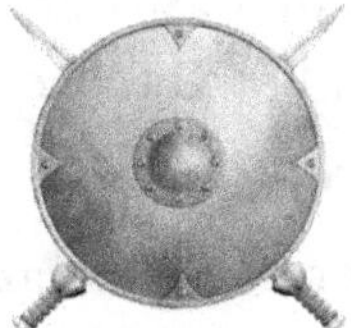

The ivy of despair had taken root in my chest months ago. There was nothing specific that had happened that brought on my depression; at least not that I can remember. I didn't lose my job, or a boyfriend; no one had died. Still, it had taken root, somewhere in the center of my chest, somehow, and as the days grew shorter and the rains had come, the vines had grown, constricting my heart and blocking out all light and cutting off anything that was good, warm, and comforting. Things I had once taken great pleasure in doing, the restoration work I did at the museum, painting, and going to the theater, all of it suddenly seemed dull, boring, and lifeless and I felt restless.

I just didn't know what to do with myself, but couldn't bring myself to do anything.

Some of my acquaintances had stopped calling altogether. I call them 'acquaintances' rather than 'friends' because true friends wouldn't give up on someone simply because they were feeling blue, even if that blue period lasted longer than a few days or weeks... would they? No. I don't think so. Roxanne, my oldest and longest friend, my best friend, hadn't given up on me. At least, not yet. She'd said to me: "Gracelyn, I'm here for you. No matter what, you just call me." I had smiled and we had hugged, but I didn't know how to quantify what it was that I was feeling at the time because secretly, terribly, I hadn't felt anything.

I was sad, all the time, but I didn't know why. I hurt for no reason, cried for no reason, and I was tired all the time, for no reason.

I had finally gone to my doctor who had diagnosed me with depression. She'd given me pills, which I dutifully took, but they didn't help. I felt lost and adrift and therapy wasn't an option; not only was it not covered by my medical plan, but you had to have a problem to work the problem out, didn't you?

I didn't. I had a wonderful job full of amazement and discovery that I was in no danger of losing. I had friends, I had a decent apartment, and lived well within my means. I had a good life.

So why did I constantly feel this way lately, and why was it getting worse?

The heels of my boots clicked sharply against the pavement as I made my way home. The January wind bit along the exposed skin of my face and I scrunched down further into the collar of my black winter peacoat. I lived in a nice, safe, secured building, with an elevator, which was a huge improvement from the walk-up I'd used to live in when I'd first taken a job in New York. At the moment, I couldn't wait to get back to it and out of this miserable cold. I admit my preoccupation while I walked, wasn't the brightest idea as a single woman on a New York City sidewalk, but I couldn't stop worrying at the problem in my brain.

Just what the heck was my problem?

I mean, I had no real problems until this strange depressive episode had started. I grew up in a loving home, raised by my grandparents after my parents had passed in a bad car accident, but that was something I had come to grips with a very long time ago, and so it wasn't a part of what was eating at me today. While I hadn't been one of the super-popular girls growing up, I hadn't been unpopular. While there were kids bullied throughout my school years, I hadn't been one of them. I'd had a small but good circle of friends, excelled academically, gone to college on a decent scholarship with the help of grants and student loans to get me the rest of the way, gotten my Master's degree in Science and Historic Preservation, was certified by The Academy of Certified Archivists, had already paid most of my student loans off by continuing to live rough my first few years out of college, and was now working on a dream project: preserving historical artifacts from an archeological dig. What was more exciting than preserving artifacts from a Viking raid in Scotland? For a history and science nerd like me, not a whole lot.

I turned mid-block and clacked up the few steps to the lobby of my building, letting myself in. It was a modest high-rise building in a relatively quiet neighborhood. Well, as quiet as any neighborhood in New York could be. It was relatively close to the museum I worked out of, being only two subway stops away, and I could walk if I wanted to. Most days I did; life as an academic isn't exactly the most active one, so I walked to and from work and ran two or three times a week to stay in shape.

Or – at least, I used to.

It was getting harder and harder to resist the call of the subway as all the joy in my life slowly leeched away, worse than the colors of a painting left too long in the sun. I just didn't have the heart to drag myself out of bed on time to make the walk anymore and I couldn't remember the last time I'd gone running.

I didn't even take the stairs anymore, but rather waited for the elevator. I stepped on-board with a heavy sigh, disappointment in myself weighed me down. I was a hot mess, and I needed to get it together, but, I just didn't want to. I didn't have the energy to, and it wasn't like I was seeing anyone and had a reason to other than for just me, which I know, should have been more than enough, but, *blah*.

I unlocked my apartment door and closed it heavily behind me, locking the deadbolt and leaning heavily against its worn surface. I dropped my purse and tote bag off to the side in the entryway and my keys into their dish on the little hall table near the door. I hung my coat and scarf on the back of the door itself, with its hook and, before

I did anything else, unzipped my stylish riding boots from knee to ankle and toed them off, wiggling my toes in the carpet through my socks.

Ah, much better.

"I'm home," I called to no one in particular. I lived alone, hence why it didn't really matter if I left all my stuff in front of the door, which I did. But points to me, at least it wasn't in a total heap this time.

I padded in my tights and sock-clad feet to the kitchen and opened the fridge, then closed it with a groan. *Who was I kidding? I wasn't hungry.* I used to enjoy cooking for myself, but not since the black ivy of my depression started choking the life out of me last year. I went into my bedroom and undressed, hanging my deep green blouse and black pencil skirt and matching jacket back in their places.

I peeled out of my socks, tights, and underwear after casually flipping my bra into the dirty-laundry basket. The tangle of undergarments followed the torture device of lace and underwire, the whole mess sulking on the top of the out-of-control laundry pile and I let them. I had hated doing laundry even before my depression; now it usually had to get to the point that I needed to root through the pile to find something clean enough to wear for me to get it done.

I padded across the hall into my bathroom. I turned the shower on and let it heat up, pulling some towels down out of the linen closet which doubled as a hall closet. I climbed in, letting the hot water beat my tense shoulders into some semblance of submission.

Today had been meeting after meeting with the walking wallets that were funding our project. I hated dealing with the suits with a passion, my time was better spent in the lab with the tools of my trade, brushing dirt away, recording details and small discoveries about whatever artifact happened to find its way to my worktable. Instead of following my passion, however, I'd been stuck kowtowing to project investors. It'd made my day especially frustrating because what currently occupied my worktable was the hilt and a good third or more of a genuine Viking blade, circa the ninth century. That's right, the ninth century! You know it gets exciting for a history nerd like me when you start dropping into the single digits before the word 'century'.

I plucked the hair band off the end of the long golden braid hanging over my right shoulder and worked the strands of my dishwater blonde hair out of their thick rope. The water against my scalp felt good, but maddeningly, I remained numb and indifferent.

It frustrated me that all I seemed to feel anymore was either nothing or negative emotions. There just wasn't any joy to be had anywhere anymore, not even a little bit. I missed it so much and I felt like I was beginning to forget what it even felt like to have something good, to smile genuinely and not feel like it was a caricature or a mask.

I scrubbed my hands over my face and stuck it in the shower spray, huffing out a sigh. It was late, I was tired, and all I wanted was my bed. So, I decided to make some seriously quick work of this shower and get to it, wanting nothing more than the sweet oblivion that only sleep brought anymore. Lathering my hair was a chore and rinsing it quickly was a joke, I had so much of it and it was so long, though there was no way a haircut would make me feel better. I skipped the conditioner and used my honey-and-milk bodywash quickly in a fast head-to-toe lather with my bath pouf. I rinsed fast, almost as fast as I had washed, and shut off the water.

Reaching for a towel, I could feel the storm of a meltdown brewing. I could feel it in my chest, and behind my eyes, a pressure that was becoming too familiar and really, really old. I didn't want to cry. I hated crying. I didn't want to be alone, either, but I certainly didn't want to drag anybody into this. I couldn't help how I felt, but I wouldn't subject anyone else to it. That wouldn't be fair to them. I'd found myself growing increasingly lonely as a result and that keen sense of loneliness only egged this meltdown on harder.

The tide of emotion was rising and I was about to be swamped no matter how hard I tried to fight it down. This was becoming a losing battle the more times it happened. I bowed forward and wrapped the regular-sized bath towel around my hair, twisting it to wring it out, straightening up and flopping it back so it would stay in place, turban-style, on my head. I used the bath sheet to dry my body, starting with my face before finally wrapping it around myself twice below my arm pits and tucking the corner tight so it wouldn't slide off. I may not be running or exercising like I used to anymore, but I was still losing weight. My clothes were loosening, some even needed a tailor to take them in; another chore I had been neglecting.

God, what was wrong with me?

I wiped a streak in the steam coating my bathroom mirror with my hand and looked at myself. Cornflower-blue eyes stared back at me, high cheekbones and a narrow chin bracketed a full mouth. I was pretty by the generally-accepted standard, but I had never relied on it. I valued brains over looks and didn't have time for people that wanted to base their opinion of me on my packaging rather than what I had to offer in the intellectual department. Sometimes it felt like my standards may have been too lofty with those expectations, but I still clung to my self-respect where any potential relationship was concerned. I had no desire to date any more losers, even though I hadn't dated in over a year at this point.

Because you're too much of a wreck.

I used my Tuscan honey lotion on my hands, arms, and legs to ward off the physical discomfort of dry winter skin. Wringing my hair tightly one last time with the towel before letting it down, I contemplated just skipping blow-drying it. But it was a tangled mess of snakes and there was no way I could sleep on it this wet. If I did, it would be a total disaster to work with in the morning, so, reluctantly, I brought out my hair dryer along with my brush.

I shouldn't have skipped the conditioner. The brush snarled painfully in my locks and the sharp pain in my scalp brought the sting of tears to my eyes. That did it. The floodgates opened, the tide rose into a tsunami and crashed into my careful walls destroying them with so much force I didn't think I could ever rebuild them. Tears poured out my eyes as I stood there staring at my reflection in wide-eyed shock.

Goddammit, I couldn't do anything right!

I cried my tears and did my best to brush and dry my hair despite them, working through the snarls and the pain on autopilot. Once it was dry, I pulled it over my shoulder and braided it quickly to keep it from being another tangled disaster in the morning.

I tossed the towels onto the overflowing dirty-laundry basket once I was back in my room and slipped a satin-and-lace nightgown over my skin. All of my sleepwear was sexy like that; an indulgence. My underwear was pretty much the same. It was something Roxy had talked me into trying, an attempt to drag me out from beneath my black clouds. At first it had been a marginal success, but the clouds had just rolled right back in again.

What was wrong with me? I asked myself the same question, ad nauseam, day in and day out.

I crawled into bed beneath my thick down comforter and lay in the fluffy marshmallow softness of my bed. The tears, which I thought I'd beaten back, welled hot and immediate again, spilling over, and down my nose onto the pillow.

I just wanted this to end, so badly. I wanted the hurt to stop, I wanted to sleep forever. Nothing helped, not my friend, not my work, not the pills from the damn doctor, nothing. I felt like I was going mad and the fight, well, the fight to just get out of bed in the morning was becoming an all-out war versus a skirmish anymore. I just didn't know how to cope with these feelings, and I didn't know how much longer I could live like this. So I sobbed into my pillow and hugged another to me, helplessly caught up in the storm of my emotions.

I don't know how long I lay that way, weeping brokenly, alone in my apartment, but eventually, I fell asleep.

CHAPTER TWO

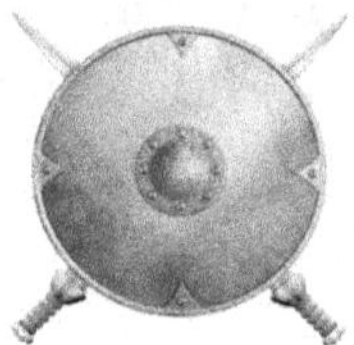

"Gracelyn, do you have a moment?" Jared's lyrical voice emanated from directly from behind me, causing me to nearly come out of my skin. I had been entirely focused on the sword on my bench and hadn't heard him come up behind me. I pressed a gloved hand to the chest of my lab coat and urged my thundering heart to be quiet.

"Jared, you scared the life out of me!" I exclaimed breathlessly.

"Obviously! It was not at all my intent, however. Are you all right?"

"Yes, yes, I'm fine."

"Again, my deepest apologies, I hadn't realized how engrossed you were." He took off his glasses and polished a lens with his handkerchief, a habit that had always endeared him to me; the fact that, as young as he was, he used a handkerchief at all. It seemed quite the old-fashioned thing.

Jared was in his early- to mid-thirties and was typically clad in an Oxford shirt and chinos with a pair of loafers on his feet. Today, it was a light blue Oxford and khaki-colored chinos. On most people, it would look like they were trying too hard or like they were some kind of rich arrogant ass... Not Jared, though. Oh, yeah, he *was* rich, and could be arrogant if the occasion called for it, but he was also a passionate academic and a very sweet soul. He was also my boss.

I smiled at him tiredly and put my hands on my knees, the brush I'd been using hanging limp in my cotton-clad fingers.

"What can I do for you, Jared?" I asked, and smiled tiredly.

He put his tortoiseshell glasses back on and frowned at me, pushing his-ever present flop of dark blonde bangs off his forehead. His hair was short, a crew cut, I think they called it, except long enough on top that it swept down across his forehead in front. When he went too long without a trim it would brush the top of his glasses, and he would be forever sweeping it off his face, until he finally got annoyed enough with it to actually do something about it.

Story of your life, with just about everything anymore, I thought derisively.

It was true, even if it stunk. I didn't generally do anything about anything unless it was to the point it was annoying me, but then again, by the time it reached that point, it was usually enough of a problem to be overwhelming when I finally did go to deal with it. I sighed inwardly and tuned in to what my boss was saying.

"Gracelyn, are you getting enough rest?" he asked, concerned. He reached out, trailing an index finger in a light touch against my cheek, just under my eye. Both my eyes were ringed in dark circles that were bordering on a deep purple, reminiscent of a bruise.

I winced and gently pulled back away from the touch. Jared was sometimes too familiar with me. For the most part, I chalked it up to the social awkwardness that many academic personalities harbored, but sometimes, I'd catch him looking at me, and well, it wasn't how a boss should look at an employee, but at the same time, it wasn't exceptionally creepy, either.

"Sorry," he mumbled, and had the grace to look embarrassed. There was a momentary awkward silence between us.

"Sorry, you needed something?" I closed my eyes and shook my head, a frown of my own furrowing my brow. My concentration was horrible today.

"Yes. I was wondering if you would accompany me tonight to the investor's dinner. Several of them were quite taken with you, yesterday." He was watching me, a wrinkle of concern between his eyes.

I let out a breath I hadn't realized I'd been holding and slumped a little on my stool.

"I…" I opened my mouth, closed it, and then opened it again. I didn't want to go, I was tired. Exhausted, in fact. It felt like I hadn't slept a wink last night and that I'd woken up just as tired as when I'd gone to bed. That being said, the investors were looking at financing an exhibit of our historical find. It could be the first step up when it came to generating enough interest and funding to really get our preservation efforts going, both at the Fernyness Wood site and beyond it, and opening up a permanent exhibit here at the world history museum and allowing the research to go on for years.

There were things at the Fernyness Wood site that were challenging *everything* we knew about the Vikings thus far, not only their travel patterns, (where they'd traveled to and where they'd come from before landing on Scotland's shores,) but their weaponry and how they'd lived. There were indications that the swords they'd carried were of a makeup that originally hadn't been thought to have been invented until well after the time we were dating them to. All in all, when it came to what we'd found in Scotland, we'd barely scratched the surface, but finding out more wholly depended on the almighty dollar, so continued funding was a top priority.

Damnit, I need to do this.

Jared blessedly saved me from my predicament of the here and now by saying, "No, forget I even asked. There will be other dinners and events." He plucked the brush I'd been using to separate dirt and debris from the sword on my bench out of my loose hold and set it down with its mates. He took my gloved hands in his lightly and shook them back and forth. I felt my shoulders ease down from where I'd had them shrugged and tensed. I hadn't even realized I was maintaining such a defensive posture.

"Go home, Gracelyn, you're done for the day. Get something to eat, sleep; this will all be here tomorrow." He tugged on my hands and with a groan I slipped off my stool and onto my feet.

"I'm sorry Jared. I slept last night, I guess I just didn't sleep very well." His hands were warm through the cotton of my gloves and I quickly took mine back, making a production of pulling the white cotton off my hands, stripping off the latex gloves beneath them, and pitching them into my waste basket. My hands were cold despite the latex but still clammy with sweat. I wiped them on my lab coat. Jared took a reluctant step back out of my personal space, though I didn't think he was being inappropriate with his proximity, I think he was genuinely worried about my wellbeing.

My thoughts were confirmed when he said,

"Well, you should sleep well tonight. You look as if you're ready to collapse. I'll see you tomorrow, hopefully much more refreshed."

He gave me one last once-over, his expression gravely concerned, and turned on the heel of his brown loafer and walked away crisply. I sighed, it wasn't that Jared wasn't attractive, he was. It was just, I wasn't attracted to him. Okay, maybe I was, a teensy, tiny little part of me wondering what he might have been like in bed. But still, he was my boss, and those thoughts were very fleeting.

I really wanted no part of a scandalous workplace affair. I'd worked too hard to get this far on merit and I wasn't about to put my reputation in any sort of jeopardy, allowing anyone to think to the contrary. My thoughts and speculation on the matter would remain just that. Thoughts and speculation.

Jesus. I was tired. I had to be, to be even remotely thinking about what it would be like to be with Jared. I quashed those thoughts, immediately dismissing them. I needed to go home and sleep; get a grip, because having any thoughts at all about having any sort of affair with my boss was far more self-destructive than I wanted to be. I really had worked too hard for this; I looked around and thought, *for all of this.*

I peeled out of my lab coat and hung it on the old-fashioned wooden coat tree beside my station. Stepping well back from my ninth-century baby, I plucked down my winter peacoat and shrugged into it. I lifted down my grey infinity scarf and wound it around my throat, before buttoning my coat. I sighed and pulled on my black leather gloves to warm my chilly hands and tried to ignore the tickle against the side of my neck from some strands of hair that had come loose from my braid.

Finally, I lifted down my purse and hung it across my chest, making for the exit to the lab, the heels of my low pumps clacking smartly against the linoleum. I left the well-lit laboratory for the dimly-lit hallway, the tone of my footsteps deepening, echoing off the much-higher ceilings as I made the transition from linoleum to the marble flooring of the hall. I took the stairs carefully in my tired state and used the museum's employee exit to step out into the freezing side alley. I thrust my hands in my pockets and burrowed my nose into my scarf, breathing out into the material to warm the lower half of my face.

I caught a flicker of shadow out of the corner of my eye and startled, thrusting my back against the door I'd just come out of, but when I looked there was nothing... I would have sworn whatever I had seen had been big, man-sized at the very least. I'd thought I was going to be attacked – mugged, purse-snatched, or worse. I swallowed my rapidly-beating heart back down into my chest and moved quickly out of the darker alley and onto the bustling street. I gave one last lingering look down that corridor between buildings, but seeing nothing, moved in the direction that would take me home.

I would swear on a stack of bibles that the shadow had come from the direction of the mouth of the alley and moved further back into it, which didn't make sense; the alley had no outlet so if someone had moved past me as I exited the door, I would have seen them on looking back... *Wouldn't I?*

I strode with purpose down the sidewalk and shivered a shiver which had absolutely nothing to do with the bitter January wind at my back. I couldn't shake the itching feeling between my shoulder blades, that sensation we have all had at one time or another of being watched.

I turned at the last second and slipped down the stairs to the subway.

Depression, meet Paranoia! Paranoia, this is Depression. You two should get along fine, I thought to myself as I clattered down the steps and lost myself in the crowd of commuters.

Still that creeping feeling couldn't be shook. I got onto the train, the doors hissing shut behind me, and grabbed onto the overhead rail. The car wasn't overly crowded, but I always felt better standing on the train than sitting. I don't know why, it just was what it was.

I held on against the rock and sway of the subway car as it sped along the tracks and got off at the second stop. With a great sigh, I moved toward the stairs and the surface. I was feeling pretty silly at this point about jumping at shadows, yet I still couldn't shake the unnerved feeling it had brought on. After my parents had died, I'd had anxiety attacks for a time. This felt much the same, though on a vastly smaller scale.

My parents. I hadn't thought of them in a while and that fact had me suddenly feeling a bit guilty. I was thirteen when it'd happened. We had been to visit my grandparents, my mother's parents, and were on our way home. It was dark and raining, well, storming... wind and rain that came down in sheets. No thunder, no lightning, just the awful howling wind, that, when it would gust, would force the car sideways along the narrow highway. My father hit a patch of standing water and we had hydroplaned. It was awful, the car spinning and spinning before crashing nose-first into the Jersey barrier. The car had flipped, coming to rest on its roof. My dad had been killed on impact; my mother, for whatever reason, hadn't been wearing her seatbelt. She'd been thrown from the car.

I had been knocked unconscious, my leg had been broken and I'd had a deep cut up under my hair on the side of my head that had required stitches. I'd had a pretty bad concussion, but I had miraculously survived the wreck intact, otherwise. To see the car, we still weren't quite sure how.

It had taken years of therapy to come to grips with my survivor's guilt, and I still had a small bout with it on occasion, but it had been a long while. Like I said, it was something I had come to terms with years ago. Still, the familiar rasp of guilt started along the underside of my breastbone as I pulled open the door to my building. I hadn't thought of them in a while, and for some reason, that bothered me. Making sure no one tailgated in behind me and that the building's lobby door was secure behind me, I moved to the elevator and pressed the button to call it. My phone began buzzing in my purse and I gave an exasperated sigh as I finally dug it out. I answered it without looking, expecting it to be Jared needing something he'd forgotten to ask me before I left, or telling me I was on the hook for dinner after all.

"Hello?"

"Gracie-lyn!" I smiled. Nope, not Jared at all.

"Hey, Roxy, what's up?" I asked.

"You okay, girlfriend? You sound fried."

"I feel fried, I didn't sleep well." The elevator doors opened and I ignored them. If I boarded now I would lose the call.

"Oh, well damn, I was going to see if you would come and see me read tonight, but just listening to you makes me want to crawl into bed and never come out again. Next one?" she asked and I felt guilty again for an entirely different reason. It had been a long while since I had gone to see Roxy read any of her stuff. She was a good writer, poetry mostly. I was torn, but my exhaustion finally won out.

"I swear to you, on a stack of bibles, I will be there for the next one. I had to skip a dinner with investors, I'm so tired. I just can't do it." My shoulders slumped.

"Next time, Gracie. Get some sleep." Concern colored her tone a darker shade of gray through the line and I felt a pang of disappointment, mostly in myself. I was letting Jared down and I was letting Roxy down, again. I silently sighed.

"I promise, Rox, I'm really, really sorry," I moaned into the phone.

"Hey, don't sweat it. I still love you. Next week." Her voice was cheerful but tremulous with some other undefined emotion. It sure as shit wasn't excitement and pretty much just affirmed that I was indeed letting her down.

Damn it.

"Next week," I affirmed meekly. We said our goodbyes and I punched the button to the elevator harder than I needed to. The doors slid open and I boarded, hitting my floor with less force.

Goddammit, I was worthless today! Of course, it was becoming a regular thing as of late.

Who am I kidding? I've been a waste of space from the day I was born.

Whoa...

Where in the hell had that thought come from? I swallowed hard and exited the elevator. I pulled my keys from my purse where I'd stashed them while excavating for my phone and unlocked my apartment door, shutting it firmly behind me.

Sanctuary! The word popped into my head the way Quasimodo had cried it out in the Disney movie and I laughed to myself. I threw the deadbolts into the locked position and slid the chain home. You could never be too secure, right?

I kicked off my modern-day torture devices and stooped, setting them on the shoe rack by the door. Granted, they were pumps, and the heels on them were relatively short, but after being in them all day they still hurt. I pressed a thumb into the arch of my stocking-covered foot and groaned in pleasure. I gave the other similar treatment, hopping up and down on one foot in my tiny foyer.

"Okay, enough of that," I said aloud, to no one in particular. I went through the usual motions, keys in bowl on entryway table, coat and purse on back of door, phone on charger in kitchen and set to ring rather than silent. I stood in my kitchen and came to the unequivocal conclusion that damn... my life was boring.

I fixed some curry chicken salad out of some leftover baked chicken breast in the fridge. Mayo, curry powder, chicken; mix; throw in some golden raisins, some slivered almonds and plop the mixture onto a bed of Romaine. *Voila!* A dinner I didn't have to think about for longer than two minutes in my tired state.

I flopped onto my gray microfiber couch and ate mechanically with my feet up on the large square leather ottoman that doubled as a coffee table and extra linen storage... *Wait, wouldn't that mean it tripled? Ottoman, coffee table, linen storage...* I ticked the uses off on my fingers. *Well, whatever!* I was being neurotic on top of not firing on all cylinders. I shoved the last bite of my salad in my mouth and got up, rinsing the bowl and fork in the sink. I placed them in the dishwasher and kicked it shut, heading straight for the bedroom.

I shrugged into a peach-colored satin nightgown that brushed the tops of my feet, ivory lace running along the hem and up the side in a Victorianesque pattern. Seed beads glimmered in crystal accents here and there, and the sweetheart neckline was similarly decorated with lace along the edge. There was a lace appliqué with more clear seed beads sewn in clusters here and there at the top of the slit high on one thigh.

It was one of the nicest things I owned and the nightgown made me feel pretty, sexy even, and I liked the feel of it against my skin. Sometimes I needed a boost of confidence, no matter what form or direction it came in. Roxy had been absolutely right about that.

I plucked a tube of my Tuscan honey lotion off of my dressing table and pulled back my blankets. Crawling into bed, I used a liberal amount of lotion on my winter-dry skin; legs, hands, and arms. I set the tube down on my bedside table and clicked off the lamp, settling back into the cloud that my bed resembled. I must have been out the moment my head touched the pillow, because I don't remember struggling to fall asleep at all.

CHAPTER THREE

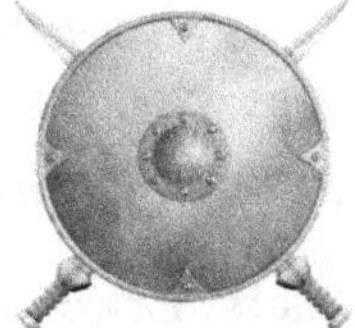

*I*t was cold, goosebumps raising on my flesh. A siren wailed and the traffic noises were far louder than they should have been inside my apartment walls. I opened my eyes and stumbled, pinwheeling my arms in the frozen air to keep myself from pitching forward... *and off the edge of my building's roof.* I threw myself backwards and landed badly on the gritty rooftop; my elbow banged painfully against the rough material and I knew I had lost some skin.

Fear fizzed through my veins like sour champagne and tears started in my eyes.

What was I doing up here? What's more, how did I even get up here?

I looked around in confusion and picked myself up off the ground, hugging myself, my teeth chattering. The access door to the roof was ajar and I bolted for it, slamming it closed behind me. I leaned heavily against it and sobbed. A terrified and confused scream clawed its way up my throat, but I clenched my lips between my teeth and wouldn't let it free.

I dragged in deep lungfuls of air and slid down the icy metal door, crouching on the cement floor of my building's stairwell. I don't know how long I spent like that, but when the panic had subsided and I heard no thunder of feet on the stairs to come fetch the crazy woman on the roof, I stood slowly. I was still shivering, though from adrenaline, shock, or cold I couldn't tell you. Maybe a combination of the three?

I bit down on a bitter sob and put one foot in front of the other, descending the stairs quickly. My bare feet stung with cold, my hands were pins and needles where they gripped each opposite arm across my chest. I folded in on myself when I reached the door to my floor. I opened it, a marginal crack, and peeked out. I let out a sigh of relief upon viewing the empty hall and bolted for my apartment door.

It was open, a dark crack an inch or two wide. I pushed against it and the chain caught, barring my entry. I stared at the chain in bewilderment. I didn't understand – I couldn't comprehend...

If I was out here and the door was chained from the inside...

I stumbled back, the doorknob leaving my hand. The door creaked on its hinges as it swung towards me, the gap narrowing. I put my face in my hands and scrubbed away the salt from my tears. I didn't see it, but I heard it, the sharp click and rattle of the chain as it was let loose. I brought down my hands and looked up and down the deserted hallway.

Should I call the police?

I snorted at myself in derision.

And tell them what? I came to, moments before taking a swan dive off my roof? Oh and I think someone is in my apartment?

The chime on the elevator pinged, and it was loud in the deserted, silent hallway. It galvanized me into action. I thrust open the door to my apartment and dashed inside, shutting the door tight behind me. I peered into the gloom, my eyes frantically scanning the dark interior of my small home for the unknown presence.

"Hello?" I whisper-shouted into the dark. I stood stock-still against my front door and listened, ears straining into the dark as much as my eyes had been a moment ago. Nothing moved. No one answered me back. I lunged into my bathroom and switched on the light, the soft luminescence washing out into the entryway, reaching across the little hall into my bedroom. I hit the switch inside my bedroom and the added light stretched to my little kitchen.

I still couldn't see the corners of my living room. I darted into the kitchen and hit the light. Empty, the rest of my apartment was empty. I pulled my loose hair away from my face and behind my ears and tugged down on it until it almost hurt.

I was awake.

I let out an explosive breath and sat down on the floor right there where my living room started. I looked at the clock on the cable box. 3:12 am. I squeezed my eyes shut and rocked in place, trying to process, and it wasn't going well.

The only conclusion I kept coming around to was that I was seriously losing my shit. As in, gone off the deep end, one flew over the cuckoo's nest, men wearing white coats were coming to take me away, ha ha!

I've certifiably lost my mind!

I sucked in a breath and held it as long as I could, then did it again, fighting the tears that were forcing their way up from deep inside me. Finally, I got up and went into my bathroom. I looked like hell. My eyes were bloodshot and red-rimmed from crying; my hair a crazy, tangled mess; there was blood dripping down my arm from my elbow; a few smears along the satin of my nightgown. I looked down. My feet were dirty and I was cold. I started the shower and stripped off the nightgown, relegating it to my little bathroom trashcan. The blood would never come out. Neither would the memories.

I got into the shower and hissed as the water stung my scrapes. I used the comb I kept in the caddy to work through all my tangles and grimly stayed under the hot spray until it went lukewarm and my fingers were raisins.

I got out and pulled the decorative towels off the towel bar, not even caring. I looked at the raw red skin of my elbow, still oozing blood, and winced, then dug the antiseptic and a large Band-Aid out of my medicine cabinet and set to work doctoring it up. I dried and braided my hair and decided I needed to do something normal, that going back to bed wasn't going to be an option. I got dressed in form-fitting jeans and a thick salmon-colored cable knit sweater that hit me at mid-thigh. I pulled on brown flat-heeled riding boots from the rack in the entry way and retrieved my keys, phone, purse, and coat. Leaving all the lights blazing in my apartment, I locked up behind myself and went to work.

Something steady, something normal. Work was just the thing.

CHAPTER FOUR

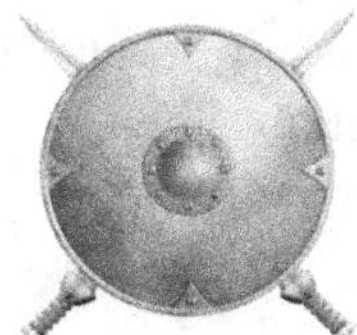

I stared down at the remains of the Viking sword on my workbench but didn't really see it. I didn't really see anything to be honest; I was staring off into space, which is why, when Jared touched my elbow, I let out a deafening shriek and damn near fell off my stool.

"Are you all right?" he exclaimed, his eyes wide, a bewildered expression on his face.

"Yeah." I tried to catch my breath and corral my racing heart. "Just a lot on my mind."

"Did you not get any sleep again?" he asked and stepped into my personal space, searching me over, cataloging my state as I did the artifacts on my bench.

"Yeah, no... I don't know." I shook my head as if to clear it.

"Gracelyn, what's the matter?" he asked gently and placed a hand on my shoulder. I looked up at him.

"I think I was sleepwalking," I answered solemnly.

Jared's brows drew together.

"Sleepwalking?" he echoed.

"Yeah. I went to bed like normal, and when I woke up, I was on my building's roof, just standing there," I admitted, totally omitting the fact that I was 'toes over the edge, poised to jump' when I snapped out of things. I rubbed my arms up and down as if I was cold, but you can't warm that kind of chill with a rub of your hands.

Jared sighed and took his hand back, but not before tucking a stray strand of my hair behind my ear in what should have an uncomfortably overly-familiar gesture. Right now, Jared was trying to be my friend more than my boss, and for once I could appreciate it. I scrubbed over my face with a hand.

"What did you do?" he asked.

"I was freezing, so I went back inside." I winced. "Tripped on the roof and scraped my elbow pretty good, but other than that, and being really cold, I was fine. Nothing a hot shower couldn't cure." I was *so* not telling him about my temporary entrapment out in the hall. Or that the chain barring my reentry into my apartment had suddenly come loose of its own accord. This story was crazy enough.

"What's wrong, Gracelyn?" he asked gently, and I realized I was frowning.

"I've never sleepwalked in my life," I admitted.

"Well, the project has been running out of money and it's been very stressful for all of us. They say sleepwalking can be brought on by stress..." He was looking me over again.

"That's probably it," I conceded a little too quickly, before changing the subject. "Speaking of money... How did the investors' dinner go?" I asked and Jared positively beamed at me.

"Very well!" he gushed. "I wish you could have been there, perhaps it would have alleviated some of your worries. I'm happy to say that the investments we received will fund an exhibit showcasing our finds for at least a year."

I stared at him and waited for the good news, but it appeared that what he'd said was it.

"What about further research and preservation efforts?" I asked, and he looked taken aback.

"We're still working on that," he hedged, and I sighed.

"So have we tapped out on the investment front? Is it time to start straight begging for donations?" I asked.

"Not quite yet, but don't you worry. This is just a first step." He smiled but it wasn't quite as bright.

I silently kicked myself for ruining his happy with the ugly reality that if we couldn't secure more funds for research and even more for preservation efforts, that we were pretty much sunk. Well, sunk when it came to both unearthing more of the story, not only of this particular raid, but also about the Vikings themselves and the people they were raiding from. We would also be done when it came to maintaining the artifacts we'd already recovered for countless future generations to learn from. He knew that as well as I did, probably even better, as he was the one to deal with the numbers on a daily basis, numbers which included my salary.

"I'm sorry, Jared," I muttered.

"For what? Caring what happens to the history? The people you work with?" He smiled.

"No, not that. Still, it doesn't mean I have to piss on your parade," I said and watched his eyebrows shoot up into his hairline. I immediately recognized my mistake.

"I'm sorry, Jared. That was crass." I closed my eyes and tried not to sway in my seat.

"Not at all, you're tired. Perhaps you should take the rest of the day?" he suggested.

"No, no. I'll just get some coffee. I'll be fine, and I *want* to work." I put on a smile that I hoped would convey everything that I wasn't feeling. He looked suspicious, but grudgingly nodded. We went over a few lab results and parted ways, him to his office and me down to the coffee stand in the museum's café. I needed a caffeine fix something fierce if I was going to make it through the rest of this day.

CHAPTER FIVE

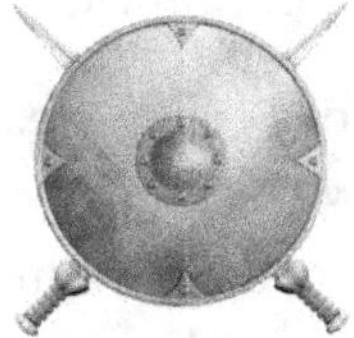

$\mathcal{I}$ leaned back from my careful inspection of the Viking sword's hilt and gave a low whistle.

"What is it?" Jared was coming out of his office, flipping through pages on a clipboard.

"I'm not sure yet," I hedged, leaning in for a closer look. "I *think* I might be looking at runes..."

Jared leaned in over my shoulder for a closer inspection, his breath was warm on my neck and I tried not to shift in my seat. We stared at the place on the hilt where I had been cleaning. The leather wrapping was long gone and the bare metal of the pommel, which had been protected for so long, was markedly less corroded than the blade. I squinted at the incised lines.

"I think you may be right." Jared turned to look at me, our noses were almost touching and he was grinning like a fool. He stood up abruptly.

"I think you may be right!" he exclaimed.

"What could it be?" I wondered aloud, staring in wonder at the blade.

"Do your best to photograph, document and transcribe after you get it cleaned up. I know a Norse language expert who specializes in the ancient runic alphabet. As soon as you have it uncovered we can send it to them." He was smiling and I found it terribly infectious, grinning back at him like a loon.

"Will do, boss," I murmured, stifling a yawn. Jared gave me a look over the rim of his glasses.

"Off with you! Have a good weekend. The sword will be here on Monday." He made a shooing motion with his hand.

I rolled my eyes and nodded, getting wearily to my feet. I shrugged into my peacoat and took my phone out of my purse. It was after six. The sky outside was dark already. I wound my scarf around my neck and pulled on my gloves, after settling my headphones into my ears. I pressed the little button in the center of the wire and held it; a soft chime sounded in my ears and I spoke aloud.

"Call Roxanne."

My phone chirped its assent and the line began to ring as I pushed out the side door and into the alley. Thankfully, there were no creepy shadows this time. The call went to voicemail and I left her a short message that I was stopping at McNaughton's for a drink on my way home and to call me.

I let music flood my ears as I finished my walk to the little bar and eatery near my apartment. It was crowded, but Tony, the bartender, waved me over to a vacant stool at the end of the bar.

"Food, booze, or both, sunshine?" he asked.

"Both!" I called back over the din.

"Usual?" he asked.

"Yeah!" I shouted back and he set to work, drawing me a Strongbow and punching my order for fish and chips into the system. He gave me his winning grin, plunked the cider in front of me and wandered off to do what he did best, serve drinks and flirt his tips into the stratosphere with the ladies.

Too bad for them he was a happily-engaged man to his one and only love, Simon.

My phone chimed in my ears that it had received a text but before I could check, arms went around me and Roxy was hoisting her large frame onto the stool beside me. Her hair was dyed black with red, as in fire-engine-red highlights, and framed her face in a short 'do, a fringe of perfectly-cut straight bangs across her forehead above her brown eyes. She smiled up at me through her rectangular, black-framed glasses and heaved out a sigh. She wore a hooded sweatshirt over the black blouse and ankle-length black flowing skirt that was her trademark weekly attire.

"Tough day at the office?" I asked over the crowd, shoving my headphones away in my purse to join my phone. She made a face.

"Got your message!" she deflected, and I laughed.

"Sorry about last night," I started, but she waved me off.

"Next Thursday." She leveled her gaze on me, and I held up my fingers in the Boy Scout salute.

"Next Thursday!" I affirmed.

"Did you get any sleep?" she asked, frowning, looking me over. Tony set down her usual drink in front of her and she shot him a grateful look, blowing him a kiss. He laughed and moved down to the other end of the bar.

"Yes and no." I told her about my little sleepwalking episode. The abridged version, of course.

"Oh, my God!" she exclaimed. "What do you think that was about?

"I have no idea. Jared thinks it's stress."

At his name she scowled.

"That's the creeper, right?" she asked.

I rolled my eyes.

"He's not a creeper! He's interested, I'm not, and he hasn't done anything to make me overtly uncomfortable yet."

It was her turn to roll her eyes.

"Do you hear yourself?" she asked.

"What?" I exclaimed.

"*Yet*, he hasn't done anything to make you *overtly* uncomfortable *yet*! I'm telling you, if he makes you any kind of uncomfortable and you really think there needs to be a 'yet' then you aren't paying attention! You need to say something to whoever is above his head before something happens and it's too late." She took a drink of her girly concoction and raised her eyebrows at me above the rim of her glass. I took a large swallow of my cider.

"I don't have anything I can really go to anyone about, Roxy. Maybe he's just a friendly guy? He's an academic, and we're notorious for our shit interpersonal skills; social awkwardness is par for the course!"

She raised one eyebrow, made a face, and then changed the subject.

"So, what are you doing tonight?" she asked.

"Dinner with you then I'm taking myself home, to sleep. I feel exhausted." I took another swallow of cider as Tony set my fish and chips in front of me.

"Your dark circles have dark circles," Roxy remarked. "Might not be a bad idea for you to sleep in tomorrow." She gave me a pointed look.

"I think I'm going to, but I hate skipping my run." I mock-pouted. "I've been skipping way too many lately."

"Skip it, girlfriend. If I could give you some of this, I would; you look like you could use it." She patted her ample middle and I shook my head at her, but couldn't stop myself from smiling. Self-deprecating though it might be, Roxy knew how to deliver her humor.

"I'm not that skinny," I protested, and it was true, you couldn't count my ribs or see the knobs of my spine or anything like that.

"You're not on the holocaust diet like some of these other bitches but you could still use some extra padding. It's cold here in the winter!" I gave a laugh at her audacity and ate my dinner, listening dutifully as she gave me a play-by-play of the poetry slam the night before. It sounded like it had been pretty good. I was sorry I'd missed it. Especially sorry because of my detour to crazyville.

Finally, exhausted and satiated from food, drink, and company, I paid my tab and bid my friend farewell and went off in search of my bed. I could barely keep my eyes open by the time I shambled onto the elevator and truthfully, I just dropped all my crap inside my door, stripped out of my boots, and let myself fall into my bed fully-clothed.

CHAPTER SIX

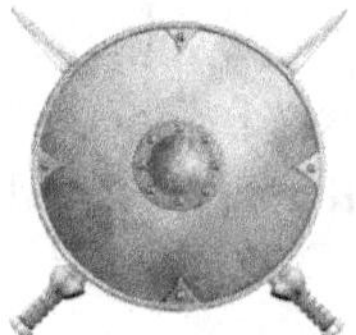

"I was in the kitchen, the knife slipped," I repeated, for probably like the thousandth time since coming to the Emergency Room.

The doctor suturing my wrist looked up at me as if she didn't believe me, but my story had not changed since I'd arrived. They kept asking me if I had any suicidal thoughts, and though I was distressed, I remained firm that no, no one had done this to me and that no, I hadn't done it to myself intentionally either. I told them I was in the kitchen cutting an avocado when the knife had slipped... but it wasn't true.

The last thing I remembered was falling into bed still fully-dressed from the day before. The next I knew, I was standing at my kitchen sink, bloody knife in the bottom, watching blood drip onto the stainless steel. I had been horrified, wrapped the injured wrist in a dish towel, and rushed downstairs, where I had hailed a cab.

The cut had been deep enough to require stitches and had bled a lot, but I hadn't damaged anything important; the tendons and nerves were safe, as were all the major veins and arteries. I stared at the top of the doctor's head while she did her work. Needles freaked me the hell out, made me squeamish, so this was not my idea of a good time.

I had been here several hours and all I wanted to do was go home. What I didn't expect was Roxanne to show up, all dressed up, with a date on her heels, looking frantic.

"Oh, my God!" she exclaimed and turned around, looking woozy. I blinked owlishly at the back of her head.

"What are you doing here?" I blurted.

"I'm your emergency contact!" she exclaimed, then blurted right back, "What did you do?" Her date was staring at my wrist in fascination. I took in his black attire and frilly shirt and sighed inwardly. Goth, probably a vampire groupie type at that.

"I was in the kitchen, the knife slipped..." I answered dully.

Make that a thousand and one times that I'd had to say it tonight.

"Damn!" she exclaimed. "Well, the hospital called and said you were here and would need a ride home." She peeked back over her shoulder and then looked quickly away. I rubbed my forehead with my good hand and huffed out a sigh.

"I could have taken a cab, I took one here," I protested weakly.

"Babe, you look like you murdered someone with an axe. I don't think any cabbie in this city would pick you up looking like that," her date pointed out.

I didn't know if I liked him calling me 'babe'; it wasn't like he knew me past the past two minutes or so. I frowned at him.

"Sorry," Roxy said, and made introductions, even though she wouldn't turn around and look at me. "Josh, this is my best friend, Gracelyn... Gracelyn, this is Josh." Roxy waved her hand in the air over her shoulder in our vague direction.

"Nice to meet you, Josh," I murmured, not wishing to be rude, and he grinned, flashing an acrylic pointed fang.

"Likewise." He inclined his head dramatically.

"Josh has a car, we'll take you home," Roxy said, and her tone brooked no argument. Good thing I didn't want to argue. I just wanted to go home. So, I simply nodded my agreement while the doctor carefully bandaged my wrist. Aftercare instructions were given, a tetanus shot was jammed in my arm, and prescriptions were written and handed over. After all of that, we were, the three of us, on our way and not a moment too soon; I hated hospitals.

We hurried through the corridors to the parking garage, and I followed along behind Josh meekly. I stopped cold in the parking garage's aisle and muttered in disbelief, "You have got to be kidding me."

"Yep, that's my baby." Josh smiled with pride.

I looked up at him, he was tall, over six feet and broad-shouldered with dark hair that curled at his shoulders and dark eyes that I couldn't tell if they were contacts or not.

"It's a hearse," I stated.

"Yep, and since you ruined my date, your skinny ass is sitting bitch." Roxy smiled maniacally at me and despite her intended humor, I groaned inwardly. Josh gallantly held open the door to his hearse and I crawled into the center of the bench seat one-handed. Too soon I was uncomfortably squeezed between the two of them, and I prayed the drive to my apartment would be a short one.

When we reached my apartment, I tried several times to convince them both I wanted to go up alone, but in the end, Roxy was having none of it. I finally capitulated and let them escort me up.

The kitchen wasn't too bad, a few drops of blood on the tile, some smears at the edge of the sink. The knife sat sullen, gleaming dully in the bottom of the sink. I would be throwing that one away. I shuddered. Josh, for getting off on the wrong foot with me initially, was being fantastic. He left without being asked to go fill my prescriptions, and Roxy looked me over critically once the door had shut behind him.

"Yeah, those clothes are dead," she stated flatly. I had to agree. I went into the bedroom and stilled. The bed was made. Perfectly made, no indentation on the comforter or evidence that I'd been on it or in it, at all. I blinked and fought the swell of tears choking off my air. I forced in several deep breaths, in through my nose, out through my mouth, and stripped out of my bloody sweater.

I swiftly changed into a black silk nightgown and pulled on my emerald green, Asian-silk robe. Golden tree branches stretched across the back and along the sleeves, lighter yellow-green leaves falling from them. It was my favorite, so much so, I only wore it when I needed comfort. I loved it so much I didn't want to wear it out prematurely.

I belted it tightly at my waist after drawing it across my chest to ensure I was as modest as I could be for Josh's return and went out into the living room, stopping only long enough to toss my ruined sweater and jeans into the kitchen trash under the sink. Roxy, for her part, opened the door and held the can out for me. I appreciated it, the less I had to use my hand and wrist the better. The numbing agent was wearing off and it was really starting to hurt.

"Where did you find him?" I asked her of Josh.

"Isn't he to die for?" she asked, all dreamy-eyed.

"Goth guys aren't really my thing," I said with a light laugh, "but yeah. I had my doubts at first, but he is kind of amazing," I conceded. I mean seriously, who is cool with having their date ruined to pick up their date's best friend from the hospital? Oh! And not only does he not gripe about it, but volunteers to run out and pick up said friend's prescriptions? A soft tapping at my door heralded his return. Roxy heaved herself up from my couch and went and got it.

Josh came back in and held up the prescriptions in their little nondescript white bag. His smile was sweet and had only a hint of his acrylic fangs. I smiled back grateful.

"Thank you," I murmured taking the bag from him. Roxy got me a glass of water and I told Josh to make himself at home. He bowed gallantly at the waist and took a seat on my loveseat. Roxy handed me the glass and twisted off the caps on my pill bottles, doling out both a pain pill and an antibiotic. I swallowed them down and we talked until I couldn't hold my head up anymore.

"Okay, girl. To bed with you." Roxy fluttered her hands at me and I dragged myself to my feet. My wrist was throbbing but didn't hurt nearly as badly, the pain medicine doing its job twofold. I suspected that might have been why I was so drowsy all of a sudden; my head was all fuzzy from the meds.

I padded into my bedroom. I hung my robe back in the closet while Roxy pulled the blankets back on my bed for me. I got in, my best friend tucking me in while Josh set a glass of water on my night table, my medications beside it within easy reach.

"I'm taking your spare key to lock up behind us," Roxy said and I nodded my assent. She switched out my light and I was asleep before I could hear the door shut behind them.

CHAPTER SEVEN

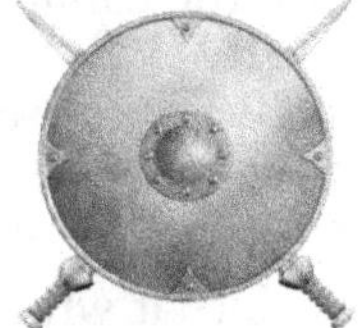

I woke late on Saturday morning and felt well-rested.

Hurrah for painkillers that hit you like a truck, I thought to myself as I threw back the blankets.

I rose and dressed for the day in a comfy pair of running capris and an oversized tee shirt. I gathered my laundry and spent the rest of my day reading, and waiting for the spin cycle and dryer to end down at the laundry room.

Roxy called to check on me a few times and I asked if she wanted to go shopping with me the next day. She had enthusiastically agreed and I felt a little less guilty about the night before. I took another pain pill before going to bed. I didn't really need it, my wrist didn't really hurt, but I took it anyways and prayed for a dreamless sleep that kept me firmly in my bed.

My prayers seem to have been answered because when I got up, I was still in bed, no further damage done. I showered and dressed warmly in jeans and a sweater. I even did my makeup, lining my eyes in warm bronze liner, using a touch of mascara on my lashes. With a final swipe of gloss to my lips, I felt as ready to go as I ever would. Truthfully, I just wanted to stay home. To hide from the world while I tried to figure this out, but I wasn't about to disappoint Roxy.

I met her at our favorite coffeehouse close to the shops we liked to go to. She had her big bug-eyed sunglasses on and her usual black attire. I smiled and sat down at the little table she had procured by the front window.

"Burned a little too much of the midnight oil?" I asked and she gave me a grin to rival the cat that ate the canary.

"Yep," was her only reply, which was really odd of her.

We went over what stores we wanted to shop at. I confessed all I was really after was clothes to replace that which had been unsalvageable. I left the story of the nightgown from my midnight rooftop sleep-walking episode out of it, though it was on my list, too.

"Let's do this, girlfriend!" She rose with a brisk sigh from our table and I couldn't help but feel that something was *off*. I got the distinct impression that she all of a sudden didn't want to be here, but I had no idea what had changed from our initial plan to go out and now.

We went to several boutiques that were more Roxy's speed than mine, yet still she seemed irritated. She wouldn't really talk to me, and her moodiness was leaving me feeling on edge. While it wasn't unusual for her, it was unusual for that moodiness to be directed at me like it was. Finally, I stopped her and asked her point-blank what was wrong.

"Nothing!" she'd snapped at me, but the longer we were out, the more sullen and angry she became. It was as I was being rung up after buying a nightgown identical to the one ruined on my roof, that the dam she had pent up all her emotions behind all afternoon finally broke. We were exiting the store when she rounded on me.

"I don't think we should hang out anymore," she blurted and I almost tripped over my own feet with the shock of it.

"What? What do you mean?" I asked, my voice as hollow as I felt. Her proclamation had absolutely gutted me. I mean, we'd been friends for years! Thick as thieves since the second grade, hell, maybe even the first. I honestly couldn't even remember back that far to know which.

"Josh and I were up fighting all last night, because once he saw you all he could do was ask about you. I'm sick of every guy I go out with meeting you and suddenly I'm not good enough anymore!" I stared at my friend in wide-eyed disbelief. *She couldn't be serious!* Yet, she was.

"What an asshole!" I exclaimed. I immediately took up for my friend in her defense because that was, indeed, an asshole thing to do to her.

"No, no, no! You do not get to change the subject." Roxy shook her finger in my face and my confusion went up a notch. This was about Josh's behavior, right? How was that changing the subject?

"Roxy, I don't understand, I can't change the way I look..." It sounded pathetic even to me, but Rox and I had been friends since literally longer than I could remember.

"I can't do it anymore..." she was saying. "I'm done, Gracelyn. Besides that, you're just not very much fun to be around anymore. I just don't think you're good for me," and with that, she thrust my spare key at me, turned on her heel and strode up the sidewalk away from me. Just like that.

I stood there mute and watched her go and wondered how many times I could break this week before I would completely shatter beyond repair.

I pulled in a deep breath and hailed a cab. I just wanted to go home. If what I was feeling right then were a physical wound, I'm pretty sure I would be bleeding to death. The tears sprang up and slid down my cheeks and I choked on a low wail, determined not to let it get free.

I must have made some sort of sound, because the cabby frowned at me in his rearview mirror. I dug a Kleenex out of my purse and tried to stem the tide of my emotions, embarrassed. I sucked it up, held it in until I was safely in the elevator of my building. The tears started first, and by the time I reached my front door I could barely see to get my key in the lock. I slammed the door behind me and locked it, sliding with my packages to the floor. I huddled in my entryway and sobbed and sobbed.

You deserve this, you're a horrible person and no one wants to be friends with you.

The thought felt foreign in my head but it didn't stop there, it went on, an entire inner diatribe...

Your parents would be ashamed if they were alive. Your grandparents were so unlucky to be burdened with the likes of you. You're a disgrace, mediocre at everything you do, a total drag to be around, you're lucky Roxy didn't dump your ass sooner. You're crazy and no one needs the crazy you bring to their life. You should have just pitched yourself off the roof, then none of this would be happening.

I staggered to my feet and hung up my coat and purse, forcing myself through the motions. I brought my packages into my bedroom, withdrew the nightgown and took off the tags. I laid it across the foot of my bed. All the while, darkness invaded my heart and my soul. My chest felt thick with it and I couldn't breathe...

Worthless, selfish, cocktease, why were you even born? Oh that's right, to bring some more misery to the planet...

I fetched towels, started the shower and got in. Never minding that it was too hot, I forced myself to stand in the punishing heat and scrubbed, but it wasn't like I could wash off my mind or cleanse the sorrow from my heart.

No matter how clean you are on the outside you'll always be black and dirty on the inside.

"No! I'm a good person! I am. I'm a decent human being." My voice sounded harsh in the enclosed space but despite the conviction behind my words, the inner diatribe continued. I was at war with something inside my own head that brought all my darkest fears, my deepest buried concerns to the fore.

That I wasn't good enough, that I would never be good enough for anyone, at anything. That I would be forgotten by the world just like my parents had been. Forgotten like the past I struggled to unearth and thrust into the light.

I sat on the floor of my shower and sobbed, rocking myself, hugging my knees. How did I manage to fuck all of this up so badly? Was it even my fault?

That awful inner voice hissed through my mind *Yes*.

CHAPTER EIGHT

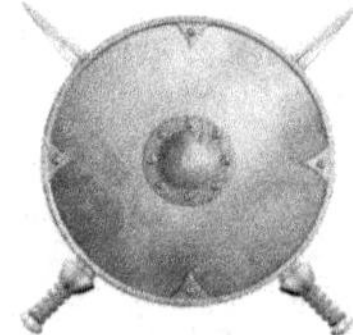

I don't remember falling asleep.

I must have, though. That, or I must have completely come off the rails, gone off the deep end, because as I lay there crying to myself, I either dreamed the most real dream or crossed the line into full-on hallucinations.

A puddle of blackness was on my bedroom floor between my dresser and the closet. It wasn't right, though. The moon and city lights that made their way through my bedroom curtains clearly illuminated the cream-colored carpet in a strip, and there was nothing obstructing the light to cause such an irregular shadow in that particular spot.

Yet the pool of darkness remained and, come to think of it, it was too dark to be a simple shadow. It appeared liquid and alive, which didn't make any sense at all.

The irregular darkness swirled, lifting and curling back in on itself at the edges, fluid in its movements, wafting up like smoke, but not, at the same time. It was more like what would happen if you dropped a spot of black ink into a clear glass of water. It plunged and roiled up from underneath, bulging at its center and expanding, twisting and stretching into a tall pillar before drawing down and seemingly falling or peeling away from a crown of snow-white hair, rushing down off the long straight strands as if they were abhorrent for the darkness to even touch.

That inky darkness continued rolling down the emerging figure of a man, a tall man, clad in very black, very thick, scale mail armor. His already-wide shoulders were made mammoth by the terrifying black metal pauldrons that sat heavily on them. The hilt of a sword rode over his shoulder as the dark continued to make its way down his frame, disappearing into the carpet at his feet as if it had never been, my eyes following it in morbid curiosity.

When the blackness had completely fled, my gaze instead fixed on his feet, traveling back up his legs, taking stock all the way. He wore greaves on his legs, both shin and thigh, and solid boots. A helmet was tucked under one arm, a round shield with a raised shield boss rode on the other, his fist hidden behind it.

I *must* be hallucinating, because it was all wrong. What bothered me, you know, other than having a giant of a strange man with long, straight white hair and equally white skin standing in my room, was the armor. It didn't match. Any of it. It was a scatter of different time periods and my scientific historian's brain rebelled. I bravely finished looking over my hallucination and met his eyes, which took me aback greatly.

They glowed a monstrous red, the color of garnets, and I'm not talking just the irises, either. His eyes were wall-to-wall, bright, glowing red, the whites, irises, pupils all swallowed in rich, glowing, gemstone red, drowning in fiery blood. The light faintly reflected off his ghostly-pale skin surrounding them.

What the hell was my subconscious trying to tell me?

He stepped free of the last vestiges of the pool of darkness on my floor and set his helmet on my dresser. The sound was very real and made my breath still in my chest.

Did hallucinations come both visually and audibly in a way that complimented each other?

I couldn't remember. I tried to remember my high school and college psychology courses, but nothing detailed about hallucinations of the mind would come back to me. I wanted to blink, wanted to squeeze my eyes shut and count to three, open them, and see nothing was there, but I couldn't look away.

He was still watching me with those terrifying eyes, like he couldn't take them off of me as much as I couldn't bring myself to stop watching him. The tears that tracked down my face were uncomfortable, and yet I was frozen, unable to move even to wipe them away. I think it was fair to say my fear had caught up and I was absolutely, one-hundred-percent paralyzed by it.

He unfastened the large buckle at his chest that held his sword to his back, carefully laying the giant blade lovingly on the carpet along the length of my antique dresser. He leaned his round black shield against the old wood's surface beside it before he straightened and pulled the gauntlets from his hands.

He watched me still, deliberately laying his gauntlets beside his helmet on the dresser top. Everything about his movements was careful and calculated to be as non-threatening as possible.

I thought to myself, *Good luck with that* as I managed to sit up, pushing against the mattress, yipping and drawing my injured wrist up, cradling it against my chest.

He froze when I made the sound, neither of us moving, neither of us breathing. When he was sure I wouldn't start screaming, that I was rooted to the spot I was in and that I wouldn't bolt, (how could I when he was between me and the door?) he started pulling at the straps and buckles holding his leather shoulder pieces in place.

As he worked his armor off into an ever-growing pile, his gaze never wavered from mine. His every movement was slow and precise. I waited and watched, feeling panic swell in my breast even though he was being so very careful. He was moving in such a way that I understood perfectly; he was trying not to spook me, which in turn made me panic, made my me fear what he wanted, what he was doing here, all the more.

I began to silently will myself to wake up again, even going as far as to speak, low and intense: "Come on Gracelyn, wake up. This isn't real. Wake up. Wake up, wake up, wake up!"

It wasn't real, this couldn't be real, but with every creak of leather, click of buckle, and rattle of scale, I was growing increasingly concerned that my sanity had completely fled and that perhaps, just maybe, I wasn't asleep at all, but awake and indeed hallucinating.

How could you even tell? I worried.

He worked off his greaves one leg at a time and shucked out of his scale mail with a loud rattle. I pushed myself back into the corner where my bed met the wall, careful of my wrist this time, and hugged my knees.

"This isn't real, this can't be real, wake up, Gracelyn. Wake up!" I had abandoned all pretense that I was asleep and dreaming and was pretty certain I had just lost my mind completely.

The man put a hand out and approached me, his bare feet a whiter shade of pale against my cream carpet. He wore black leather pants and a billowing black linen shirt. I squeezed my eyes shut, forcing yet more pent-up tears to slide down my cheeks, and though I wanted to simply stay that way, not looking, I forced my eyes to open. I somehow fully expected him to be gone, but nope, he was just that much closer.

"Shhh," he soothed, and, gripped with terror, I tried to push my way back through the wall, my feet sliding against the sheets, my back pressed firmly into the damnably unyielding drywall.

Hallucination. It's just a hallucination. He's not real, this isn't real. I thought desperately.

The bed dipped where he placed his knee on the edge, allowing it to take his weight. I squeezed my eyes shut again and cringed. Hallucinations wouldn't make the bed dip. Hallucinations could be visual, could be auditory, but they couldn't affect the physical world around you. Of that, I was certain.

"Who are you? What's happening to me?" I wailed and put my hands over my face. The bed moved beneath me again and strong arms pulled me against a granite chest. I sobbed.

Oh, my God, he was going to rape me. I thought savagely to myself, *Only in New York City could you be attacked in your apartment by a Lord of the Rings fanboi decked out in full armor!*

"Shh, Gracelyn, shh, you're safe now."

I jerked in his hold.

Safe? Safe? How did this classify as 'safe'? How did he know my name?

"Who are you?" I demanded, remaining stiff within his embrace.

"I am Alrekr Hakon Frithjof, and I am here to protect you," he murmured against my hair. I sucked in a breath; the tang of burning metal came off of him, an acrid smell, sharp but not unpleasant.

"I, I don't understand," I stammered, and his chest rose and fell in a sigh beneath my temple and cheek. "P-p-protect m-m-me from what?" I slowly lowered my hands, which still shook, from my face, and he took one of them in his large hands and pressed it flat to his chest beside my face.

"That doesn't matter now," he said, gently, and I swallowed hard, trembling. "Sleep, Gracelyn," he commanded and the rumble of his voice beneath my ear made me gasp.

"I don't understand..." I repeated, "Who are you?"

He sighed and gave a slightly exasperated growl. I flinched, and his hold tightened on me.

"I told you, I am Alrekr Hakon Frithjof, and you will understand in time. Right now, you can rest. I will stay here as long as you need me to."

It should have creeped me out with a creep factor of twelve on a scale of one-to-ten, but I can't for the life of me explain why it didn't. I huddled stiff in his arms and struggled to pronounce his name.

"I will, All-however-you-say-it."

He chuckled and I startled, not expecting that from him.

"Your modern pronunciation would be Alaric. Use that if you prefer."

"Alaric," I whispered, and I swear the sigh that emanated from the giant in my bed was of contentment. I swallowed hard and finished, "I would, but this is crazy. Like, really batshit, off the walls, crazy. This isn't real, is it? You're not really here, I'm asleep, and when I wake up this will all be a bad dream, right?"

"No," he said, "I promise you, this is real. I am real. I also promise that I mean you no harm. Quite the opposite, in fact. I am here to protect you."

"Protect me? Protect me from what?"

"Hush, that doesn't matter now." His hand found the back of my head and smoothed along my hair.

"What do you mean it doesn't matter? It most certainly matters to me."

He sighed again, only this time, the sound held impatience. "It is a long story, one which I do not have time to tell if you are to get any sleep. Do you not work tomorrow?"

Of course, he wouldn't tell me. There was nothing to tell. He was a hallucination, after all. I pressed my lips together and asked, "Are you going to hurt me?" mostly because, I don't know, I just needed to hear him say it.

"No," he said gravely. "If I am here to protect you, then why would I harm you?"

"Good point," I said softly, and swallowed hard. "You promise?" I asked.

"I swear it," he said and I tried to place his accent, but couldn't.

I was silent for a long time and his tight hold on me loosened, but only slightly. One of his arms moved carefully to drag the blankets up over me. I stiffened, unsure, and he'd stilled for a moment.

"You will grow stiff if you sleep like this," he said.

"I'm not sleeping, how can I?"

He chuckled and said, "You must. You must do your work on the morrow, remember?"

"This is kind of more important," I tried to argue.

"The only thing that is important now is that you find and reclaim your joy. Your work brings you the most joy, does it not?"

"Well, yes, but how do you –"

"Enough questions, sleep now," he said firmly and when I opened my mouth to say something else, a word in a language I had no name for slipped from his and it was as if the pressure, the very atmosphere in the room changed. Like the oppressive dark somehow grew *less* dark, though there was no change in the quality of light.

My eyelids grew suddenly heavy and I murmured, "What did you *do*?" but I don't know that he ever responded.

I went to sleep. Just like that.

CHAPTER NINE

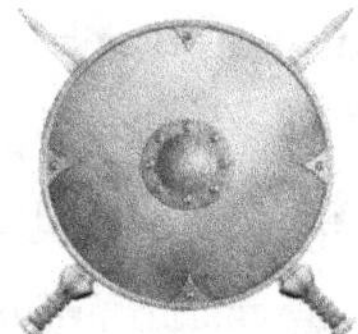

My alarm shattered the peaceful, restful spell I had been under with its incessant screeching. I slapped at it with my good hand from beneath my warm nest of covers and successfully silenced it. I lay still for a moment before the scene from last night played across my mind's eye in high-definition weirdness. I sat up sharply and clicked on the bedside lamp.

Empty.

My bedroom was just as it should be, no weapons, no armor, and no hyper-masculine mysterious mystic warrior.

I swallowed hard and breathed out a harsh sigh. After warring with myself for several moments, I let myself declare that it was officially one very realistic and weird dream. I flopped onto my back and lay there, staring at the ceiling. I know it was ridiculous, but admitting to myself it was just a dream? Well, I felt my heart crack, pieces of it falling away. What had happened last night was just a dream, sure, but what had happened with Roxy hadn't been. Losing my best friend had been all-too-real.

You're alone now, Gracelyn. For real, this time.

Yes, I was. I sniffed back the threatening tears and thrust it all away as I got up. I padded across my bedroom and out to the kitchen to check my phone, hoping against hope, but no, there were no messages.

I returned to my room and sat down on the edge of my bed in a heap. I debated deleting Roxy's number, but no, it was way too soon. She would call, wouldn't she? Apologize? Let me apologize for being a crappy friend? I could do better, I know I could. I certainly hoped that I would be given the chance, but right now I needed to respect her decision, no matter how painful, and get on with my day. I got up and walked the few short steps to my dresser.

"Ow!" I raised my foot and looked down with a frown, checking the bottom. I wasn't cut but there was an angry red line on the ball of my foot from whatever I had stepped on. I looked down and nestled in my thick area rug was something black and shiny. I reached down and plucked it from the plush fibers, holding it between fingers gone suddenly numb with disbelief. I dropped it into the palm of my opposite hand and stared.

It was metal, wider at the top, tapering down into a rounded point at the bottom. Six holes were aligned across the top edge and a frayed thread hung from some of them. The thread was thick, coarse, and black like the metal scale I held in my hand. I flashed back to the night before and the dream that was apparently *not* a dream, and not a hallucination, either. I clutched the scale from Alaric's armor in the palm of my hand until the semi-sharp edges bit into my flesh.

It wasn't a dream; I'm not crazy; he was real.

I let that sink in and shook my head. It was too weird. I dug in my jewelry box and pulled out a length of silver rope chain and filtered through a myriad of charms until I found one with a suitably-sized jump ring. Using my fingernails, I pried it apart until I could get the charm off and then set to work fitting the ring through one of the center holes on the scale. It took several attempts, and finally the use of my teeth, to close the jump ring. I threaded the chain through the ring and clasped it at the nape of my neck under my hair. The black metal scale rested at the hollow of my throat, warm against my skin, and the ropes of despair constricting my chest eased slightly with the knowledge that *yes*, he was real and *yes*, something was really going on, here.

You're not crazy, I told myself, excitement fizzing through my veins. *I mean, this is totally crazy, but you aren't.*

I didn't have any idea who Alaric was, but he'd said he had been here to protect me. That meant that I at least had one person in my corner, right? That I wasn't as alone as I thought I was.

I clung to that feeble hope and got into the shower to deal with the snarl that was my hair. I shoved all thoughts of Roxy to the back of my head, dressed and went to work. Work was a solid, a consistent go-to for me. The history I uncovered had waited too long to be revealed and I saw myself as its only voice some days, which gave me purpose; gave me drive. I chose a pair of black ballet flats for comfort today and walked briskly to work. I settled at my bench, pulling my lab coat over my lavender satin blouse and gray dress slacks, the picture of professionalism. The look was solid, and far more pulled together than I felt.

I threw my braid over my shoulder and let it hang down my back as I fitted magnifying goggles, much like jewelers wear, to my face and began the painstaking process of uncovering the runes I'd discovered on Friday.

Hours later, I let out an explosive breath and came up for air. I pulled the magnification apparatus off my head and rubbed the red marks I knew it left behind on my forehead.

"Gracelyn!" Jared called and I turned. He was leading another man wearing a suit towards me. I stood, setting down my tools and stripping off my gloves as they threaded their way through the other workstations to mine.

"Yes, Jared?" I asked and put on a smile. I had no feeling backing it up and I hoped it wouldn't show.

"Gracelyn I'd like you to meet Gunnar Volund." The man beside Jared held out his hand for me to take. I looked up at him; he was very tall, over six foot, with a wide breadth of shoulders. Light, true-blonde hair in a business-like yet fashionable crew cut offset eyes that were the color of the clouded sky over a storm-chopped sea, the emotion behind them steely and calculating.

"Mr. Volund, how do you do?" I asked politely, but his vibe immediately set me on edge. He had a look that made me feel like I was treading in shark-infested waters and that there may or may not be blood in that water, it was still too dark to tell. He shook my hand and his grip was firm, but not painful. He smiled enigmatically and nodded to Jared.

"Mr. Volund wished to meet one of the conservationists on our little project, as a potential investor. I thought your current project would impress him the most." Jared smiled and I couldn't help the genuine smile that curved my own lips as I angled myself so that Mr. Volund could see the corroded hunk of iron and bronze on my bench. I turned on my saleswoman charm.

"Ah, yes, she's a beauty, isn't she?" I asked, inviting Mr. Volund to take a closer look. He leaned past me, his gaze lovingly caressing the ancient weapon. He muttered something in a language I didn't know, but it could have possibly been Norwegian or Swedish. I looked to Jared who gave a little shrug behind Volund's back... Not something Jared recognized; interesting.

"So, tell me, Mr. Volund."

He straightened and looked down on me. Not down *at* me, there was a difference, and I knew it well and good.

"Yes?" One word, imperious and heavily-accented.

"How did you hear about our little discovery?" I watched him, and he smirked. He could look down on me all he wanted, I wasn't about to let it bother me.

"Around," was his one-word reply. I darted a look over to Jared who shrugged. He rubbed his index and middle fingers together with his thumb. Apparently Mr. Volund had money; it was highly irregular for

Jared to bring investors or philanthropists by without giving me some warning first. Huge quantities of potential money was the usual reason when he did, and this was no different.

"I see." My voice was low, barely above a whisper.

"Have dinner with me," the imperious man said, and I didn't hear a question mark.

"I'm certain something could be arranged. Can't it, Gracelyn?" Jared asked, and I scowled at him. Volund must be really loaded.

"I don't know..." I began, suddenly genuinely reluctant. This man gave me the chills, internal warning beacons flashing their little red lights. Unfortunately, I couldn't tell Jared any of that, and I'm afraid he and Volund took it as me being coy. I didn't see a way to salvage the situation, so I went with the truth by saying, "Tonight is bad." My thoughts were turning toward the mysterious dream-that-wasn't-a-dream from the night before. Specifically, to the giant of a man who would rival Volund here in height. I wasn't sure what was hidden under Volund's suit but I'd felt the rock-hard muscle beneath the linen homespun shirt on Alaric last night.

My hand drifted to the scale at the hollow of my throat, hidden mostly by the collar of my blouse. I fiddled with it absently, my nerves fizzing in the presence of this stuck-up investor. I drew a strange sort of comfort from the scale even as Volund gave a slight shake of his head.

"Tonight is no good for me," Volund gave a dismissive wave of his hand. "I will have my driver pick you up on Wednesday night, the day after tomorrow, yeah?" I stared at him wide-eyed and he nodded, answering for me, "Yeah." He turned to Jared and began speaking to him, turning to go. Jared flashed a winning smile over his shoulder at me and I gave him my award-winning glare. I mouthed, "You owe me" to him and he waved me down subtly behind Volund's broad back, following alongside him like an enthusiastic puppy.

I made an exasperated noise once I knew they were out of earshot and turned back to the sword. It was going to be a while before I got all of the runes uncovered to a state they could be carefully photographed. It was a painstaking process removing the dirt and corrosion without doing more harm than good. It was a fine line between uncovering and accidentally obliterating that which you sought to uncover.

I tugged my purse off of my coat tree and went in search of some coffee or something to eat. All the while, I puzzled over the sudden appearance of a loaded investor. One who was so reluctant to say how he'd even found out about our project. He was a mystery in and of himself, much like the sword on my bench.

CHAPTER TEN

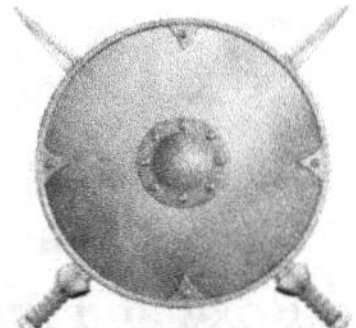

When I finally shut my apartment door, I was bone-tired. I had been a simmering pot of anger ever since I'd returned from lunch. Jared had stopped by to inform me that Volund's driver would be picking me up at 8:00 pm sharp Wednesday night outside of my apartment building... *My apartment!*

When I brought up to Jared just how wrong I thought it was that he had just given out my address to a man I didn't know, he'd waved me off as if it weren't important. I'd gaped at him, at a loss for words when he'd told me he'd given Volund my number as well. My jaw had worked up and down as I had struggled to find the words. He had simply told me not to be late, that this dinner could be worth hundreds of thousands, if not a million or more, and walked off. Dollar signs apparently were worth more than my wellbeing.

Maybe I was over-reacting. It's not like Volund had done anything untoward, he'd just been an arrogant asshole like so many other rich folks I'd dealt with in the past. Maybe it was just his size that I found to be intimidating?

I sighed, my mind a mess of confusion, and once again I found myself gripping the metal scale at my throat like some sort of talisman. I wondered, suddenly, if I would ever even see Alaric again. I was kind of amazed that I wanted to see him again. I mean, I had so many questions.

I fixed myself a simple dinner of soup and salad, and ate. I changed for bed and brushed out my hair in front of my bureau mirror, taking a little longer to braid it than usual. I crawled into bed and lay there watching the spot where he had appeared the night before. An hour went by, then two.

I turned to the wall and heaved out a sigh. What if he never came back? I punched the pillow into submission and lay on my side. I was surprised to find how much the thought of never seeing him again stung. My thoughts drifted to Roxy, and the scaffolding I had carefully erected around my heart to begin to repair it suddenly started coming apart. I sniffed as the first tear slid over my nose to join the others heading for my pillow.

The bed dipped and I gasped. I turned toward the subtle red glow over my shoulder. It was emanating from his eyes, as he settled in behind me his warmth radiating through my back. My breath caught when I realized he was shirtless. He slid a massively muscled arm beneath the curve of my neck and across the flat of my chest above my breasts. The other snaked across my middle, and he pulled himself right up against my back, spooning me.

"You came back," I whispered.

"How could I not, when I hear you cry?" he asked.

"You can hear me?" I ask.

"You are my charge. I can hear you when you are distressed, when you hurt." His warm breath stirred the hairs at the nape of my neck, caressing that sweet spot on the side of my neck below my ear and I shivered. He cuddled me back closer into the heat of his body.

"Where do you come from?" I asked softly.

"Shh, sleep now, Gracelyn," he urged gently.

I settled into the circle of his arms, the contact nice rather than sinister, comforting rather than creepy. I tried again.

"Where do you come from, Alaric?"

I didn't think he was going to answer me, he was silent for so long, but then he said, "Once, long ago, I came from the North." His voice was deep, yet soft, his tone gentle. I could tell I would be getting nothing else from him, but that didn't stop me from trying.

"Why are you here?"

He gave an exasperated sigh and I smiled, knowing full well I could be a real pain in the ass.

"I told you, you are my charge. I am here to protect you."

"Charge? What, like a bodyguard?"

"After a fashion, if you'd like to call it that."

"I'd like the truth," I said carefully and he let out a breath.

"Gracelyn..." His tone as he said my name held warning.

"Fine," I said, then hesitantly I asked, "Will you be here when I wake up this time?"

"No."

"Why not?"

"I have duties elsewhere," was his solemn reply.

"Will I see you again?" I asked.

"I will try," he murmured close to my ear, close enough his warm breath washed over my skin just so, sending a wash of goosebumps along my neck and back, and down my arm.

"I'd like that," I murmured, and his hold on me tightened a little.

"I promise nothing," he said, but I could hear the lie in his words. He would be here if he could. I just knew he would by the way his hold on me felt. Like he would let me go over his dead body. I know it was wrong somehow, that it should thoroughly creep me out or scare me, but, for some reason, it didn't do either of those things. It felt good and safe, protective in a way that reminded me of when I was small, before my parents had died, when I knew I had someone there to catch me no matter how or when I may have fallen.

I lay with my strange new friend for a long time, listening to his quiet breaths before he asked quietly...

"You are not afraid?"

"Only thing I am afraid of is that I'm crazy," I answered honestly, voice shaking with a new emotion, one I couldn't readily quantify. Gratitude?

"You are not mad, Gracelyn. That, I can promise you." He murmured this softly against my shoulder and I forgot to breathe, I don't think it was intentional on his part, but suddenly and embarrassingly I was aroused. I swallowed hard and closed my eyes, his words sinking in... *I wasn't crazy.* Oh, how I wanted to believe him...

"Then what am I?" I asked.

"You are the strongest woman I have ever seen. Now, sleep."

"I was," I said, in an effort to keep him talking.

"You were what?" His speech was accented and oddly formal, yet try as I might, I still couldn't place it.

"Afraid. I thought you were going to..." I shuddered, not wanting to give voice to the word.

"Rape you?" he surmised.

"Yeah," I whispered.

He placed his lips beside my ear and whispered gently, "Were I in my youth, I would have."

I stiffened in his arms and his hold loosened. I tried to process what he'd said, finally relaxing slowly when I realized he was as still as a stone behind me, waiting on me to see what I would do.

"You're not very old," I murmured at last. It was true. I mean, he didn't look a day over thirty when I stopped to think about it.

"I am older than you can imagine. Now please, sleep. I will not be here when you wake but I am here now and will stay to keep the nightmares at bay. You are safe with me, that too, I can and do promise."

I closed my eyes and sank into the warmth and safety he was offering, a million questions flitting through my mind, each eluding me one after the other as I drifted into a deep and dreamless sleep.

CHAPTER ELEVEN

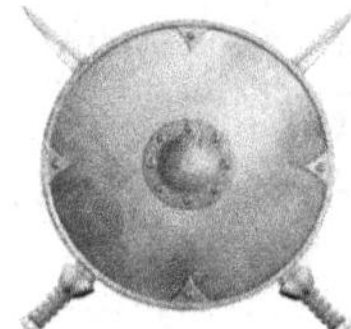

The next day I thought nonstop about Alaric. He was really real, not a figment of my imagination. As I worked on the remnants of the Viking sword on my bench, my thoughts drifted back to the night before last, the first night. Something was bothering me, and it took several hours for my historian's brain to process what it was.

His sword and shield were clearly Viking, his helmet was even Viking, but his armor, the scales; it didn't match, did it? I was about to put down my brushes and go off to my good friend the internet to look, but Jared stopped me as I was getting up from my stool.

"Don't forget, tomorrow night at eight." He tapped his watch face by way of emphasis and I scowled at him.

We'd been quietly feuding since I'd gone into his office and lambasted him over giving up my address. He firmly thought I was taking things far too seriously while I thought he wasn't taking things nearly as seriously as he ought to be. Not when it came to my personal safety. I'd tried to explain that Gunnar Volund had given me the absolute creeps, but Jared brushed me off. Then again, Jared was as privileged as they came. An affluent white male from an affluent family, like Volund. Of course their ilk would stick together. It was a regular good ol' boys club.

While I had 'white' going for me, I had neither affluence nor the preferred gender. I grudgingly had to swallow the fact that Jared just didn't understand what being a woman in New York City, hell, anywhere on the planet, entailed. He didn't know what it was like and simply couldn't relate.

He didn't grow up with the joys of being told that little Bobby picks on you because he likes you. That violence against women was a normal, accepted practice under the guise of 'boys will be boys.' He didn't understand walking through a parking lot with your keys already out and sticking out of your fist, just in case. He didn't deal with being on high alert all day every day and all night, every night, because, God forbid, something did happen to you, you'd better be willing and able to explain why you wore what you did that day and have a damn good reason for it. And let's face it, no reason was ever a good enough reason, no matter what you did as a woman.

"Wear something nice," he called back to me, just before he went through the door to his office and I know he did it just to irritate me, but him not knowing what I'd just been thinking made it much worse for me than just the mildly-irritating little quip he'd meant it to be. I fought down the bubble of rage that rose up and threatened to choke me. I was his employee, not his girlfriend, and not his damn property! *How dare he!* Still, I kept my cool; it wouldn't do to lose my temper, lest I just be relegated to the pile of 'hysterical women.' God! I couldn't believe how sexist he was being. *Or how unreasonable I was potentially being.* Which I had to admit, was a distinct possibility at this point.

I sighed and looked down at the sword. I roughly retook my seat, though I didn't immediately dive back into my delicate work. Instead, I took deep, even breaths, in through my nose and out through my mouth, making sure I had careful and perfect control before I resumed the careful preservation of the priceless artifact in front of me. My earlier goal of comparing time periods for armor and weaponry was momentarily forgotten.

I sighed, and a little more of my frustration left and a little more of my patience returned. It would be a while before I freed enough runes from the centuries of corrosion, if I could retrieve enough of them to even make sense of what they may or may not mean. It would only help us, the sooner I accomplished the goal of uncovering them all. If it was something good, like a date or a name, there would be interest and investment opportunities aplenty. Perhaps even enough we wouldn't need Volund's money.

Wouldn't that be nice? I thought to myself, knowing full well how much of a pipe dream it was. My irritation only grew with how badly my healing wrist itched beneath its fat Band-Aid, hidden beneath the cuff of my blouse and lab jacket.

I set back to work and tried to ignore Jared, and the fact that the clock was crawling around the dial at a snail's pace. I just wanted to go home. I wanted to see Alaric, speak with him some more. I fought down a bubble of panic that he might not show. I was going to be out late the next night. What if he showed, and I wasn't there?

Shit.

For months, I'd felt as if my world were tilted on its axis. Depression and anxiety were both eating me alive, from the inside out, until none of my friends wanted to be around me, and who could blame them? I set down my tools and pinched the bridge of my nose. I did not need to think about it. I didn't want to think about it, but I couldn't help it. For as abnormal as Alaric's presence was, it was his presence that had helped me begin to feel normal again, if that even made sense.

The fog of sorrow was creeping its way back into my heart. I gripped the scale from Alaric's armor in the palm of my hand and felt marginally better. Still, I needed to know more about him. With any luck, and God willing, I would, even if it wasn't tonight.

I left the museum at my usual time and headed for home, stopping for a takeout on the way. I was hungry; at least that was something. Who knew what kind of restaurant Volund had in mind for tomorrow night. Probably it would be one of those places that had artsy little food on a big plate, the kind of fancy *haute cuisine* fit for the jet-set but certainly not for a lowly pleb, like me. It was likely I would need the damn leftovers from tonight if that were the case.

I slipped into my apartment and shut the door. I didn't bother with the lights until I got into my little kitchen, and even then, I just used the light above the stove.

I ate my take-out out of the carton it came in. So lady-like, I know, but I didn't feel like dealing with the dishes and it wasn't exactly like I would be having houseguests dine with me anytime soon. Besides, I was feeling more than a little rebellious. Honestly, I was only one or two notches from downright mutinous at this point. Volund had my hackles up and Jared had just pushed me straight into feminist rawr!

I couldn't help it, once I was standing in my apartment, my thoughts drifted back to Alaric. I wasn't one hundred percent sure what the hell I thought I was doing, letting a strange man with glowing red eyes into my bed at night, especially one as big and scary-looking as Alaric was, but here I was, hoping I would see him again tonight, if only to tell him I wouldn't be home until late tomorrow.

I packed my uneaten chicken teriyaki and pot stickers into my fridge and ditched the fork I'd used to eat it with in the dishwasher's silverware basket. I stretched and went in to take a hot shower, lighting the candles in my bedroom and bathroom. Candlelight was always soothing to me, and with my head feeling as full as it did, I wanted comfort. Well, as much of it as I could squeeze out of my surroundings; I sure wasn't finding any of it within.

I showered by candlelight, dried myself, slipped into my nightgown, picked up my brush and began working it through my hair, starting at the ends. A blur of movement in the hall outside the bathroom door caused me to leap out of my own skin, a startled scream escaping my lips. I turned to see Alaric standing in my bathroom doorway. He was back in his scale mail. His pauldrons and greaves were missing, though, as were his sword and shield. His boots were planted in my hall carpet shoulder-width apart. A small smile played on his full lips, out of place with the powerful and frightening warrior look of the rest of him.

"You startled me!" I was gripping the handle of my brush so hard my fingers were starting to hurt. I loosened my grip and drew a deep breath.

"I am sorry," he said in that low bass rumble I was growing accustomed to.

I was staring, I knew I was staring, but I couldn't help it. He motioned towards me with his hand.

"May I?" he asked.

"What?" I asked and his lips quirked at the corner.

He almost had to turn sideways when he stepped forward into the doorway of my bathroom. As it was, the scales on the shoulders of his sleeves brushed against the wood of the doorframe, making a rattling noise. He plucked the hairbrush from my suddenly-nerveless fingers. This was the first time I had stood next to him, and I was startled to realize just how big he really was. He filled my bathroom, which was small to begin with, and his presence was overwhelming. I drew in a deep, slow breath through my nose and again smelled that acrid tang of burning metal. I licked my suddenly-dry lips.

"Come," he said, and I hastily blew out the candles resting on the sink and the back of the toilet. He backed out of the bathroom and I followed his hulking figure into my bedroom.

He had set my brush on my bureau and was in the process of shucking out of the scale when I entered. It landed in a heap with a dull rattling thud on my carpet and I winced, worried the downstairs neighbor might be disturbed. He kicked it aside and held out his hand, palm up. I placed my smaller one in it and he gently tugged me toward the bed. I hopped up onto it and he sat down, moving my thick wet hair into his leather-clad lap. He gently began detangling the ends. I watched him utterly fascinated.

"Who *are* you?" I murmured.

"I told you, I am Alrekr Hakon Frithjof." He continued to brush my hair and we sat in silence.

"That's your name," I said finally, then added, "Not who you are."

He stopped mid-stroke and his face rose from where he'd fixed that glowing red gaze of his on my hair pooling in his lap.

Though his eyes were that solid red glow, and it was hard to decipher where exactly he was looking at any given time, I knew he was looking right at me. His brow furrowed and he reached out his index finger, tracing the edge of the scale at the hollow of my throat.

"Where did you get this?" he asked. I swallowed hard, afraid he would make me give it back, but I told the truth.

"Found it," I said, my mouth dry. "After the first time you were here. Is it a problem?"

His eyebrows shot up in the opposite direction. Where he'd been frowning before, his countenance was now wholly surprised.

"No," he answered shortly and resumed brushing.

I had so many questions, but now that he was here, I was loathe to open my mouth and spoil this. Whatever 'this' was.

"Turn," he ordered gently.

I blinked at him in surprise, and he gently took me by the shoulders and turned me away from him. He moved the brush onto my scalp and gently pulled, and I let out a groan of pleasure. I'd forgotten how good it felt to simply have someone brush my hair. No one had done it since my mom had died.

"What is it, Small One?" he asked.

"Nothing," I lied.

The brush stilled and I sighed. I was a terrible liar. I changed tack and told the truth, my cheeks flaming. "No one has brushed my hair since my mom died," I said, and he silently continued his ministrations. I swallowed again, and took another tentative step forward by saying, "I miss it."

"Truth between us, always, Gracelyn. I will not have it any other way if I am to be your friend," he murmured in that low voice of his.

"Okay," I whispered, and in a moment of bravery, added, "That goes for you, too."

He chuckled deeply and set my hairbrush down on the bedside table in front of me. I turned to look at him but he grasped my shoulders and gently turned me away.

"I was not done," he chided and I obediently faced forward. He started at one side of my head, picking up sections of my hair, twisting and weaving it with his long fingers. The silence swelled between until I couldn't take it anymore.

"You said I was your charge What did you mean?" I asked.

"I do not think you are ready to hear the answer." His voice was husky, soft, and I suppressed a shiver.

"What if I disagree?" I asked.

"I do not care," he rumbled.

I couldn't help it. His response had been so forthright I laughed, while thinking to myself: *Oh. Well. Crap, then.* I closed my eyes, an amused smile on my lips and simply enjoyed the feeling of him playing with my hair for a time.

"You said you would protect me from myself and those who wished to harm me. What did you mean?" I asked.

"You are persistent." He was smiling through the observation, I could hear it plain as day.

"Yeah, I am," I affirmed. "Call it a scholar's curiosity."

"To answer that question, I would have to answer the first. You are not ready. Choose another."

Wow, okay then.

"How old are you?" I asked.

"I do not know the measurement by your modern calendar," he murmured.

"I'm not getting a lot of answers." I pouted.

"No," he agreed. "You are not."

"Don't sound so happy about it," I teased gently and he chuckled. Another shorter silence slipped by. "Where does that leave us?" I mused aloud, not really expecting an answer, but he answered anyway.

"I do not know."

"Finally, something we can agree on," I murmured.

He fiddled with something at his hip and tied off the end of whatever he had woven my hair into. I murmured my thanks and turned, and caught the tail end of a pleased look upon his face. He stood.

"Don't go," I pleaded.

"I am not."

He pulled off his boots and put them near the rest of his things. He motioned with his hands and I scooted over towards the wall. He picked up my brush from the bed and set it on my bedside table before turning and looking down at me. He pulled his shirt over his head and dropped it by the bed. I looked him over again.

Wow, just wow.

He might as well be chiseled from a block of white marble. He was all delicious masculine planes and angles and I quickly averted my eyes before I could be caught staring.

"Face the wall, Small One," he muttered and my gaze flicked up to the severe red glow of his eyes.

His hands rested on his hips, and I slowly complied with his wish. I closed my eyes and listened as he stripped off his leathers. I went very, very still when he slipped between the sheets. He pulled me back against his chest and I relaxed against the heat of him. He was so warm. I turned over, his arms loose around me, and I rested my cheek against his chest, my head cradled against his shoulder.

"Why isn't this weird?" I asked. "Why aren't I afraid of you?"

He smoothed his calloused palm up and down my arm.

"I do not know," he said. "I should terrify you. Why do I not?"

"You're scary," I admitted, "but you've never hurt me, you've stated you're here to protect me. *Should* I be afraid?" I asked.

"Yes," he answered and I grew uneasy.

"Sleep now, Gracelyn," he murmured against my hair, and no more was said. I closed my eyes and cuddled against his warmth, breathing in the faint scent of burning metal. It would normally be an off-putting smell, but over the last few nights, it'd become a comfort to me. I was nearly asleep when I remembered about the next day.

"Oh! Before I forget, I won't be home until late tomorrow night. My boss is making me go to dinner with an investor."

His hand drifted from my arm to my cheek and he raised my face with a gentle touch so that he could look me in the eyes.

"Why do you say it so?" he asked, scowling.

"I don't know what you mean," I said, the breath stilling in my lungs.

"This investor, what has he done to you?"

"Nothing."

"Gracelyn?" His tone was disapproving and I shifted slightly.

"I mean it," I said. "He hasn't done anything."

"They why do you dread seeing him?"

I bit my bottom lip and let out a frustrated sigh. Alaric's fingertips grazed my jaw and I looked up at him.

"I don't know, he just gives me a bad feeling," I said honestly. "He's arrogant, and used to getting what he wants, and it's off-putting."

"Do not go," he said, and his tone held finality, but not like he was ordering me.

"I have to," I said. "There are a lot of people depending on the funding he could provide. It's not just about the history, it's also about keeping us all employed."

"Hm."

I waited but he didn't expand, which was maddening. I pushed up from his chest, twisting with little finesse so that I could look at him. He was smiling a Cheshire Cat little smile and I felt myself frown.

"What's 'Hm' supposed to mean?" I asked and his smile grew.

He cupped my cheek with his hand, smoothing along it with his thumb so gently. It was completely out of sorts for how large and imposing he was that it surprised me.

"You are a sweet soul, Gracelyn."

"But?"

"'But', nothing; you think of others before yourself, are willing to do things that will put yourself in danger for people you do not know."

"I don't know if Gunnar Volund is a danger to me. I mean, not in a physical sense."

Alaric's expression darkened and he took me into his arms. I settled back down against him and he sighed.

"He had better not be," he said, and it was the first time I heard him sound intentionally menacing.

I closed my eyes and cuddled into his side. For now, I felt safe. Still, the pervading sense of unease when it came to Volund and his dinner seemed to deepen. I shook it off, thrusting it into the back of my mind, and took comfort in Alaric and his presence, while I could.

CHAPTER TWELVE

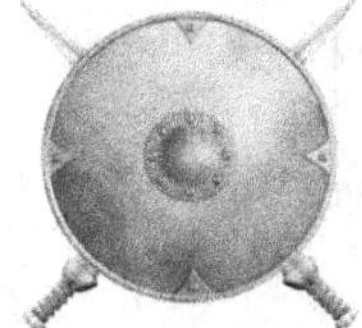

When I woke the next morning, I used my little hand mirror to check my hair in the bathroom mirror and gasped with surprise. It was lovely and intricate. Alaric had made several fishbone braids on either side and had woven them into a single fishbone braid that stopped at my mid-back. My hair, unbound, reached past my ass, so for it to be that short meant he had spent quite a bit of time and effort plaiting it.

It was beautiful and I didn't want to take it out, and it hadn't frizzed uncontrollably as I'd slept so I left it. I washed my face, brushed my teeth, and got ready for work in gray slacks, a white blouse, and an asymmetrically-hemmed heather gray cardigan. I slipped my feet into black ankle boots with a sturdy heel and zipped them, and pulled down my purse and peacoat. I turned back to my bed, which I had neatly made, and touched a finger to the scale at my throat.

Shoving Alaric to the back of my mind like I'd shoved Volund to the back of it the night before, I strode out of my apartment, locking it securely behind me and I went for the elevator.

The morning passed pretty quickly and it was promising to be a long enough day as it was, but I still had that dinner with Gunnar Volund to deal with, so you could imagine my surprise when my stomach gave a rumble of protest and I looked up to realized I'd worked straight through lunch. It was already six o'clock! I had less than two hours to get home and get dressed.

I raced to my apartment and changed quickly into a modest black dress that hung in a sheath to just below my knees. The bodice of the dress fit well and appeared to wrap and had a v-neckline that didn't disclose anything I didn't want it to. It had short cap sleeves and was the picture of professionalism, while still looking nice. I paired the dress with black stockings and midnight suede four-inch heels and called it good. I lined my eyes in smoky liner and mascara, and even did a smoky shadow for good measure. Some clear gloss on my lips and I was ready to go.

As I stood back and took stock of myself in the mirror, I looked towards my bedroom with a pang. I was going to be home super-late and I wondered briefly if he would be here when I returned. My ruminations over Alaric were interrupted by a sharp knock at the door. I checked the peephole and saw a stately older gentleman dressed as a chauffeur, smart little cap, white gloves and all, standing primly on the other side of the door like it was nothing for him to be there. Never mind I was in a secured building.

I silently fumed at the audacity of Jared. He'd even given Volund my apartment number! We would be having words tomorrow. I opened the door, purse on my shoulder and my coat in my hands.

"Ms. Adams?" The man's voice was smooth and cultured.

"Yes," I replied, and he gently took my coat from my hands, holding it open. I shrugged into it with a slight blush and locked up my apartment.

When I turned around, he turned smartly on his heel without saying a word and snapped out his elbow from his side in a clear indication I should take it. I slid my hand in the crook of his arm and we were off to the elevator. This was a trip, even for me. My nerves were fizzing in the most uncomfortable of ways.

"What's your name?" I asked, as the elevator made its descent.

"Maximillian," he replied.

"Should I call you Max?" I asked.

He shot me an imperious look and said, "I would prefer if you didn't, Madam."

All right then.

We walked to the waiting town car in silence and he opened the door. I climbed into the back and realized I had no clue where we were going.

"Excuse me, where are we going?" I asked through the open divider. I received no reply. I swallowed hard as we moved into the flow of traffic. Fear bubbled in my chest and I asked again.

"Maximillian, where are we going?" I didn't mean for my tone to come out as harshly as it did, but I wasn't fond of whatever game he was playing.

"We are going where Mr. Volund wills it," was his all-too-creepy reply.

I texted Jared that he and I would be having a serious talk tomorrow. I didn't even get so much as a "What's wrong?" from him.

We drove to the heart of Manhattan and stopped in front of a rather expensive restaurant, one of those fancy, must book a year in advance, over a hundred dollars a plate places. My nerves, already more than a bit frayed, came apart even more. Jared was right, this guy was loaded.

Maximillian opened my door and I slid out of the car stepping onto an honest-to-God red carpet at the curb. A man in a thousand-dollar suit stepped forward.

"Ms. Adams," he greeted me in a severe tone.

"Yes?" I squeaked. The guy was imposing and it had nothing to do with his size, though he stood a head above me. His blonde hair was in a short buzz cut so close you could see scalp. He wore black wraparound sunglasses and had one of those clear plastic coils behind his ear running down into the collar of his jacket.

"Come with me. Mr. Volund is expecting you." He turned and walked into the restaurant. The door was held open by a doorman in a deep red bellhop type uniform, complete with the round pillbox cap. I followed the man and swallowed hard. He was clearly some type of security personnel and I was beginning to wonder exactly what Mr. Volund did for a living.

The table was small, a four-seater but tucked into a back dimly-lit corner of the restaurant. 'Intimate' was a good word for it. Mr. Volund rose from his seat and nodded to the security man-hulk thing, and he stood aside to let me pass.

"Mr. Volund," I uttered softly and attempted to school my face into concealing my anxiety.

"You are upset?" he asked as I took his hand to shake, and I grimaced. I was a shit actress. I had never perfected the art of keeping what I was feeling off my face or out of my eyes.

"This whole experience has been highly irregular," I stated and cheered inside at how professional I sounded.

"Please, sit." He pulled out the chair beside his, not across, and I noticed the table had been set that way, and only for two. He dismissed his bodyguard, who stood facing out into the restaurant at the edge of our little alcove. I took off my coat and hung it and my purse on the back of the chair before taking the proffered seat. I let him push the chair into the backs of my knees, considering there really was no way of avoiding it when a man helped you with your chair and I didn't want to wave him off to do it myself. No need to be rude when I was sort of at his mercy... and I totally loathed that I felt that way. At his mercy was *not* someplace I wanted to be.

"Mr. Volund, I really would like to know why I am here," I said, as he took his seat beside me. I looked at him over the too-small corner of table between us.

"You are upset," he repeated, then asked, "Why?"

He didn't care how I felt, not really. If he did, he would have answered my question to put me at ease. I shifted in my seat and considered him. I held my breath and twisted my lips while I looked him over. I wasn't entirely upset with him, more at Jared and, well, "The truth was the golden path to walk by," my grandfather always said.

"This is New York," I stated. "I'm upset at my boss for just giving out my building and apartment number to someone I don't know. I'm upset at your driver for refusing to tell me where he was taking me, and I'm upset at myself for not being more cautious and demanding answers before I agreed to any of this."

Volund sat back in his chair, his blue eyes sparkling. He was smiling at least, though I wouldn't call it anything close to 'warm'.

"I will speak with Maximillian on this. As for Mr. Worth, I do not think there is anything I can do there; you will have to speak with him. My sincerest apologies for not knowing the custom in regards to this city." His voice was heavily accented, something Scandinavian, I'd bet, though I still couldn't place it. I almost felt a little bad for Max and tried to mitigate the damage. After all, he was just Volund's employee, and Volund had ordered him not to talk.

"It's fine. I'll deal with Jared. I'm sure it just escaped his mind. But I would have liked to have the option of meeting you here rather than, well, you know." I dropped my eyes to my water glass.

"As for why you are here..." He leaned forward. "When Mr. Worth sang so highly his praises about your work on the project, I simply had to meet you. I did not expect you to be so..." he waved his hands in my direction.

"So what?" I blinked in confusion.

"Beautiful," he stated and I blinked again. I never thought of myself as beautiful, ever. I mean, pretty maybe, but I would never go as far as *beautiful.*

"Uh, thanks," I said, taken aback, blushing.

"I wished to get to know you, as well as about the project you work on. I take a deep interest in what it is you are doing in Scotland."

"Why?" I asked.

"I believe that you may have found the last raid of one of my ancestors." He leaned back but his gaze on my face was no less intense than it had been a moment before.

"I don't even know how we would prove that," I said.

"My ancestor was a great Viking, ruthless, and as the old histories are told, he died upon a distant shore to the West. When I heard of your team's discovery I took an interest, especially when I heard the age of those discoveries."

"Let me guess, during the time your ancestor supposedly lived."

He inclined his head. "I am willing to donate money to further your research. If you were to find proof of my ancestor's involvement in this raid, I would be willing to donate substantially more."

Well, hell.

He was willing to donate. That was a start. I don't think he had any idea that the condition of his continued monetary involvement was pretty much impossible. Very rarely did we get specific names associated with anything we found; usually the historical site in question had to be pretty obviously a part of a story of some renown for that to happen.

Sure, sometimes you found things like specific names associated with things older than our Viking find, but those were usually extremely well-preserved, like the burial chambers of the Pharaohs or the villas of Pompeii. This was various assorted weapons, armor, small trinkets, and yes, even bones that were preserved in mud and dirt, but all of our finds had thus far been corroded, indecipherable.

I chewed my lip and contemplated my sword. There was hope there, inscribed on the hilt at the time of its forging. It was a gamble whether it would lead anywhere solid, but it was also a gamble I was willing to take to keep so many of us employed.

"Okay," I said. "Every little bit helps. If you donate, I can promise the money will be put to good use. What I can't promise is that we will find anything on your ancestor, or that this was indeed a part of his or her raid. That he or she had anything to do with it." I looked at him as food was placed in front of us and the wine was poured.

"If you do find something, I wish to be the first to know," he said as I unfolded my napkin into my lap.

I was suddenly starving. Hungry enough that I didn't care that I hadn't been the one to order my own food.

"I can't promise that, either," I said. "Those types of assurances would have to come from Jared, um, Mr. Worth."

"Understood." He raised his wineglass and I raised mine. Clinking glasses, we sipped. The wine was good, sweet and floral with just a hint of bite.

"Tell me about your ancestor." I tried what was on my plate, and died and went to heaven. Now I knew why this place was as exclusive as it was.

"He was a ruthless man, the first-born son of a great king. His name meant 'All-powerful high son', his surname was given to him and it meant 'Peace thief', for that is what he did. He stole peace from the lands to the west, to the east, and even from the neighboring kingdoms of his own lands. He was a passionate warrior known for his extraordinary cruelty. It is said that he would spend days raping and pillaging through a town and that his raids were the stuff of legend. He left nothing behind but a blackened ruin; rivers and streams ran red with blood; those that tried to oppose him on the shore, well, the tide would be thick with the remains of his enemies, and it, too, would surge with blood."

I blinked at the reverent tone that Gunnar Volund used in describing what sounded like a monster. I chewed silently as he continued.

"It is said no one and nothing was safe from him, not man, woman, nor child, and that he wore the skulls of infants on his belt. Nailed the faces of men on his shield. He brought glorious spoils back to his father and made great his reign."

Gunnar was smiling and I was feeling a little ill. How could someone idolize such a creature? I hardly thought it even appropriate to classify him a man.

"That sounds..." I hesitated and finished with, "...awful."

Volund laughed at my sour expression.

"He is who I wish to be in my business."

He speared a piece of meat with his fork and ate it.

"What exactly is it that you do?" I asked.

"I am in banking," was his short reply.

"Ah..." I let it go at that. I honestly didn't think I wanted to know anymore.

Volund and I ate in silence for a time, but all that good food had turned to ash in my mouth as I turned over what he'd said in my mind. If he wanted to be like his ancestor, then I was pretty sure I wanted to be as far away from him as possible.

"What of you, Ms. Adams?" he asked.

"Please, call me Gracelyn," I said, more out of politeness than anything.

"Then I must be Gunnar to you." He smiled and I returned it as best I could.

"What do you mean, Gunnar?" I asked.

"Why this project?" he asked.

"Honestly, it's the same reason I undertake any project. There's a forgotten story to be told, which must be told. Nobody deserves to be forgotten. Everyone has a legacy and the stories of their lives should be told to future generations. History is how we keep from repeating our mistakes. It's what makes our future brighter. History is how we attain immortality. By the deeds we do in life, by the lessons we leave behind, by the stories we tell." I folded up my soapbox and resolutely stuffed it away before I embarrassed myself with my ranting.

"You are passionate. That is a good thing." He nodded once. I couldn't help but smile.

"There's passionate and then there's overzealousness. Be grateful I could stop myself or you would have to put me resolutely into the 'overzealous freak' category."

He laughed and it was a rich, warm sound, the first of its kind that I'd heard from him. Perhaps there was hope for Gunnar Volund, after all.

We finished our meal and departed. When we stepped out of the restaurant, there was a sleek gray 1940's Rolls Royce idling at the curb. A driver who was *not* Maximillian opened the door and ushered us inside with a gloved white hand.

"I too, have a love of history, and fine old things," Volund said as he slid in behind me.

I don't know why I couldn't think of him as Gunnar; maybe it was too personal. I liked to keep my work and personal lives as separate as possible. The car pulled smoothly into the flow of traffic.

"I return to Denmark next week," Volund was saying. "I would like to call you from time to time." He searched my face and I am sure found the reluctance I was feeling there.

"All right," I finally agreed. "I will give you any updates I can on my progress."

He pursed his lips, plainly unhappy with my response. He took my hand in his and I stiffened marginally.

"I would hope that we could speak on more than simply your work. I have enjoyed my time with you tonight."

I smiled, warmed by the compliment, but all I really wanted to do was escape this luxurious car for my bedroom, so I could see if Alaric was there.

"Dinner was fabulous. Thank you so very much for both it and your contribution to our project." I remained stubbornly obtuse to his advancements. His smile became slightly feral and I felt chilled.

"I shall deliver the check tomorrow." He kissed the back of my knuckles and went to let me go, but instead turned my hand to look at my wrist. "What is this?" he demanded, looking at the fat rectangle of the giant Band-aid on the underside of my wrist.

"Oh, it's nothing," I said, suddenly nervous. "A small kitchen accident, the stitches come out very soon." He eyed me carefully. "Itches like crazy, means it's healing well." He let me go, seemingly satisfied by my explanation, though I couldn't tell you why I'd over-explained as much as I had. Ugh, God, I just wanted to go, and I was grateful when his driver opened my door. I scooted out of the car and leaned down for a last stab at a more professional goodbye.

"Goodnight, Mr. Volund," I said, my mouth suddenly dry.

"Gunnar, please. I like the sound of my name on those lips."

I simply nodded, at a loss for what else to do, and straightened. My heels clicked a sharp staccato in my hasty retreat, chasing me all the way to my building's lobby door. I coded myself into my building, but the silver Rolls didn't depart until I stepped onto the elevator and out of sight.

CHAPTER THIRTEEN

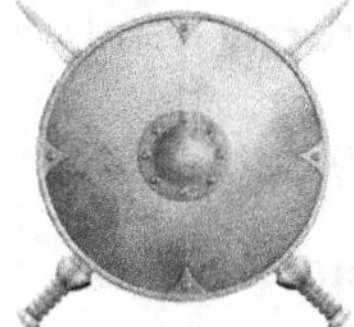

I closed my apartment door and leaned heavily against it, securing the deadbolts and chains. I turned into my dark and silent dwelling.

"Alaric?" I called softly.

I waited several moments, and my heart fell a little at the lack of response. I went into my bedroom and sat on the end of my bed, prying the heels from my feet and rubbing them. I set them in the bottom of my closet and went to work, slipping the dress back on its hangar, and ditching the rest of my attire in the laundry. I tugged on my robe and hung a clean nightgown on the back of the bathroom door. I went into my dark living room and curled up on the end of the couch, beginning the laborious process of undoing the intricate braids in my hair. It was hard as hell doing it blind when I couldn't see how it went in the first place. I was growing frustrated when warm, gentle hands covered my own, stopping me mid-motion.

"Let me." His voice was molten metal, liquid and beautiful. My shoulders eased out tension I hadn't realized they'd been holding.

"What troubles you?" he asked, and before I knew what I was doing, I was confiding in him.

"Volund gave me a severe case of the creeps is all. I did manage to secure some more funding for the project, but I don't know at what cost, yet." Alaric's hands stilled a moment before resuming unplaiting my hair. I stopped speaking, waiting for him to say something.

"Go on," he urged quietly.

"Volund is interested in our project because he thinks it might have been one of his Viking ancestors. He told me about the guy."

Alaric's hands went to my shoulders, and simply rested there.

"The way he talked about him seriously creeped me out. He said he wanted to be just like his ancestor, ruthless and cold. The things he said about him..." I shuddered. "His ancestor was the worst of the worst. I would hesitate to even call him human. It was terrifying, the way Volund looks up to him. Then, in the very next breath, Volund went on to tell me he'd like to call on me. I told him I didn't mix business with my personal life and he got this look." I shivered again. "It was like '*Challenge accepted!*' It made me super uncomfortable," I whispered the last.

Alaric's thumbs dug gently into my tense muscles and I gasped, my eyes sliding closed as my head dipped forward to give him better access. I sighed in contentment as he kneaded between my shoulder blades gently. He stopped, and went back to undoing my hair, combing his fingers through the long, long strands.

"You are safe here, with me," he said, finally.

"I know that," I said, but couldn't stop the reluctant sigh. Of course I was safe with him. I believed that whole-heartedly, but he wasn't here with me all of the time. He couldn't be, for reasons I still didn't know or understand. Still, the sentiment had been pure and so I said, "Thank you."

"For what?" he asked.

"Being here." I shrugged. "And for listening." I tilted my head way, way, back and looked up at him. He was shirtless, his leather pants riding low on his hips, that delicious 'V' marking out his hip bones disappearing into the black leather. His red eyes, as unreadable as ever stared down into mine.

The moment suddenly held a weight that it hadn't just a second before, but instead of being creepy or off-putting, it was exactly the opposite. I held my breath and almost willed him to do what I knew we were both thinking. I wanted him to bend down and meet my lips with his so badly, but instead, with a hard swallow and a strain to his voice that hadn't been there the moment before, he asked me, "You wish to shower?"

"Yes," I said softly, disappointed, but unwilling to actually talk about it because, *how embarrassing*.

"Go." His voice was sharp, but gentled when he added, "I will be waiting when you get out." He backed out of my field of vision and I got up and rolled my head on my neck, feeling a bit better. I went into the bathroom and started the shower, taking a moment to look across the hall into my bedroom. He was there, lighting the candles I had scattered about – with his fingertip.

I stared, mystified, for a moment until he said, without looking, "Gracelyn..." drawing out my name in his low bass rumble. I went to the bathroom door and flipped on the light switch on the wall beside it as I swung the door shut. My last glimpse of him, I saw him flinch, shying away from the electric glow.

Were his eyes sensitive?

I pondered this, hanging my robe on the hook beside my nightgown. I showered and dried my hair in record time, braiding it over my shoulder, nearly down to my hip. I marveled that he'd managed to get it as short as he did with all of his braids the night before as I shrugged into the black silk nightgown, which fell just above my knees. The soft material caught on my skin here and there, as real silk sometimes was wont to do. The spaghetti straps held it in place over my modest chest and I turned this way and that to make sure nothing was going to spill out, suddenly self-conscious. I turned out the light and opened the door, walking across into my softly candle-lit bedroom.

He was in my bed, the blankets bunched at his waist. His boots and pants were folded neatly between my closet and my dresser. My cheeks heated, and he patted the side of the bed between him and the wall, a slight frown furrowing his brow.

"What?" I asked, looking down at myself.

"I do not like you in this." He waved his hand up and down, and I was confused.

I crawled up the bed as modestly as possible, and he lifted the blankets for me to get under.

"You are a creature of the light," he was saying, as he pulled me against him. "What you have worn the last few nights suits you better; you should wear whites and creams, colors of the sun and your pure nature. Not black. You are not like me. You should never wear the mantle of darkness." I looked up at him, not sure what to say, I had never received a compliment so beautiful, and at the same time so backwards, in my life.

"Uh, noted..." I said. "You shouldn't be so hard on yourself, though, Alaric. I don't think you are a bad person. You've only ever been kind to me."

He scoffed, a sharp and derisive noise full of bitterness. "I am the worst kind of person, Small One. The very worst. Now sleep, if you are tired." He slid us down so that we were in a comfortable sleeping arrangement.

"I don't think you're so bad. I bet you never wore the skulls of babies on your belt," I muttered sleepily into his chest and I swear he flinched at my words. I frowned and tried to raise my head to look at him, but his hand pressed me down firmly, yet still gently, to his chest.

"Sleep," he urged, his lips moving in a warm caress against my forehead, and I did, like magic.

CHAPTER FOURTEEN

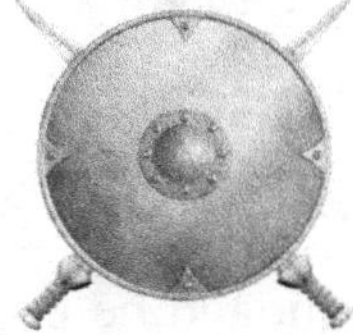

I ground my teeth in frustration at Jared.

"I don't see the problem here," Jared was saying. "You live in a secured building."

"Except that didn't stop Volund's creepy-ass driver from knocking on my apartment door, Jared! My lobby door locks, but people piggyback in all the time! Just don't give out my apartment number ever again! It's all I'm asking. Building address, fine, cellphone number, ok, but *never, ever* hand my apartment number out, no matter how many dollar signs are circling your head!" I crossed my arms over my chest defiantly. Jared looked taken aback.

"You think I would compromise your safety over money?" he asked, frowning.

"Sure feels like it," I said and felt a little guilty at his crestfallen expression.

"Gracelyn, I don't know what to say." He put his hands on the hips of his light Dockers and looked down at his loafers.

"Say you won't give out my apartment number to random investors," I said.

He had the grace to look embarrassed.

"I won't give out your apartment number to anyone, ever again. I'm sorry. I owe you an apology. Let me make this up to you?"

He was looking hopeful, I grew instantaneously suspicious.

"What did you have in mind?" I asked.

"Let me take you out for drinks tomorrow night." He raised an eyebrow.

"Jared, I don't know..." I began, and he popped his glasses off his face and pinched the bridge of his nose, closing his eyes and letting out a gusty sigh.

"Okay, well, consider it both an apology and a celebratory drink then. Strictly professional."

My brow wrinkled in confusion. "Why would we be celebrating?" I asked.

"Because Volund Equities just donated a few million to further our research." He smiled, a huge grin, and my eyebrows shot up in surprise.

"A few *million?*" I repeated.

"Single largest donation yet. I don't know what you said, Gracelyn, but it must have impressed him a whole hell of a lot." He was smiling ear to ear, polishing a lens of his glasses on the tail of his white oxford shirt.

"I think he wants to try and date me or something," I muttered.

Jared frowned and opened his mouth to say something.

"I shot him down," I continued before he could say it. "Told him I'd be happy to keep him appraised on how things were progressing with the project. I don't mix business with my personal life, *ever.*" I gave Jared a pointed look and shivered internally when he gave me a look entirely too reminiscent of the one Volund had given me as I exited his fancy car the night before.

"Of course," he said, and the tone was more-than-slightly-dejected as he realized there really was no chance. Unlike Volund's, Jared's expression had turned from deciding if I were a challenge to take on to something resembling chagrined defeat. I nodded and turned on my heel, going back to my bench and to continue the delicate work of removing that which obstructed the raised runes on the hilt of the Viking sword perched on its top.

Could it be a name?

How weird would it be if it was? How exciting would it be if it was? I sat down and pulled on gloves, coming up for air long after everyone else had gone home. I had two full runes uncovered and it looked as if there might be more.

I stretched the kinks out of my back and quickly wrapped things up and hurried home. I wanted to see Alaric, it was all I could think about. So, you can imagine my dismay when I approached my apartment to see the sleek Rolls Royce idling at the curb.

Gunnar Volund himself exited the back with a bouquet of lavender roses in his large hand, his tailored suit framed by an expensive-looking camel hair trench coat. I swallowed hard and stepped forward, keys in my hand, at the ready, though what he might do on a busy sidewalk I didn't know. He came forward with the flowers and held them out to me.

"My sincerest apologies," he said, and I furrowed my brow.

"For what?" I asked, making no move as of yet to take the flowers.

"I was under the impression I made you uncomfortable last night. It was not my intent." He held out the flowers again and I sighed, taking them.

"Thank you, they're lovely." I smiled.

"Would you allow me the privilege of taking you to dinner again, before I return to my home country?" he asked, his eyes roaming my face, searching it for answers.

"I will have to think about it," I said. "Though I have to say, I am extraordinarily grateful for your generous donation to our project." For that, my smile was nothing but genuine.

A smile curved his lips in response to mine.

"I will call you by phone at the beginning of next week, yes?" he asked.

"Sure, that would be fine," I assented. He inclined his head and got back into his car. I watched it smoothly pull away from the curb and enter traffic. I quickly entered my building and went upstairs, locking my apartment behind me.

I turned on my kitchen light and found a vase for the roses, filling it and adding the little packet of food that came with them. I spent several minutes arranging them and set them at the center of my little four-person dining table. I skipped dinner and showered and dressed for bed, anxious to see Alaric, hoping he would appear. I dried my hair, braided it swiftly, and pulled on an ivory satin nightgown with white lace edging the hem. It was a halter style and left my back exposed to the dimples in my lower back just above my ass. I contemplated putting something a little more covering on when I heard the rattle of his scale armor in the bedroom. I went in as he straightened from shucking it off.

He looked me over, raking those dimly-glowing red eyes over me. I crossed the toes of my bare feet over each other beneath the hem of my nightgown and tried not to fidget. He seemed pleased.

"Better," he affirmed with a nod.

"Hello to you, too," I breathed. He looked at me and cocked his head to the side, considering.

"Apologies, Small One," he said. I went to the bedside lamp and stopped at his sharp intake of breath.

"What?" I asked, looking over my shoulder. His eyes remained firmly on my exposed back, but he said quickly,

"Do not turn on the light."

I straightened and turned to him.

"Wouldn't you like to see better?" I asked.

"I see perfectly well. Gracelyn, *please*..."

I stepped away from the lamp and the candles in my room flared to life as he pulled his shirt over his head.

"Why no lights, does it hurt your eyes?" I asked.

"No. I do not wish to explain it." He took off his boots, first one and then the other.

"You do not wish to explain a lot of things." I crossed my arms and he stilled, a slight smile curving his lips.

"Ask me a question," he stated dryly.

"Where do you come from?" I asked. It had been the burning question at the forefront of my mind since the moment he had first stepped out of the puddle of irregular shadow on my bedroom floor.

"My encampment," he answered flatly, and I blinked.

"Your encampment," I repeated and he nodded, reaching for the thong securing his leather pants. I straightened to my full height and he smirked, undoing the leather. I kept my eyes on his, which I swore were laughing at me as he deliberately unlaced first one side then the other.

"What did you mean, you were protecting me from myself?" I asked and I was surprised that he answered me this time.

"Did you not find yourself on your roof?" he asked. "Did you not cut your own wrist?" I dropped my eyes to the fresh fat rectangular Band-Aid on the inside of my left wrist. The damn thing itched horribly and the stitches were to come out tomorrow at my doctor's. I couldn't wait for that.

"Yes," I murmured softly and looked up as he peeled out of his form-fitting leather pants. I stopped breathing for a moment, I was sure of it. I quickly looked back into his eyes, blushing furiously. He was smiling from ear to ear, enjoying my awkward discomfort, which ticked me off a little.

"So, you're here to keep me from sleepwalking?" I asked.

"After a fashion," he murmured and lifted the covers, ushering me in.

"What does that mean?" I demanded, crawling over to my side of the bed.

"It means I am here to make certain that the other side plays fair." He got into bed with me and turned on his side to look at me, propping his head on his hand.

"Wait, back up, you're really confusing me," I said.

"I am," he agreed, inclining his head. I frowned at him and was rewarded by his deep rumbling laugh. I wanted to kiss him, partially because I wanted to wipe that smirk off his face, but mostly because I was growing to care about him a great deal. His presence had become a comfort and staved off loneliness from becoming absolute.

"Tell me," I urged, then added, "please." He laid flat and gathered me to him, almost as if he'd read my mind about the whole kiss thing. I tried not to feel rejected, but it was hard.

"There are two sides to everything. Light and dark, good and bad, heaven and earth..." he paused, and it was a long one.

I thought for a moment that he wouldn't continue, but then he did.

"You are familiar with the concept of Heaven and Hell, are you not?" he asked.

I simply nodded, I had been raised Catholic, so I knew.

"You know of the constant battle between light and dark, yes?" he asked and again I nodded.

"Then this should come as no surprise to you." He picked up my hand from where it rested on his stomach and idly entwined our fingers as he went on.

"What the battle comes down to is simple," he murmured. "Souls."

"Souls?" I asked softly, to keep him talking. I mean, I suppose it made sense, but I needed a little bit more.

"Yes, the amount, and the strength of each soul is the deciding factor on which way the scales slide. In which direction the balance shifts. The stronger the souls, the better the outcome for whichever side can claim them," he murmured.

"Okay," I said, when he stopped speaking. I was beginning to feel unnerved. "How, exactly, do I play into all of this?"

"You are a strong soul, Gracelyn Adams, and somewhere along the way you garnered their attention." He held me tighter.

"Whose attention?" I asked, almost afraid to hear the answer, but I was pretty sure I already knew.

"Hell's," he said softly, and I stiffened.

"And whose side are you on?" I asked.

"Once I was a warrior of Lucifer's army, but no more... I fight for the Host now, and for my redemption, but then you were put in my charge."

"What does that mean?" I asked, my voice shaky. What he was saying was fascinating, but at the same time, was it more fantastic than how he'd come to be here?

"It means that I am on *your* side, Gracelyn." He rested his lips on my forehead as he spoke, and the tension drained from my body at the fierce sincerity of his tone.

"So the roof, my wrist..." I asked dully, a cold pit of fear in the bottom of my stomach.

"A demon's last efforts to drive you to madness, to take your own life."

"Ah, suicide." I knew suicide was a sin, had been raised with the knowledge that to take your own life was actually one of the biggest ones; a cardinal sin. Doing so wrote you a one-way ticket into Hell. Do not pass go, do not collect two hundred dollars, you go directly to a world of fire and brimstone and spend an eternity in Hell... a place I didn't want to believe was real, but I had no reason to doubt what Alaric was saying.

"So you're saying suicides are conscripted into Hell's army to fight against the army of Heaven?" I asked, putting things together.

"Yes, and so when it was discovered that demons were driving men mad, coercing them into despair and eventual death by their own hands, that is when Heaven began fighting in a similar fashion," he said.

"So you're saying you're my guardian angel?" I asked, and he barked a laugh.

"Guardian," he rolled the word, as if tasting it like candy. "Yes, I suppose I am that, but do not ever mistake me for an angel, for they are greater than I could ever be." He sounded in awe of them. I lay still against him and tried processing all of this.

"So, what are you, then?" I asked, sleep dragging at my edges. I brought my leg over his and snuggled into his side without thinking, wanting to be closer to his warmth, though I wasn't the type of chilled that it could remedy.

"I am no angel," he said, his voice suddenly strained and pretty soon I could feel why pressing against the top of my thigh. I bit my lip and decided the best course of action would be to ignore it, mostly because I was comfortable, partially because there was no denying I was attracted to him.

"We established that," I said, stifling a yawn.

"Sleep, Small One," he breathed.

"Not until you tell me what you are," I muttered and forced myself to stay awake.

He gave an exasperated sigh.

"I was a man once, and then I died and wasn't a man anymore. Now, please, sleep." He pressed his lips together and would say no more, slowly letting out the breath he was holding as I slipped off into oblivion, safe in his arms.

CHAPTER FIFTEEN

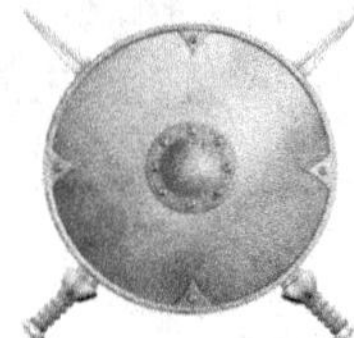

Everyone goes through a point in their life where they wish they were special in some way. Whether it be through an accomplishment, or to be a special someone to someone, it doesn't matter. Everyone wants to be special. So why did my special have to be because my soul appeared extra tasty or looked extra sparkly to some kind of demon horde?

For the first time since his appearance in my apartment, I had not slept well in Alaric's presence. Twice, I had woken from nightmares, and twice he had held me to him, making soothing noises, his calloused palm rubbing aimless circles on my back, until my breath had evened, my tears had stopped flowing, and I drifted once again into a fitful sleep. The last time I'd woken was just before my alarm had gone off, and the first time I had seen him leave. I'd watched as he sank back into the darkness in the corner of my room, his glowing red eyes dimming into the black, the shadows lessening gradually until it was simply the corner of my bedroom again.

I don't think he knew I was awake. I wondered off and on throughout the day, if he had known, then would he have stayed with me?

I had uncovered another half of a rune. This work was painstakingly slow, but it would be worth it, not just if it spelled out a connection to Volund's ancestor either, that's not what I meant. Whatever these runes were, whatever I could uncover enough to decipher, they would be invaluable in a historical context for constructing a clearer picture of who may have owned this sword, or the belief structure of the wielder. It could be so many things.

Jared stopped by my bench as I finished clicking off the lights.

"Are you ready to go?" he asked and smiled, a bit too eagerly.

"Yes." I smiled and tried not to let on how tired I was. He put out an arm, and trying not to read more into it than there was, I took it and we departed the workspace.

We chatted amicably about my sword and theorized what was written on the hilt, laughing and making up silly things as we waited for our table at the little Italian place halfway between the museum and my apartment.

"It's probably something vulgar on par with Roman graffiti," I surmised.

"Speaking as a friend and not a boss, an ode to the wielder's penis perhaps?"

My eyes widened and I didn't even bother to fight down the bubble of laughter that flowed out into an all-out riot of it.

Jared laughed too, and then admitted, "I didn't think it was that funny! Your reaction though, that was gold." He was grinning and I was grinning, and we were taken to our seats.

"Honestly, I almost hope it's our boy Volund's ancestor's name," he said as we sipped our wine and waited for our food.

"Stranger things have happened," I said, and of course my thoughts drifted to Alaric and our conversation of the night before. Stranger things indeed...

"That was an intense thought, whatever it was. Care to share it with me?" he asked. I absently rubbed my wrist beneath its patch of Band-Aid hidden beneath my sleeve. The stitches had come out this morning, but it still itched as it healed.

"Long, long week is all," I successfully lied and pushed back my shoulders.

"What's that?" Jared asked and leaned across the table, his eyes focused on my chin – no, not my chin, on the scale from Alaric's mail.

I brushed it absently with my fingers. "Guitar pick," I lied again, and saw Jared's eyes narrow in suspicion.

"I didn't know you played," he said.

"I don't," I replied, and the silence settled between us, somewhat uneasy. Our food was set between us, and I smiled up to our waiter and thanked him. Jared's eyes were still on me, rather intensely.

"Gracelyn, may I ask you a personal question?" he asked.

I swallowed what I was chewing and looked at him square. 'Strong soul', huh? Well, I think I was about to need that strength.

"You can ask, but I don't promise that I will want to answer." I gave him honesty.

"Fair enough," he answered, composing himself. "Do you not find me attractive?" he asked, and I blinked.

Well, hell, that was forthright, and it *did* deserve an honest answer. I set down my fork and folded my hands.

"Jared, as far as men go you are very attractive. However, to answer your question, while I find you attractive in a physical sense, no, I am not attracted to you. A big part of that is because you are, indeed, my boss." I waited for the hurt, or for the anger, but neither of them came. He seemed to mull this over for a long time.

"If I may be forthright," he said and I nodded my assent. "You are a lovely woman, Gracelyn Adams."

I blushed and opened my mouth to speak but he held up his hand with a pleading look, so I shut my mouth and let him continue.

"I am not just speaking physically, though you are quite attractive to me. I mean you are lovely in that your passion for what we do captivates me. I wish to know you, all of you, and if I cannot do it as your lover, I am here to tell you that I wish to be there for you as a friend. Always." He took a sip of his wine and we sat in silence for several moments.

"Whoever captures your attentions will be a lucky man indeed," he murmured, and I blushed again when my mind drifted immediately to glowing red eyes, spider-silk hair and a certain carved-marble physique.

"Thank you," I murmured at last. "Friends I can do, but I won't do anything else. I can't do anything romantic with you, Jared. I've worked too hard to be where I am to flush it away with a scandal." I met his gaze with mine and was overjoyed to see him smile, even if it was a little sadly.

"Friends it is, then." He raised his glass.

"Friends," I said, and we clinked glasses, and a weight I hadn't known I'd been bearing lifted from my shoulders.

Maybe life after Roxy wouldn't be so bad after all. Maybe I would make new friends and even if it wasn't the same without her, that was still something, yeah?

CHAPTER SIXTEEN

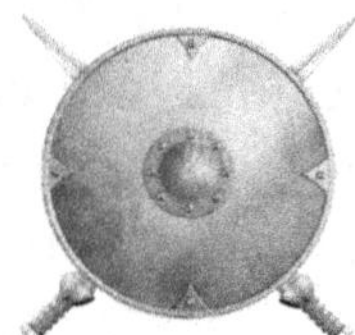

My apartment smelled heavenly of roses when I entered it, and I remembered the lavender roses on my dining table. I went over to them, switching on my little kitchen light over the stove so I could see them. I pulled out my phone and google-searched 'rose meanings' on a whim.

I stood still, an unpleasant creeping sensation crawling up my spine. Lavender roses did not mean an apology. I stared down at the four words and swallowed hard...

Love at first sight.

"Gracelyn, turn out the light." I startled, then rushed to do as Alaric asked.

"What is wrong?" he asked, striding to me, grasping my elbows and looking me over, stepping into my space as if to shield me.

"Nothing," I lied, and plugged in my phone at the wall outlet near my counter.

"Do not lie to me, Small One; I feel your unease." I went back to him abruptly and wound my arms around his waist, laying my head on his chest, the linen of his shirt coarse beneath my cheek. At five-foot-eight, I still fit perfectly beneath his chin. The man was massive.

"I am here. Now, what is it?" he asked. His arms wound around me and he smoothed a hand over my hair, a soothing motion that nearly made me melt.

"I'm probably just overreacting like I did with Jared." I explained about Volund and then about Jared. Alaric listened carefully to all I had to say, standing stoic, simply holding me.

"I do not like this Jared you speak of, but I like this Volund man even less, now. He is ambitious and has a raider's spirit; that which he cannot have, he will take. I do not wish you sullied." He crushed me to him and I closed my eyes.

You can sully me any day of the week and twice on Sunday, thank you very much, I thought to myself.

Alaric pulled back to look at me, face impassive and I blushed and wondered to myself, *Did he hear me?* I stood still while he scrutinized me, his mouth pulling down in displeasure or dismay. I looked down and realized what I was wearing was the cause, black slacks, charcoal blouse, and a black cardigan.

"I should go change," I said.

"I shall draw you a bath."

"A shower would be quicker," I said to his retreating back.

"Yes, but I wish to draw you a bath," he called lightly over his shoulder before disappearing into my tiny bathroom. The sound of my clawfoot tub filling filtered out to me. I went into my bedroom and selected a light mint-green satin nightgown from the drawer and turned to see Alaric watching me from the doorway. His arms were crossed and he leaned against the door frame nonchalantly, one boot propped on its toes in front of the other leg. I smiled at how relaxed he looked.

"So what are you going to do while I'm in there?" I asked.

"Join you," was his short and very serious reply. I swallowed the sudden lump in my throat. Maybe he *had* heard my thoughts.

"Okay," I whispered, laying the nightgown on the end of my bed.

I hung up my cardigan while he took off his boots. I chewed my lower lip a moment and unthreaded the slender black belt from my slacks, hanging it on its peg at the side of my closet. He was working his shirt over his head and I was suddenly glad all my bras and underwear were lacy and pretty, one of those confidence boosters, you know? I peeled out of my blouse, reached down and unzipped my boots, stepping out of them and peeling off my socks. I slid my slacks down my legs and stepped out of them, tossing the entire bundle in my hamper which was half-hidden by hanging clothes in my closet. Alaric was watching me, stoic and unreadable, hands frozen at the ties on his leathers.

"Is something wrong?" I asked.

"I am a man still, in many ways," was his hushed reply. He shook his head as if waking from a dream and peeled out of the leather pants. I didn't bother to hide my confusion, but decided to let it go because honestly, the only thing that sounded better than a bath right now was a bath with Alaric. I was suddenly glad of the large old clawfoot, because it had a hope of accommodating both of us. For once, it was going to be a boon. Usually, its size meant that I would just spend that much more time cleaning the thing.

I tossed my bra and panties into the laundry and fetched clean towels out of the hall closet, clutching them to my front. His hands descended on my shoulders.

"Do not hide from me," he murmured and the tension in my shoulders eased when his lips met the back of one. His hands slid from my shoulders, caressing down my arms before leaving my skin. A pleasant tingling was left in their wake as if my body had come alive from his touch. He stepped back, and the cooler air of the apartment swept over my skin in the absence of his warmth. I shivered and went across the hall, into the bathroom lit with candles.

I set the towels on the closed lid of my john and heard the water slosh as he got into the tub. I turned around and he was settled, holding out a hand to me. I took one of my arms off from covering my chest and let him help me down in between his legs, leaning back into him, the water rising dangerously but not quite to spilling over from the displacement of our bodies. I turned off the tap with my foot and lay back against him.

His hands drifted to my shoulders and kneaded the tight muscles along my neck. I groaned in pure bliss and closed my eyes.

"This is nice," I murmured, and my voice came out huskier than I intended.

"Agreed." The bass rumble from his chest vibrated along my spine and things gave a pleasurable little throb low in my body. I let him turn me to pudding, and sighed in contentment, which I was surprised he echoed.

"When did you die?" I asked quietly, curious, and picking up our conversation from the night before.

"Hmm? Long, long, ago. I understand your modern calendar now, someone explained it to me." His arms crossed over my chest and he cradled me against him.

"So, how long ago?" I asked.

He was so evasive.

"It was around your year nine hundred and eighty-four, if the mathematics are correct." My breath stilled in my lungs... *The late tenth century, incredible.*

"How?" I asked.

"In battle," he said, uneasily, and I swallowed any further questions for now.

"I see," I murmured and did my best to let it go. This was entirely too nice and I didn't want to ruin it.

"You have many questions, Small One. Why can I not simply enjoy the time I have with you?" he asked, an almost echo of my own thinking.

I cocked my head to the side, craning my neck back as far as it would go to look up at him, looking down at me.

"Can you read my mind?" I asked.

"No."

I narrowed my eyes, playfully suspicious and was rewarded with his smile, which was quite endearing.

"How come you never ask any questions about me?" I asked.

"I have watched you for a very long time; I do not believe there is anything I do not know about you," he murmured quietly. Still, the vibration of his bass voice through his chest and along my spine made me want to go into delicious shivers.

"Oh, yeah? What's my favorite flavor of ice cream?" I asked and he quirked an eyebrow.

"I do not know what that is."

"You don't know what ice cream is?"

He raised that eyebrow slightly higher like, *'Really, Gracelyn?'* and I laughed.

"No, I suppose that was after your time."

"Go on, ask another," he said, his hands smoothing down my arms, his fingers finding the spaces between mine, his palms engulfing the backs of my hands. I sighed happily and let my head drop back onto his chest. I was getting a crick, holding it like I was to see him.

"My favorite color?" I asked, and he moved our entwined hands so that his arms were around me and I was hugging myself, too. He didn't answer, silently pondering the question and I smiled.

"See, you don't know everything," I said, victoriously.

"I know what matters," he murmured, his lips brushing the shell of my ear, sending a wash of delicious tingles sweeping down my neck and further down my shoulder and arm. "I know the beauty you harbor within yourself; that it is only a fraction of what is reflected on the outside. I know your passion for your work, the depth of feeling you have for those around you. I know you are bold, unafraid, and that your heart is always visible in your eyes. There are many times you could have been broken, should have been broken, but you are resilient. A true warrior spirit. I admire you, Gracelyn Adams, I see you for who you really are. What else is there that I need to know?"

I didn't know what to say. My eyes misted with his beautiful words, and truthfully, I didn't feel worthy of such praise, but there it was, and, ever the polite daughter my parents and grandparents raised me to be, I said the only thing that came to mind.

"Thank you. You're being too kind."

He chuckled.

"'Kind' is something I have never been accused of being." He heaved a great sigh, my whole body rising and falling with the motion of it.

"Are you ready to get out?" I asked.

"No. Are you?"

"No," I murmured back, and so we stayed until the water grew tepid and I was all but a prune.

CHAPTER SEVENTEEN

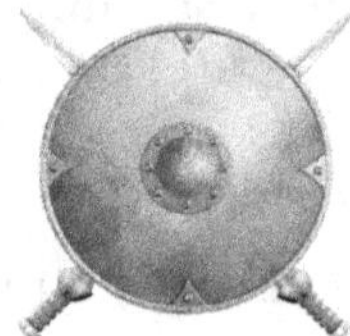

I wrapped a towel around my hair after stepping out of the shower. After the tub had drained, I'd showered to get my hair clean. Alaric had stood in the bathroom doorway and we'd talked; he'd asked me what ice cream was. I'd spent the time it took to soap, rinse and condition my hair explaining in great detail how ice cream was made and how different things could be added to it to make different flavors. He'd stood there, mystified, and that had tickled me to no end.

"So, what is your favorite flavor?" he asked nonchalantly, and I grinned.

"I thought it didn't matter," I teased, slipping my nightgown over my head, letting the towel fall from beneath it. *Modesty preserved*, although it was probably a moot point, seeing as I'd just taken a bath with him and he'd been nude in my bed with me for almost a week now.

"It does not, but I am curious now."

He pulled back the blankets on my bed and I got in.

"Black Cherry Amaretto; Häagen-Dazs makes it," I said, climbing in.

"What is Amaretto?" he asked, sliding in beside me.

"A sort-of almond-tasting Italian liqueur," I answered, then asked, "What do you like?"

"Venison and mead; bread warm from the hearth." He settled and raised his arm so that I could cuddle close in what was becoming our typical fashion. I yawned and settled against him.

"What was it like?" I asked. "Way back then?"

I was unable to suppress my curiosity any longer. It was a miracle I'd suppressed it this long.

"It was then as it is now, brutal..." he began. I listened to him as he spoke of harsh winters in a new settlement, of life under the rule of his father, and of battles fought and lives lost over greed and honor.

It was fascinating as well as sorrowful and horrific. To listen first-hand to his accounting of conditions left me feeling both low and utterly grateful to be born in the twentieth century and to be a part of the twenty-first.

It also brought home the realization that, though he didn't look over the age of twenty-five or so, in his time, Alaric had been at his peak, and was one of the unlucky fifty-percent of men to die between the ages of twenty-one and thirty. Still, if he'd managed to survive past his thirty-first year, he would have been considered in the twilight of his prime and by age forty would have been in the twilight of his years. Not many men lived past the age of fifty, which was considered old just before the early Middle Ages. Today, fifty is considered middle-aged, period, for most.

"What is it that has you thinking so hard I can almost hear it?" he asked and I smiled.

"We have it easy in this day and age," I said.

"Yes."

"I'm sorry life was so hard for you."

"Do not be. I do not deserve such a sentiment. I was not what could be considered a good man."

"That was then, Alaric. This is now, and you've been pretty good to me." I pushed myself up and laid a gentle kiss at the corner of his mouth, which was better than his chin, which was the only other thing I could reach at this angle. He flinched and I lay back down; his expression grew distant and I worried I'd done something wrong. He smoothed a hand over my hair and I was reassured.

"Sleep now, Small One." His voice was low and troubled.

"Okay. Goodnight, Alaric."

"Goodnight, Gracelyn," he purred, and I stopped fighting it and fell fast asleep, warm and safe.

CHAPTER EIGHTEEN

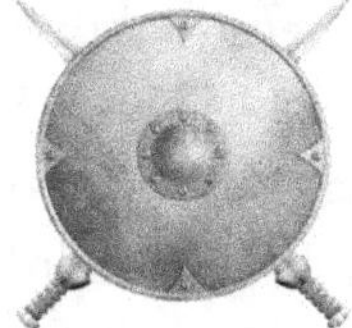

Saturday dawned a little warmer than it had been lately, and for the first Saturday in a long while, I felt enough energy to go run. I dressed appropriately for the weather in my cold-weather running gear, chuckling as I pulled on the black Under Armor cold gear compression leggings. I pulled on a royal blue, moisture wicking, long-sleeved, mock-neck top and pulled it down over my lean hips. I tugged on my socks and running shoes, lacing them up tight.

Running gloves, with my spare apartment door keys in a secret compartment on the heel of my left palm, and I was almost ready to go. My hair hung over my shoulder in a long braid and I added a black fleece band that wrapped around my head and covered my ears, tucking the earbuds from my headphones under it and into my ears. I plugged them into my phone and started the music playing before pulling on my black runner's hoodie. I slipped my thumbs through the loops in the sleeves and zipped it up the front, tucking my phone into the pocket on my upper arm where it was meant to go, and finally was ready to make like a baby and head out! Okay, yeah, that was crude and corny, but whatever.

I locked up behind myself, did some stretches in the hallway, took the stairs down to the lobby in a light warm-up and stretched some more before going out into the cold. It was rough going at first, but I soon found my rhythm. My breath plumed the air as I exhaled, and I turned into Central Park after several blocks of fast-paced power-walking along the sidewalk being jostled by other city-goers. I broke into a longer stride once I reached the running path and the press of bodies was quickly left behind.

My lungs burned with cold as I ran and it took me longer than usual, from my couple of weeks of inactivity, to really find my zone, but soon enough, I was settled comfortably into a runner's high. I was enjoying the euphoria as I passed dog walkers, mothers and strollers, and the occasional old couple out for a walk when I caught sight of a man in a suit standing by the path; a very familiar, very tall man in a very expensive suit. I slowed to a cool-down walk and Gunnar Volund fell into step beside me.

"Mr. Volund, what are you doing here?" I asked, between breaths.

"I was told I must see Central Park before leaving the city. I had time before my next meeting. It is magnificent." He smiled, but it was wooden to me.

"Yeah it's pretty impressive," I muttered, but what I was thinking was *Yeah right, you just happened to decide to check out Central Park as I ran by?* I grimaced inwardly at what I was thinking, it did sound awfully damned paranoid. It probably really was just a coincidence.

"You are through with your run?" he asked, eyeing me.

"Yeah, I think so." I had my breath mostly back and was stretching my quads, bringing my heel to my ass and grabbing the front of my running shoe with my gloved hand.

"Would you care to join me for an early lunch?" he asked.

I tried to think of a way to decline and came up empty.

"Sure," I finally caved. "As long as it's no place fancy," I amended, looking down at my runner's gear. If I took off my hoodie, there would be obvious and unattractive sweat stains and my hair was thoroughly damp at my temples and the nape of my neck.

He chuckled, his hands in the pockets of his very expensive-looking gray trench coat and looked me over like he was imagining what was underneath. It was creepy, and I plastered on a polite smile.

"Do you know of a place nearby?" he asked.

"There's a really good coffee house and café near here." I jerked my head in the general direction and he fell into step beside me.

"Did you uncover anything new this week?" he asked.

"Yeah, actually, a couple more runes. It'll still be a while before I can piece anything together to send out for translation, if there's even enough there," I said. "Jared and I were speculating what they might say last night."

The moment the words left my mouth I wished I'd never uttered them. Volund's eyes went dark the way the sky does when a thunderhead rolls in. I shivered, and his perfect mask slipped back in place.

"Oh?" He sounded innocent enough, but my alarm bells had already started clanging in my skull.

"Do you and Mr. Worth share a relationship outside of work?" He leveled his gaze on me, and I laughed and hoped it didn't sound as nervous as I felt.

"No, not at all. Jared is my boss, and after years of working together, maybe my friend, but no more." I waved my hands back and forth in front of me by way of emphasis. "I try to keep my work and personal lives as separate as possible." There, I had said it.

That feral look was back on his face, like I'd just upped the challenge for him with my declaration.

"I see, so you and Mr. Worth are not, ah, seeing each other?" he asked plainly.

"No, most definitely not," I answered, my mouth dry.

Again, "I see," was his only answer to what I'd said.

I cringed inwardly and thought to myself, *Well played; you may have gotten me to admit I wasn't involved with Jared, but that doesn't mean I'm not seeing someone.*

I led the way mutely, crossing the street in the direction of the café I'd mentioned, the gears of my mind whirring and clicking at a furious pace. True, I wasn't seeing Jared, but how exactly could I imply that I was seeing Alaric?

Well, you know, Gunnar, I may not be diddling my boss, but I am sleeping beside a giant of an albino man with glowing red eyes who died in 984, every night. I have to think he likes me. I mean, he's been in my bed every night this week... naked. We even took a bath together!

I choked down a bubble of hysterical laughter. Maybe I was insane. I felt my chest constrict with my self-doubt. Maybe I had been dreaming Alaric all along... I reached for the scale and grasped it beneath my shirt, comforted by the outline of its edge against the restrictive material. I led Volund into the crowded café and took up a little two-seater table by the front window. A waitress came by and took our order; I went with a salad. I needed something light after running, and would get something more substantial later.

"Tell me about yourself, please," he said as soon as our waitress left us.

"Ah, well, I hold a Master's Degree in the Science of Historic Preservation, and I, uh, I'm certified by The Academy of Certified Archivists. I'm twenty-nine years old and moved to New York City from Connecticut when I was twenty-five when the museum I am working for now reached out to me with a job offer." I drank deeply from my water glass.

"I asked for you to tell me about yourself. While your resume is impressive, I was hoping for a little more insight into Gracelyn the woman, not the historical preservationist." He smiled and it wasn't unkind, but rather as if he were trying to be patient with me.

"I... I, uh..."

Truth was, I didn't know what to say.

"My parents are dead," I finally blurted.

"Oh?" he asked. No look of sympathy, no empathetic platitude, just a cock of his head and a curious look that made my insides twist with a mixture of fear and revulsion. As pretty to look at as this man was on the outside, I was pretty damned sure ice water flowed through his veins.

"Car accident, I was thirteen," was the only elaboration I was willing to give him. Something about him was off, way off, and I just wanted our food to come, so I could eat and go my separate way as quickly as possible.

"Where did you go?" he asked.

"My grandparents on my mother's side took me in," I replied as the waitress came back with our food. She was getting a huge tip for promptness from me.

"No siblings?" he asked.

"Only child."

I put my napkin in my lap and drizzled salad dressing over my greens from the little cup they provided on the side. He picked up his sandwich and took a healthy bite. His charming mask back in place, he smiled at me. I returned it and munched happily on my garden salad. If I was busy eating, then I wasn't talking, which seemed to be toward my benefit with this man.

It was about then, and too late to do me any good, I might add, that I realized I'd pretty much just admitted to this predatory man that I was in New York alone with no nearby family. Even if my grandparents lived in the city, which they didn't, an old couple in their late seventies wasn't much to get around.

For the first time I found myself wishing Alaric were a normal man and someone I could really be with. I didn't really know what we were to each other, I mean, friends didn't sleep nude night after night, or bathe together. We hadn't so much as kissed, either, so 'lovers' sure wasn't what you'd call us. He'd called me 'his charge', and he certainly acted as if he were my guardian. I sighed and felt the disappointment cloud my heart. I really didn't know what I was dealing with when it came to Alaric, but at the same time, it was as clear as day to me that he had my best interests at heart... I mean, didn't he?

"You look sad," Volund observed.

"I get that way, sometimes, when I think about them." It wasn't exactly a lie; I did miss my mom and dad, and I did get the occasional pang of sadness, but for the most part, thoughts of them brought me comfort and happiness. I'd had a good childhood growing up. Even after they were gone, my grandparents' efforts at making up for them being gone had been nothing short of spectacular. We all knew it wasn't the same, but Grandma and Pappy Wright had been at every school debate, every science fair, and every track meet. They hadn't missed a thing, even with Pappy's failing health. He'd passed when I was in college.

"Your parents?" Volund's smooth voice broke my reverie.

"Yeah." I put on a false smile. He smiled back, and this time it reached his eyes.

"Tell me about them?"

I did. They were gone, and I loved them, and was proud of them, so what could it hurt?

"My father was an engineer, my mother was his high school sweetheart and worked at a daycare. She had a degree in early child development and education. That worked out well for them because after I was born, I just went to work with my mom. It meant free daycare for them and plenty of other kids to play with for me." I smiled, and was surprised to see what appeared to be a genuine curve of his lips that warmed his eyes from chips of ice to warm spring skies. It was when he looked like that, that I could see him as Gunnar, rather than Mr. Volund, or just Volund, in my mind. I wondered briefly what might have happened to him to make him so cold and to want to emulate his horrible Viking ancestor so much.

"Your mother. That is where you get your kind nature?" he asked.

I blushed.

"I suppose so. I know I got my love of science from my dad. He was always explaining things to me and was always so excited. He would take me up on the roof of our house in the summertime and set up his telescope, and we would spend hours up there, staring at the sky, and planets, and make up stories about how life was on other worlds until my mom would call us into the house again." My eyes became unfocused and I stared out the window, belatedly realizing they were misting up with the fond memory.

"What about you?" I asked and tried to subtly dash the moisture away. He wiped his mouth with his napkin and turned his neck to the side until it gave an audible pop. It was the first sign of discomfort I'd ever seen him display.

"I grew up in a privileged home."

I waited for more, but none came.

"And?" I prompted, resuming the demolition of my salad.

"My father is a great man. I made him proud the day I built my empire." The ice was back in his expression, his lips curved into that unsettling feral grin. "I do not know how he felt when I crushed his business beneath my own, but to me it felt good. I rivaled his greatness and using what he taught me, surpassed it. Our ancestor would be proud."

And the monster was back. I wished he'd stayed away...

"What about your mother?" I asked quietly.

"Like me, my mother was but a decoration for my father. Something pretty to be seen with, to have on his arm." He waved a dismissive hand in the air. His accent had thickened when he talked about his family, his mother, especially. I think he may have felt more for her.

"What was she like?" I asked, and his expression shut down.

"I do not wish to speak on this anymore," he said, and the tone of his voice was final.

"All right," I murmured. So, Gunnar Volund had daddy issues. Interesting. Something had definitely happened. I wasn't sure I wanted to get close enough to find out what. Something about the large Dane scared the shit out of me and set the warning bells in my head to clanging, and after he spoke about crushing his father's business, the expression on his face, well, the air-raid sirens were adding their wail, and red flashing lights were there, too.

I suddenly wanted to go home and take a long, hot shower.

Gunnar Volund was obviously a man who was used to getting what he wanted, and I was beginning to think my paranoia of earlier wasn't so paranoid. I finished my water and excused myself to the restroom. I took a few minutes to get my wits about me. When I came out, the pleasant mask was back on Volund's face and our bill was paid.

"I will see you home," he said, with that perfect smile on his lips that went nowhere near his icy blue eyes.

"Oh, that's okay, I'll walk." I smiled back.

"Nonsense, this New York City of yours, I understand it has crime, violent, not like Denmark. You would be a prize to this criminal element." He held out his arm.

"I've lived in the city for over four years, no trouble yet." I laughed and his expression hardened.

"I insist," he declared, and rather than make a scene, I took his arm.

We stepped out onto the sidewalk and sure enough, there was the black town car, Maximillian holding the door open, his expression grim. He looked at me and, I swear to God, flinched. I slid into the back seat, perturbed. We rode in silence to my building. I opened the car door before Maximillian could get out to open it for me. I smiled sweetly at Volund and thanked him for lunch.

"I will call on you early in the week about that dinner," he said, and I nodded, my eyes felt a little wide. I wanted to go to dinner with him as much as I wanted to shoot a lethal dose of heroin.

"Of course, I look forward to it," I answered and rushed to my building's lobby door, slipping one of the hidden keys from the palm of my glove and letting myself in. I turned and waved as if nothing was wrong and Volund grinned at me like a fox from the back seat of the town car through its window. I suppressed a shudder and got into the elevator, letting it whisk me to my floor, my lunch surging and pressing threateningly at the base of my throat.

There would be no dinner with Volund and I was beginning to not care if I had to be rude about it.

CHAPTER NINETEEN

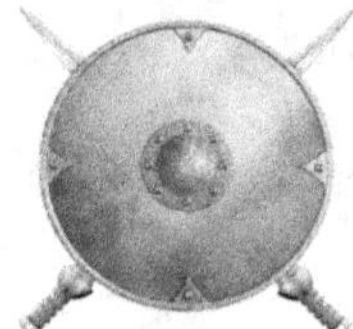

laric didn't come that night. It was the first night since he'd first appeared that he didn't show, and I stood in the center of my bedroom at three in the morning and wrung my hands. Was it something I had said? Had I done something to make him not want to come? I really wanted to tell him about Volund, to get his thoughts on the situation. Well, mostly I just wanted to know I wasn't imagining things. The last time I'd told him about the man, he'd said he didn't like him; that he was ambitious; and that if he couldn't have something he wanted, he would take it. Those were pretty much precisely my thoughts on the subject, too, but it bothered me I had no one to voice them to.

I paced back and forth across my bedroom floor and chewed my lower lip, rolling it under my teeth until I could taste copper from doing it too much. I scrubbed my face with my hands and grasped the scale from his armor. With a final sigh I got into bed and lay there, worrying about him.

"Where are you?" I asked my silent bedroom. I sighed after long moments, and murmured into the dark, "Well, wherever you are, I hope you're safe."

I closed my eyes and fell into a restless sleep full of dreams that made no sense but were still terrifying.

CHAPTER TWENTY

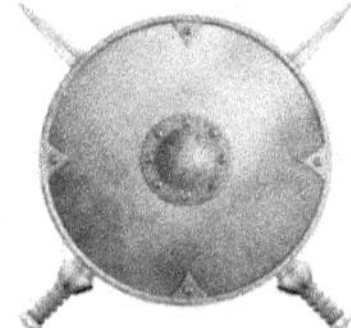

*S*unday was sorta rough. I woke in a pretty foul mood and decided to hole up in my apartment with a book. I was so not fit for public consumption, being a terrible Ms. Grumpy Pants. I read, took a nap, ordered some takeout for dinner and binge-watched the entire first season of *Treasure Quest* on my Kindle huddled in comfortable warm clothes on the end of my couch. I was really disappointed to find out that there hadn't been a season two of the show. It had been fascinating, all about recovering historical finds off the ocean floor using deep sea remotely operated vehicles, or ROVs. Granted, they were looking for treasure, not history, but the crew had a deep appreciation for the history involved with their finds, too, and I felt kindred with some of them.

I sighed as I moved around my small kitchen, cleaning up after my takeout meal, and froze.

Had I heard that or was it just my imagination?

I stood still, ears straining and there was no mistaking the heavy thud of scale on my bedroom carpet. I shot around the corner into my small hallway and caught a glimpse of his large black clad frame moving the mail out of the center of my carpet.

"You didn't come last night."

I couldn't keep the edge of hurt out of my voice. He turned and sadness crossed his features for a split second.

"I told you, it could not always be so." His voice was soft as fur, his eyes flaring, the light growing then dimming from some unknown emotion. I went to him and wrapped my arms around his waist and hugged myself to him. There was no hugging him to me, he wouldn't be moved unless he wanted to be moved, but that was okay. That was just Alaric. His arms went around me after a moment and he enfolded me against his chest with an unidentifiable sigh.

"I was worried about you."

My voice was muffled by his large chest, but he'd heard me. He drew back and looked down at me a solemn expression on his face.

"Truly?" he asked.

"Yeah. Why wouldn't I be?" I asked, then went on with, "You come to me most nights wearing armor, with a weapon strapped to you. I know you fight something, somewhere. I'm not stupid. When you didn't come, I was scared something had happened to you." I was surprised to feel the prick of tears at the backs of my eyes.

"I would never think you a stupid woman, Small One." His long fingers tipping up my chin, he smoothed his thumbs across my cheeks, wiping my tears away.

"I was well, no harm befell me on the battlefield. I was..." he stopped, thought better of whatever it was he was going to say, and then finished with, "...There was another matter that needed my attention."

"Okay."

I knew better than to pry, his expression had closed down enough to tell me that it would get me nowhere. He let go of my chin and hugged me to him, his lips resting on the crown of my head.

"I bought ice cream," I said, my voice once again muffled against his chest.

He smelled good. Masculine, warm and spicy, with that edge of burning metal. His laugh was rich and rumbled through his chest, and it was like being drenched in a fall of dark chocolate. It made me smile. The candles flared to life in my bedroom. I'd replaced them all and added more in anticipation of his arrival yesterday. In fact, I had candles in every room of my small dwelling. Bathroom, bedroom, kitchen, dining area, and living room. I gave a gentle but excited tug on his hand in the direction of my kitchenette, but he was unmovable.

I'd done quite a bit of shopping after I'd showered and changed from my run the day before. After paying my bills on my trusty laptop, which rested at my dining table, I'd gone out and bought candles, some more candle holders, as well as ice cream and one other surprise.

"Turn out the light," he said, shying back from the doorway.

"Oh! Right."

I went out into my kitchen and turned out the electric light I'd been cleaning up by. He came out of my bedroom and looked around, noting the candles. His lips twitched with a barely suppressed smile and they winked to life. I smiled and took the ice cream out of the freezer. A pint of Häagen-Dazs Dark Cherry Amaretto Gelato. I peeled off the plastic cellophane holding the small carton closed and pulled off the cardboard top. He looked down at me, a frown wrinkling his brow as I dished it into two bowls.

Grinning, I handed him one and a spoon, which looked very, very small in his large hand. I took a bite of my ice cream, the rich flavor dissolving over my tongue and he followed my example. I laughed out loud at the expressions that played over his face.

First, there was sort of this *What the...?* look at the cold, then his eyes widened and flared a bit brighter in surprise, then, my favorite one of all, his eyes became hooded in pleasure as the flavors played out.

"That was seriously the most fun I have had watching you so far," I said. He swallowed and cocked his head to the side considering me.

"Oh! Wait! I have one more thing." I went to the fridge and opened it, retrieving the bottle. I shut the door on the tail end of his sharp intake of breath. I turned around to see his hand raised in front of his face. Oh, crap, the light.

"Sorry," I mumbled.

Excitement had gotten the better of me; I had to remember next time. I wasn't sure what it was about electrical lights that got to him, but I was distracted pretty quickly by my new mission.

"What is that?" he asked around another mouthful of ice cream.

"You'll see." I used a corkscrew to open the bottle and brought down two wine glasses.

"I'm not sure how it's going to taste with cherry amaretto ice cream, or how it compares with how it was back then, but I figured if I was going to make you taste something that was a favorite of mine, well, turnabout is fair play."

I turned and held out one of the glasses. Alaric's look was one of pure suspicion. He set down his mostly-empty bowl and I picked up my glass. He smelled the liquid in his and his expression was one of awe.

"Is this...?" he trailed off and I nodded, grinning. He closed his eyes and breathed deep.

"It was, surprisingly, easier to find than I thought it would be," I said. He opened his eyes and his face was very serious as he regarded me.

"Drink," he commanded, spearing me with his gaze, and I didn't even hesitate.

I took a mouthful. He moved lightning-fast, closing the gap between us, his fingers curling around the back of my head and his mouth crashing down over mine, and he invaded my mouth before I even had the chance to swallow.

My wine glass crashed to the floor and I knotted my fists in the front of his shirt – but not to push him away, oh no. I pulled myself flush against him and kissed him back.

The mead was sweeter than I expected it to be and complimented the burn of alcohol that came with it. Rich, complex, and full-bodied, that was how Alaric tasted, and a moan escaped my throat, one that he swallowed greedily as he kissed me like he was going to devour me from the mouth down. He pulled back abruptly and I staggered in place.

"Holy cow!" I blurted.

He growled and turned away from me.

"I should not have done that," he grated.

"I'm glad you did."

The small kitchen was filled with the sound of our mutual heavy breathing. We stared at each other for long moments and the small space between us suddenly felt as if it were a yawning chasm.

"That will not happen again," he said, and looked stricken.

"I really want it to."

"Gracelyn –"

I went to him, halting whatever it was he was about to say by wrapping my arms around his waist, resting my head against his broad back.

"I mean it," I said. "I want this, I want you more than anything I've ever wanted in my life."

He turned and I backed off enough to let him, stepping into his embrace to look up at him even as he searched my face, his own emotions completely unreadable.

"It cannot be between us," he murmured and he pursed his lips to keep from saying more, his expression shifting from unreadable to pained.

"What? Why?" I asked, my heart breaking from the look on his face.

Could he get in trouble? If he did, what would happen?

"It is forbidden, but I have been careful," he said. "I have avoided all suspicion to this point, but understand me, Gracelyn; I should not be here, it goes against every code, but I..." he looked so frustrated and it tore me apart. "I could not resist being near you. When I thought you may have been lost, when the demon entered the physical realm to coerce you into doing those things, to drive you mad, you fought so well! So stubborn, a warrior's will, unbreakable. I could not resist. I destroyed him and I came to you." He set his glass on the counter and looked almost ashamed. "I was weak," he finished.

I stood there for a long time trying to process. Finally, I stooped and began cleaning up the shards of glass from my floor. He knelt beside me and took my hands between his own. The glass I had collected fell back to the floor with a few sad musical chimes.

"Say something." His brow was creased in worry.

"You're one of the best things to ever happen to me."

My eyes welled with tears; if what he was saying was true, our time together could end at any moment. I didn't even spare a thought to what could or would happen to me, I was more scared for him, and I said as much.

"If they, whoever they are, find out what's going to happen to you?" I asked, those tears collecting in my lower lashes, causing his image to blur.

He pulled me up into his arms against his chest and sat down. Long legs out in front of him, down the narrow length of my kitchen tile, his leather pants shielding his leg from the spilled mead and broken glass, he pulled me into his lap, but I twisted, straddling him so I could see him clearly.

"Don't cry, please. I am not worth your tears, Small One."

I gasped in outrage and pounded a fist rather ineffectually against his chest. It was more to make a point than anything.

"How can you say that!?" I cried. "You're worth everything to me!"

"It is ever the truth," he murmured and tucked me back against him.

I huddled there, miserable and frustrated with his evasive lack of answers. He was right about one thing. I was a fighter, and I wasn't about to give him up without one. I pressed my mouth against his and he made a surprised sound but didn't stop me.

"If this could end at any moment, then I want to make every moment count," I said breathless with emotion.

He closed his eyes and finally nodded once, and I brought my mouth back to his. He kissed me and I held onto him and we let our emotions carry us. This kiss was something gentler, building slowly like a flame that was struggling to catch. We warmed ourselves by it, holding onto each other until Alaric's hands drifted to his leather pants and worked frantically between us to unlace them. He was hard. I could feel him pressed between our bodies, his cock begging to be freed and I understood the sentiment.

I gathered my nightgown with my fingers, hitching it up my thighs and planted my knees against the tile floor. A piece of glass dug sharply into my shin, but I didn't care. Alaric freed himself and I moaned into his mouth as the scorching, silken flesh of his cock grazed my inner thigh. He wrapped one strong arm around my lower back and I rose up on my knees a little more.

God, the feel of him pressed against my pussy's lips, sliding along my slit towards that ultimate goal was enough to drive me crazy. With a small excited cry from my lips, he pressed against my opening and I let myself drop carefully, taking him inside me, gliding down the length of him until our bodies met. I closed my eyes, even though I wanted badly to watch him, because the feel of him was near overwhelming. He was longer than any man I had ever had before, which wasn't saying much. I hadn't had many lovers before him. He was thicker, too, stretching me nearly to the point of pain.

He tore his mouth from mine and gasped when he was rooted as deeply as he could go inside me and I smiled, biting my swollen bottom lip, my breath rushing out of me in a close to satisfied and pleased rush.

"You feel so good," I declared, and he wrapped his other arm around me, cradling my head and pulled me down onto him tighter. I cried out and bowed my head, forgetting to breathe for a moment.

"Gracelyn," he moaned, and the sound of my name on his lips caused me to tighten up, bringing another slight cry from him.

I rose slightly and fell, working a slow and controlled rhythm, rolling my hips and guessing at what he would like, watching his reactions, doing a little more of this and a little less of that as his reactions called for.

His hair was softer than I could even imagine as I held it back from our faces. My thighs trembled with the unfamiliar exertion our position put them through, but I wasn't willing to stop. I was getting closer and I could tell he felt good, and I didn't want to stop. He didn't make me. He got his feet under him and stood up in one fluid motion, his hands gliding down my back, supporting me under my ass as he set me on the edge of the kitchen counter. He was taller than me, and I scooted closer to the edge, further onto his cock as he stared down at me with a grave expression. It was an expression that promised me silently so many beautiful things.

"I don't want to hurt you," he whispered, and he sounded almost afraid.

I smiled despite his fear, I couldn't help it. I reached up and drew his mouth down to mine for a lingering kiss.

"Then don't," I said in a hush across his lips.

He groaned and kissed me with a passion I had never known before now and cautiously, he drew back and thrust forward.

Oh, my God, the sheer power contained in his body was like nothing I had ever felt, but at the same time he was so careful of me, drawing back and surging forward, his cock driving deep, but almost agonizingly slow. I reveled in the feel of him against and inside my body, clutching myself to him, wrapping my legs around his lean hips. Each of us breathed the other in and out; our warring, panting breaths were a symphony of love and devotion as he took me high and higher towards a heaven only he could provide.

"Alaric!" My voice was foreign to me, breathy, high, and tight.

I leaned forward, and he held me, my lips finding his chest and shoulder. He cradled me against him, lovingly, protectively, and yet still didn't break his slow and careful thrusting cadence. I held onto him, trembling with emotion, overwhelmed with sensation, pleasure zinging along every fiber, every nerve ending in my being, until I arched back, my palms flat to the countertop to keep myself from falling completely backwards.

He took my orgasm as permission to let himself go just a little bit. His thrusts became harder and more passionate, though not at all painful or too much. I bit my bottom lip and met his gaze with my own, and with a startled gasp of almost-surprise, he thrust into my body one last time, powerfully, and I came all over again.

I came back to myself slowly, gasping and panting, and he eased from my body, both of us shuddering at the sensation of him leaving me, though he didn't go far. He moved one of my knees, closing my legs, and leaned a hip heavily onto the edge of the counter beside me.

"That was... Wow."

He grunted an agreement, but his gaze had left my face and was on my left leg. He dropped to his knees in front of me and said tersely, "You're bleeding."

"Must have been the glass," I said faintly. "It doesn't hurt."

He looked up at me sharply, and I looked down at him. I touched the side of his face, cherishing this moment, even as I hissed lightly when he plucked the piece of glass from my skin.

"Okay, now it stings," I said with a little laugh.

His expression was so very serious, so very grave as he bent, his gaze never leaving mine and placed the flat of his tongue against my ankle, just above my foot. He laved my leg with his warm, velvet tongue in a straight line to just below the cut and there was something so intensely primal, so beautiful about the red of my blood against it as he sat back and closed his mouth, his eyes slipping shut as he seemingly savored tasting me.

It was a terrible sort of beautiful that tightened things low in my body with desire and longing.

He opened his eyes after swallowing and murmured, "Let us clean up."

Our ice cream had somewhat melted by the time I'd cleaned up the mead and broken glass, but it was still good. We finished it and the honey wine at my little dining table. I'd gone to wash the sticky off my ankles and feet in the bathroom and the rest of the blood off my leg while he turned down the bed. I'd changed into a different nightgown, too. Leaving the first to soak in cold water in my bathroom sink after treating it with some hydrogen peroxide solution to, hopefully, lift the few spatters of blood from my freshly doctored leg. It'd only required a small Band-Aid. The cut wasn't very big at all. I'd worried more about the backs of Alaric's legs, but his leather pants had been thick enough to protect him.

I cuddled against him beneath the blankets and clean sheets and suddenly felt as if I had on too many clothes.

"So how long have you been watching me, or been my guardian or whatever?" I asked after several moments of silence.

"When did your sadness come?"

"A little over a year ago," I answered.

"That long." His voice held no humor and he didn't joke about these things. I let him hold me, smoothing his hands along my body while I stewed on this bit of information.

"You said I was assigned to you…"

"Yes," he huffed a sigh as if this were hard for him. I felt a tad guilty. Alaric had been there for me for over a year, keeping whatever influence that had been drowning me in sorrow for that time from swallowing me completely. He had been my silent savior and I didn't even know it. Then, when the bad guys had upped their game he'd broken the rules for me, to keep me safe.

"Yes, all of this is about right." He nodded and I realized belatedly I'd been speaking aloud like I sometimes did while processing through information.

"Now, if you're caught, you'll be in trouble."

He chuckled but it was dispassionate.

"Yes."

"What will they do?" I asked again.

"I do not know. Likely, I will be denied my final test," he said.

"Final test? For what?" I asked.

"Redemption," and the way he said it made it sound absolutely huge.

My heart sank. I wasn't ready to let him go. I wanted to know so much more.

"Alaric..." I said, finally.

"Yes, Gracelyn?"

"Don't get caught."

"I have no intentions." He drew me tighter against his body, comforting me, when it was he who faced the consequences of our tryst. "However, what I did, it cannot happen again, nor can it ever go any further." His lips moved against my forehead and his voice just sounded so... pained.

"What we did. Together. It wasn't just you," I murmured.

More silence and he sighed, as if in defeat.

"Rest," was all he said.

"Alaric?" I said, after a while of quiet contemplation.

"Yes?" he asked.

"Why'd you finally kiss me?" I asked.

"After over a thousand of your years without the taste of it, I could not resist tasting my long-lost mead from your sweet lips," he murmured, and I about melted from the sentiment.

It was the most romantic thing any man had ever said to me. Ever. I felt things low in my body give a throb and silently told them to shut up... If Alaric had any idea how his words affected me, he gave no indication.

"Oh," was the only thing I could say for a minute or more, then softly, "I'm still glad you did."

He chuckled and it was that rich dark sound that was so, just, him, that I loved to hear it. The candles in the apartment extinguished, plunging us in to darkness absolute, the faint glow of his eyes the only illumination.

"Sleep," he repeated, and I did.

CHAPTER TWENTY-ONE

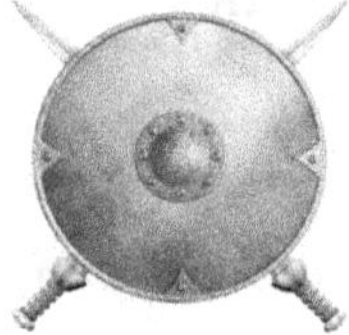

$\mathcal{M}$y mood gradually lightened over the next few weeks, and I felt as if I was thriving. When Volund had called, I had rejected going to dinner with him before his departure back to Denmark. His voice had held a thrill of anger when I cited that my calendar was simply too full that week. I'd apologized profusely, not meaning a single word of it, promised that I would call with any developments regarding the project's progress and had gotten off the call.

The only call I'd made since was to let him know that we'd done what we could with the sword when it came to brushing the surface dirt away, but now it needed further work to remove some of the corrosion to see if we could get any further with the runes. That had been a week after my refusal. The sword had gone into an olive oil bath and I'd been working diligently on it but sometimes the best thing you could do was give an object time to reveal itself. After as long as it had been in the dirt, it wasn't in a real big hurry to give up all of its secrets.

It had been photographed using alternative light sources with varying wavelengths. My favorite nerd in the whole wide world, Germaine, was using computer software to pile those images one on top of the other in some form of fancy techno-widgetry that was way above my pay grade. We were hoping to see if there was enough there to send it out for translation.

It was Friday and I was wrapping up for the night when Jared came by. I wouldn't know if Germaine's work would bear fruit until the middle of next week.

"Gracie," Jared said – he'd taken to calling me Gracie since our dinner where the terms of our relationship had been firmly established. He had adhered to those terms with grace and we had been becoming cautious friends.

"Yeah?" I asked, winding my scarf around my neck.

"A bunch of us were going out for a drink, you want to join us?" he asked.

I looked outside, the days were beginning to get longer, which saddened me as my time with Alaric would be cut shorter. The sun was just most of the way through setting now, as opposed to it being completely dark.

"I think I'll pass tonight. I'm beat." I smiled. Jared smiled back and turned to go, but at the last second stopped and turned back to me.

"Hey, Gracie," he said.

"Yeah?" I asked.

"Whoever he is, I'm really glad for you. He makes you happy. It looks good on you. Someday I hope you'll let me meet him."

I stood mute for several heartbeats... Finally, a sad smile curled my lips and Jared looked stricken.

"I didn't mean to upset you!" He held up a hand as if to ward something off.

"I wish you could meet him," I said and this was the biggest obstacle to my joy. I wanted Alaric to experience all of me, not just physically, but everything. My friends, my family, which really was just my gran now, and my work. I wanted to share so much more with him than I was able to; I yearned to, but I couldn't, and so we did our best to steal what moments of time we could with one another and cherished them for what they were.

"What is it, Gracelyn?" Jared asked, gripping my elbow lightly.

All I could see on his face now was concern, and it warmed me down to my toes. He really was a good friend.

"It is complicated." I blew out a breath. We stood for a long pause and I finally smiled and said, "I've got to go," then did something I had never ever done before. I hugged my boss. "Thank for being such a good friend," I said.

"No problem." He patted my back and let me go, and with a final smile I went out the door.

The air was bone-chilling when I stepped out into it. I hustled up the sidewalk and stopped at the corner waiting for the light to change so that I could cross the street. I leapt lightly off the curb and strode across the cracked asphalt, buoyed by thoughts of Alaric. I quickly walked toward my building and punched in the code to my lobby door. I grew impatient waiting on the elevator and took the stairs two at a time instead, gasping for breath as I unlocked my apartment door.

The faint smell of burning metal wafted out as I opened it and I smiled. I stepped inside and shut and locked the door, turning to face him. He stood, eyes glowing softly, lips curved in a smile, a single red rose hanging loose in his fingers.

"Happy Valentine's Day," I said and he smiled.

I took off my coat and scarf and hung them and my purse on the back of the door, tossing my keys into the dish on the hall table.

"I still do not fully understand the tradition," he said with a frown, which was ruined by his smile that just wouldn't quit. "This is for you."

He held out the rose and I took it with a smile. He stepped forward and pulled me to him. I went willingly. Our lips touched in an almost-chaste kiss but knowing us, it wouldn't stay that way for long. At least, not if we weren't careful.

"Is it just me, or is it getting harder and harder to be good?" I asked.

"It is not just you." His voice was husky and low and did horrible things to my hormones, what he said next pretty much sent me to my knees emotionally rather than physically. "Please accept the rose I give you as a token of my love and devotion on this day. It is not nearly what you deserve. Would that I could tear my beating heart from my own breast and lay it in your hands, I would, Gracelyn, I would." I rested my ear against his chest and listened to the slow, steady throb of his heart.

"I like your heart right where it is," I murmured, then surprised myself by saying, "Alaric, I will never love anyone the way I love you. Not ever. Why do things have to be this way?" I shivered as my throat grew thick with unshed tears.

"I was an evil man when I lived. I was the foulest and most depraved soul in death and a warrior of Hell for a little over five centuries of your time. I could not tell you what it was, my beloved Small One, but one day the killing held no more joy for me. I grew tired, could not stand it anymore. I realized how wrong I had been for so very long."

He sighed and it was a sound of utter exhaustion.

"On that day, I threw down my arms, and myself upon the mercy of the Host. I was prepared for them to end my existence, but they stayed their hand. They returned my weapons, my sword and my shield, and they told me the path to redemption would be a long one. They told me that I fought on the side of the angels now. I became no better than a grunt in Heaven's army, but I was pleased to be there.

"I spent the next five hundred and thirty years fighting, climbing throughout the ranks, working on becoming the type of man I should have been from the start."

He drew back and looked into my face.

"My point is, I know now that I have spent that time becoming the man you needed me to be for you. I feel that in my damned state I am wholly undeserving of you, your kindness, and your love. I am twice-damned for bringing you the burden, the pain, of loving a man that cannot completely give himself to you. My punishment for my deeds has come full circle. I now feel the agony a thousand-fold that I dealt to innocence in my mortal span, with every look, with every touch, knowing that I cannot have you and that I have ruined you for future happiness with my purely selfish deeds. Yet I cannot bring myself to give you up until I am forced to."

He smoothed my tears away with his thumbs and for the first time ever, I did the same for him.

God's work, the Devil's work, I didn't care. Right then I just wanted with everything in my heart and everything in my soul for Alaric to know even a slice of the happiness I felt when in his arms. I stood on tiptoe abruptly and placed another kiss on his lips then backed away slowly.

"I love you, and I will take you any way that I can," I told him.

I left him standing in my entryway and went into my kitchen, filling the empty mead bottle I'd kept with water and placing the long stem of the rose into it. I turned to find him watching me and I smiled.

"What shall we do tonight of all nights?" he asked, and I bit my bottom lip.

"Valentine's Day is supposed to be about the one you love. I think I would very much like to spend it with you in bed, if you don't mind."

"I take it you do not mean to sleep."

I laughed and shook my head. "Sleep is overrated," I told him.

He stepped into me, big hands going to my waist and murmured, "Someday this will all end."

"Today's not that day," I whispered back, really wishing that he would stop reminding me.

"No. No, it is not," he replied with a sad little smile, and he bent to kiss me.

I wrapped my arms around him and kissed him back with everything I was. I understood why, with the quiet little reminders that this wasn't something that could last forever. He wanted me to be prepared. He wanted me to not be hurt, but I knew that was impossible. I knew that there would be pain, but I also knew that everything leading up to it was so pure, so good, that there was no way the universe could or would let me get away with it scot-free. There would be payment owed and I would just have to hold on and remember that with every tear, every throb of my broken heart, that I had known it was coming and that I chose it anyway. How could I not?

I twined my fingers in his silken-soft long hair and held it back from our faces, molding myself to the front of his body, his strong arms around me. There was seriously no safer place that I felt I could be, in this world or the next.

He was so careful of me when we were like this. His hands were gentle, his touch light. He treated me as if I were made of glass, and I could somewhat understand why. His size and strength in comparison was immense, and he would be all too capable of hurting me, even if it were unwittingly. It was nice that I could trust him so completely, that I didn't have to worry about it. Even at his most passionate, he was always cautious, always, with me.

His broad hands slid along my ass appreciatively, a low groan of pleasure rumbling through his chest. It made me smile against his lips, even as his touch became more intimate, sliding along the outside of my slacks and delving between my legs from behind. He leveraged me up, easily, and I wrapped my arms around his neck, bracing against his broad shoulders as he straightened, my legs twining around his lean hips. I could feel him pressing against his leather pants, long and hard, the heat from his body incredible, branding, scorching my pussy even through our multiple layers of clothes.

I was hot for him, wanting, and groaning into his mouth, whining wordlessly about how we were far too dressed for this. He and I were so in tune with one another, he didn't even have to ask what was wrong. Instead, he carried me to the bedroom, staring into my soul from inches away, the expression on his face reverent, as it ever was when he looked at me. It was an expression that made me melt inside every time I saw it.

Despite how desperate we were to be skin on skin, we took our time undressing, kissing and licking along every inch of exposed skin as it was revealed. Lips to shoulder, to throat, to chest. Fingertips caressing along limbs and teasing more intimate places. He groaned when he discovered how wet and ready I was by the time my slacks and panties had found their way to my bedroom floor.

I loved the feel of his over-warm body against mine, the sweep of his large hands, rough with callouses from his sword and shield, against my skin. I pressed a gentle palm to the center of his chest and nudged him toward the bed. He smiled down at me and lay down, reaching for me and helping me up. I straddled him, and reached between us, wrapping gentle fingers around his long, thick cock and stroking him. He was already as hard as he was going to get, but it was worth watching his head fall back onto the pillows his eyes close and his lips part in pleasure.

It was even better when I positioned him at my body's opening and slid down his length, taking him in slowly, letting my body adjust, though it was as eager as I was to have him. His hands went to my body, above the swell of my hips, sliding over my ribs, my stomach, cupping my breasts. He played his thumbs back and forth across my nipples and I bit my bottom lip, rolling my hips in an easy motion.

It was perfect. The feel of him in me and around me was unparalleled by anything I'd ever experienced before. I struck a gentle cadence, rising and falling; the movement of him stroking against my walls, the intimate play of his hands and eyes over my exposed flesh set me at a sort of peace that was hard to describe. It was wonderful and amazing having this beautiful man beneath me and I would willingly do anything and more that he asked.

He moaned, his eyes closing, the light from them gone, plunging the room into deep blue shadows. The candles flared to life and I gasped as he thrust up to meet my downward stroke. Pleasure unfurled low in my body and an almost tickling sensation flitted through my body in sparks from a campfire, swirling high into the night and disappearing somewhere out above my head.

I loved it when we got like this. The pleasure seemingly suspended time and space, holding us in the palm of its hand. It could have been hours or mere minutes, but it felt like it was infinite. Days or weeks could pass and it was just him inside of me, the enjoyment rolling along like surf, lapping gently at our shores, eroding our inhibitions and drawing a primal, base nature out of each of us that spun into a wild passion.

It felt so good, *he* felt so good, that no matter how long we were together like this, it was never long enough. I always came in such a way that it felt like I was spiraling out of control, but Alaric was always there, his touch grounding me.

I loved him so very much, and deep down inside, I knew I would love him forever. It was the perfect Valentine's Day evening.

CHAPTER TWENTY-TWO

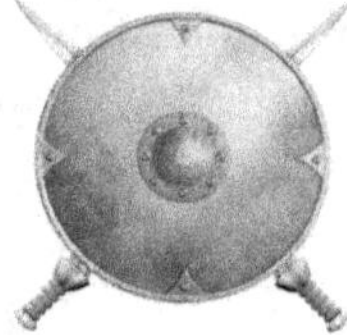

I was excited.

I had just emailed the images of the completed runes to Jared's Norse language specialist and would likely know what they meant in a few days' time. My excitement was a bit tempered by the fact that Gunnar Volund deserved a call to update him on the progress. I heaved a big sigh and sat in front of my workstation's computer anxiously waiting for the Skype call to go through. I wanted it over with, badly.

Though it was six in the afternoon here, it was midnight in Denmark. Still, when the call connected there he was, looking as relaxed as I'd ever seen him. His suit jacket was missing and the cuffs of his expensive dress shirt were rolled back over his forearms. He was leaned way back in his expensive looking leather desk chair and a highball glass of amber liquid was held loosely in one hand.

I forced a smile, greeting him and asked, "Long day?"

"Very, and what have I told you about calling me Mr. Volund?" he chided. It wasn't playful or warm; in fact, even through the image on the screen, his eyes turned into chips of ice. I suppressed a shudder.

"Apologies," I said. "A habit of my profession."

He inclined his head and took a sip from his glass.

"So what is it you have to tell me, Gracelyn?" he asked.

I cleared my throat. "Well, ah, I completed cleaning the Viking blade as best I could and uncovered what runes there were. We went through extra measures of scanning a three-dimensional representation of the hilt into the computer, as well as subjecting the surface of the metal to several alternative light sources, carefully photographing all the way. One of our technical geniuses, Germaine..."

"Yes, yes, this is all well and good; please get to the point!" he snapped and I swallowed back the bitter bite of anger that almost came free from my mouth.

"Yes, well, the point is that compiling these images has yielded a clear result and the runes are indeed readable. The images have been sent to a Norse language expert. He -"

"And what do they say?" he asked.

I frowned at the interruption.

"We should know in a few days," I bit out sharply and terminated the call before he could say anything else. My computer immediately began the notification process that he was trying to reconnect the call. Well, forget that. I turned off my speakers and my monitor, and gathered my things.

I just wanted to be home.

CHAPTER TWENTY-THREE

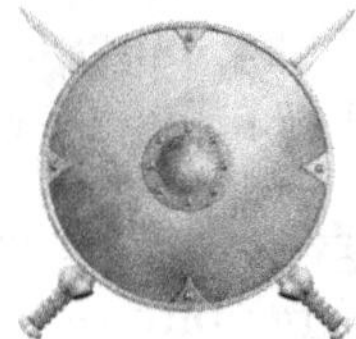

"*D*id you hang up on Gunnar Volund?" Jared screeched from my phone as I let myself in to my apartment.

"Yep," I answered.

"Oh, my God! Gracelyn, why?" He sounded like that was a total disaster.

"He was rude," I answered simply.

"He's threatening to pull our funding," Jared wailed.

"Oh for goodness sakes!" I scoffed. *What a big damn baby.*

"You need to apologize."

"This coming from Jared-my-boss or Jared-my-friend?" I asked.

"Your boss..." and then, "Your friend says 'well done' for hanging up on that arrogant S.O.B., still, make it right Gracie. As much as I hate to say it, we need that money."

I rolled my shoulders. I wished for Alaric and sighed into the phone.

"You got it, boss," I said dejectedly and hung up the phone after some quick goodbyes.

I opened up my laptop and drafted an email apologizing and making some excuse or other about a tough day. My inbox pinged almost immediately with a response.

I will be in New York next week. Dinner. I will send a car. Accept and all will be forgiven.

Pushy bastard. I heaved a sigh and hung my head. *Okay, fine.* I could deal with one more dinner if it meant saving our funding, even though I was loathe to accept. I emailed back with my acceptance, though with the stipulation I would meet him. Again, with an instant return.

I will send a car. I believe you are in no position to make any stipulations.

What a child! I ground my teeth and replied as sweetly as possible that that was fine. I huffed out another sigh and shut down my computer. I didn't think I was being totally unreasonable, but "'to-ma-to, ta-mah-to', I suppose.

To top my evening off, it was one of those rare nights there was no Alaric. I tried not to worry and got ready for bed after a quick dinner of salad and leftover lemon pepper chicken breast. Tomorrow was another day, right?

CHAPTER TWENTY-FOUR

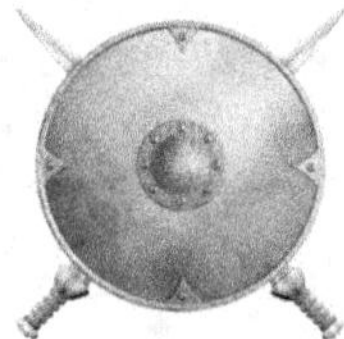

The week flew by.

Alaric had returned the next night, with word that the fighting had intensified and that meant there would be nights he couldn't come. I'd nodded and said I'd understood, but a small part of me mourned a little. I knew in my head that this wouldn't... couldn't last forever but I wasn't one to ever give up until the bitter end.

I leaned back and took stock of myself in the mirror. Lavender satin blouse, gray pencil skirt, smoke-colored hose, and smart black pumps that were all business. I'd tortured my long, long, dishwater blonde hair up into a business-like French twist and had pinned it in place to within an inch of its life. My makeup was conservative and I nodded to myself. There would be no mistaking this for a romantic dinner. I'd made sure of it. I looked nice, professional; 'businesslike and professional' was precisely what I was going for. No room for misinterpretation from anyone, least of all Gunnar Volund.

I stuck my tube of pale lipstick into my clutch, along with my ID, debit card, and what little cash I carried in case of an emergency cab ride or what have you, just as a resounding knock came at my door. I pulled down my lighter, spring raincoat and shrugged into it. The gray complimented my skirt. I opened the door to a dour Maximillian and gave him a dazzling thousand-watt smile.

I skipped being pissed at him. He'd actually buzzed my apartment to let me have him come up this time, which was a vast improvement in and of itself.

We went down to the lobby and there was the black Lincoln town car. I felt a little sullen as I got into the back. This little misadventure had been the catalyst for mine and Alaric's first real disagreement. He had not wanted me to go, had wanted me to cancel, and, honestly, I had wanted to do what he'd suggested, but I would be letting Jared and an entire department of people down if I did.

When people hear that money goes for research, they never really appreciate what that means. Sure, it sometimes means more fancy gadgets or a new method of dating an object, or imaging something to check out what is under the surface; and sure, some of those toys can be expensive; but what that donation sometimes really means is that you are paying someone's wage, allowing them to tinker, restore, and promote a project; write about it all so that future generations can learn from it and not repeat things that have already been done. So that new information can be brought to light, the story can be fully told. And the people whose lives were integral during the time that history was made? Well, so that they will never be forgotten. Immortality is real and attainable by the action of really living during the time we are alive.

If that makes any sense.

People like me, people like Jared, and even people like Germaine with all of his uber fancy modern technology, got that. I was pretty certain that people like Gunnar Volund didn't have a freaking clue.

His donation was a means to his own end, of finding out if one of his relations had been on that distant shore and sure, I suppose that had a certain sense of nobility to it, but mostly I was pretty certain, *that* aside, his donation was nothing more than a tax write-off, that he could honestly get anywhere else.

I was snapped out of my reverie when the door to the town car popped open and I was ushered out. We were at a fancy place on Broadway near Central Park. So, not far from either my museum or home. A few subway stops or a long walk; well, long in these heels. I allowed Volund's security muscle to escort me to his table, which again, though it was a different restaurant, was still as secluded as you could get.

Volund rose and, acting the perfect gentleman, took my coat, hanging it on the back of my chair. I tried my best to school my face into a pleasant and professional mask and took the seat, allowing him to shove it into the backs of my knees. Sometimes I wish I could just scoot in my own damned chair. My thoughts drifted back to Alaric and I think my face fell.

"Oh, come now, Gracelyn. As I said before, attending this dinner ensures my forgiveness for your rude behavior." He chuckled and it oozed arrogance. Maybe I was just being unforgiving. Ending the Skype call had been kind of rude, and unprofessional... I'd known I'd be eating crow when I did it, but that still didn't excuse his bad behavior. Blargh, I hated these things.

"Apologies, Mr. Volund. That look had nothing to do with you, or dinner." I attempted a small smile, which fell flat at his darkened expression. I realized my error and said lightly, "Ah, sorry. Gunnar."

His expression smoothed, if only a little, and he took his own seat.

"What bothers you?" he asked.

"Well, I was hoping that I would have something to tell you by now on what the runes might say, but alas, nothing yet. Our language expert hasn't gotten back to us." I took sip of water.

"As you can tell, I am not always a patient man."

He smiled, but I wasn't fooled. I thought that was supposed to be an apology, but what he said next chilled me right to the bone. "But that is all right. I always get what I want, in the end."

He gave me a pointed look, and I all but squirmed in my seat.

"So, your work with the sword, it is done?" he asked, as the server poured the wine.

"No, no, I have a long ways to go yet. Weeks, maybe months." I took another sip of water.

"Please, taste the wine. It is an excellent vintage."

He took a sip and watched me over the rim of his glass. I took a hesitant sip just to please him, though I wanted desperately to keep my wits about me. Something about this meeting was just plain off, though I couldn't tell you exactly what it was.

"It's excellent," I said and I wasn't lying.

He nodded, as if satisfied.

"So, what do you do when you are not playing with your little artifacts? Hmm?" he asked as the appetizer was served.

I gritted my teeth and bit back what I wanted to say, which was that I didn't appreciate his condescending tone.

"Read, mostly," I answered vaguely, and he gave me a withering look.

I took in a breath and let it out slowly. "Poetry. I read poetry."

He nodded and finished chewing.

"Fools, the lot of them, but I will humor you. What is your favorite poet?" he asked.

"I like Frost," I replied tersely, and then I couldn't help myself. I added "...and it's not foolish. Poetry is part of what makes us human."

He laughed outright. "Tell me a poem by this Frost, then." And he sat back expectantly.

I suddenly wished I'd kept my mouth shut and longed to be safe and sound back at home with Alaric, curled in my bed, reading Frost to one another by candlelight. I sighed.

"I have been one, acquainted with the night.

I have walked out in rain – and back in rain.

I have out walked the furthest city light.

I have looked down the saddest city lane.

I have passed by the watchman on his beat

And dropped my eyes, unwilling to explain.

I have stood still and stopped the sound of feet

When far away an interrupted cry

Came over houses from another street,

But not to call me back or say good-bye;

And further still, at an unearthly height,

One luminary clock against the sky

Proclaimed the time was neither wrong nor right.

I have been one acquainted with the night.”

I took a careful sip of wine. The poem was Alaric’s favorite and a deep ache had settled in my heart at the recitation. I missed him.

“And just what is that supposed to mean?” he asked.

I fiddled with the scale from Alaric’s mail and twisted my lips back and forth as I thought about it.

“What do you think it means?” I asked finally, taking a bite of my cuisine.

He pondered this a moment.

“I think the man is a weak, maudlin fool who cannot do for himself,” he said finally.

“I don’t think so,” I said. “To me it speaks of great pain, of loneliness. He walks the night alone, sees things the rest of us don’t see under a great burden of...”

Volund's roar of laughter stopped me mid-sentence.

"You have a soft heart," he said, and the way he said it, it was so not a compliment. I'm not one-hundred-percent sure what it was that flipped his switch from wolf in sheep's clothing to just full-on, not-even-trying-to-hide-it predator with me, but flip it had, and I was not impressed.

"I think the world needs more people with soft hearts," I said and leveled my gaze at him. His eyes narrowed.

"Do not think to insult me." His voice was low, menacing even.

"I wouldn't dream of it, Gunnar," I said, and at that particular moment with him, looking at me, like that... I meant it.

Dinner was, of course, fabulous. Company notwithstanding, I enjoyed the food, which was something, I guess. Volund took a few more pot-shots at me, and I let him without remark, though I was simmering and wondering what he was trying to play at. We exited the restaurant and I was surprised there was no car waiting.

"I thought you might join me for a walk in the park," he said, holding out his arm.

"I really must be going..." I attempted.

"Nonsense, you will walk with me," he said in his imperious tone, and I'd pretty much had it with his bullying ways.

"You know, I appreciate greatly your donations to the museum I work for, but I am really not caring much for this." I waved my hand by way of emphasis. "Or whatever this is. From now on, I think it best that you go through Jared, my boss, for any information regarding your ancestor or his involvement in the raid we are researching. Thank you for dinner, the food was lovely. Good night."

With that, I turned on my heel and strode up the sidewalk in the direction of the park.

I should have taken the subway or gotten lost in the crowd, but I didn't. I needed to cool my head, and walking among the trees, through the grass, had always done the trick before, so I strode into the park and down the path towards home.

I was lost inside my own head, bitter and furious in my thinking when a hand crushed over my mouth and yanked me hard back against a solid chest. I bit down savagely on the hand and heard Volund curse; he dragged me kicking off the path and I lost a shoe. I was equal amounts furious and scared as we delved back deeper into shadow across the grass.

"I told you, Gracelyn. I get what I want, and I am not accustomed to anyone getting in my way, telling me no, or giving me disrespect. You have done all three. I would have liked to have waited, but I think your lesson must be learnt now."

Adrenaline spiked through my veins and I fought like a wildcat, but I had nothing on him, not size, not weight, not muscle mass... nothing. If I could get loose, which I couldn't, I'd most definitely have speed, and maybe endurance on keeping that speed up, but at that moment, I was sunk. I had never dreamed he would come for me, that he would risk so much, but he did, and it was both terrifying and beautiful. We were deep in shadow beneath a copse of trees and Volund had spun me, slamming my back against the gnarled bark. I gripped my clutch tighter as pain radiated out from my back into my chest and ribs.

I thought I was imagining it when I saw the twin points of red over Volund's shoulder, but no, it *was* him, and relief flooded through my veins, making my knees go weak.

A deep, intimidating growl emitted from Alaric's chest and Volund was ripped off of me. He stumbled back and ass-planted in the beauty bark around the base of the trees. Alaric towered over him in his scale mail; his pauldrons and greaves were absent, but he still made one hell of an imposing figure. Volund went white and put up his hand as if to ward off the vision of his impending doom.

"You dare to try and sully that which is innocent and pure?" Alaric asked, in a snarl I had never heard come from him before.

"What are you?" Volund sounded scared, and for a split second I was scared for him.

Alaric advanced on him. I stopped and grabbed my clutch, that I didn't remember dropping. I went forward and wrapped both of my arms around one of Alaric's.

"No," I said and gave a tug, but it was like pulling on a granite statue. He was fixated on Volund, and the look on his face... it was like he was going to rip him apart.

"No!" I repeated a bit more forcefully and leaned my full weight on pulling him back. "He's not worth it. Please! I'm okay."

Alaric turned to me and his face softened. He touched the side of my face and tracked his fingertips through the dampness on my cheeks.

"I should kill him," he stated flatly.

"No, those days are over for you, it's not worth it; he's not worth everything you've worked towards. I love you, and I am telling you I'm okay."

We stared at each other a hard moment while Volund sat there and shook. He didn't bother to get up. I was glad; I wasn't entirely sure what Alaric would do if he did. He turned those blazing red eyes on Volund.

"Remember this, human, it was Gracelyn's gentle heart that stayed my hand this night. There will be no repercussions on your part. You will not contact her, you will not punish her by withdrawing funds which you have already pledged to her cause." He paused, then finished with, "You will retaliate in no way upon her person. To her you are dead. If I find otherwise, I will make you dead for real. And when you reach Hell, I will visit more suffering upon you than you could ever have imagined in this life. Am I understood?"

Alaric's arms went around me and he pulled me to him, I went gratefully into his embrace and watched the emotions play out over Gunnar

Volund's face: fear, rage, uncertainty, anger, and then finally resignation. Reluctantly he gave a hard nod.

"Go." Alaric commanded, and Volund hesitated.

Alaric swept me up into his arms and barked the command again. Volund stood, and he was almost as tall as Alaric.

What he did next, well, he sort of impressed me. Rather than run, like I probably would have in his position, he dusted off his suit and straightened his cuffs and tie before turning and striding back to the walking path without another word. I let out an explosive breath I hadn't known I'd been holding. Alaric vibrated beneath me with barely-suppressed rage.

"I should have slaughtered him..." he began, and I stopped him.

"Shhhh, I said I'm okay," then I broke into a wide grin.

"What is so funny?" he asked.

"If I'd have known that was what it would take to get you out of my apartment with me, I would have done it a long time ago," I joked, and his frown deepened, the furrow in his brow deepening into a canyon.

"I fail to see the humor in this," he said.

"I have to, or I'll start crying," I said honestly.

His expression crumpled into concern.

"I cannot walk with you back to your apartment; I can only go as far as the darkness permits me. Which way?" He looked to me for guidance and I pointed.

He strode in that direction. I kicked off my other shoe and let it drop. I was so not going back for the other one. As soon as I was near enough a street, I would hail a cab. Thank God I had hung onto my purse for dear life. I might have dropped it, but I had kept track of it. That was important.

"I can't believe you came. I mean, how did you know?" I asked.

"I will always come for you, Small One. For as long as I am able. You are still my charge, I know your feelings." He brushed a gentle kiss across my forehead and I closed my eyes, cherishing the moment.

"I love you," I whispered.

"And I, you, Gracelyn; and I, you."

CHAPTER TWENTY-FIVE

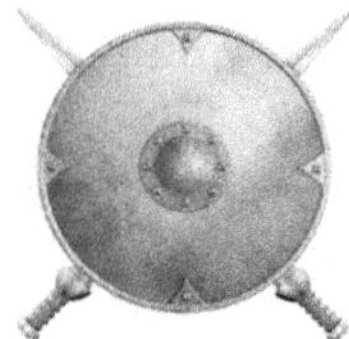

laric had set me down as close to the street as he could. I could see his eyes watching me from the cover of darkness and smiled back at them as I got into the cab. I don't think the cabbie even noticed I had no shoes; if he did, he made no comment. Either way, I tipped him well. When I unlocked my apartment door about twenty minutes later, Alaric was waiting. Traffic in New York was a bitch, it turned a five-minute walk into a twenty-minute cab ride, but with no shoes on, it was kind of necessary.

I went into his arms immediately and stayed there for several long moments. Neither of us spoke, neither of us needed to. I was safe. I was safe because Alaric had come for me.

"How in trouble are you?" I asked, finally, and he shifted slightly but didn't answer. I swore softly.

"I do not know," he said honestly, plucking at the pins holding my hair. I looked up at him, searching his face. He was frowning. "I do not like what you have done with your hair," he said and I smiled. He was always honest, never sugar-coated anything.

"Let me change and you can take it out." My voice was soft.

"Yes, I want you in my arms." He reluctantly let me go and followed me into my bedroom, where we both set about getting ready for bed, though truth be told, I wasn't the least bit tired. Still too jazzed on adrenaline, I think.

I slipped into my nightgown and heard Alaric growl behind me, but it wasn't the usual sound he made when wrestling with himself over touching me; this was feral and deep with the thrum of fine, burning rage. I turned around.

"What's wrong?" I asked.

He came to me, shirtless and barefoot, black leather covering his powerful legs, moving with him like a second skin. He lightly gripped my shoulders and turned me back around.

"Does it hurt?" he asked me and my brow wrinkled in confusion.

I sucked in a hissing breath when his fingers lightly trailed across my back, following the edge of what promised to be one seriously mighty bruise.

"It does now."

I yelped when he hit a particularly tender patch. It must have happened when Volund slammed me into the tree. I'd been under the effects of too much adrenaline and must not have realized how hard he'd slammed me into the bark. I mean, I didn't feel it at the time, but now? Owie.

"You should have let me kill him." Alaric's voice was dispassionate and low.

"He wasn't worth it."

"He hurt you. He should die." He was being stubborn and I turned to face him.

"Things don't work like that anymore," I explained, gently.

"This is a softer time. While I enjoy it because it made you, this is one time I long for sword and shield, and the right to face that worm in combat."

He led me to the bed and we made ourselves comfortable. He was gently plucking pins from my hair when the shaking started.

"I am so, just, blessed that you came when you did. I didn't know what was going to happen to me."

My voice broke and Alaric pulled me back against his warm chest, careful of my bruises. He cradled me to him and murmured gently in a language I didn't know. I broke down and cried.

"Better?" he asked, when I'd been quiet for a time.

"Better," I affirmed.

He gently ran his fingers through my unpinned hair and then brushed it until I was as relaxed as I could ever be. I loved it when he brushed my hair almost as much as I loved it when he allowed me to brush his. He spoiled me.

"Do you think you can sleep?" he finally asked.

"Read to me?" I cuddled into his side, laying my head on his chest. He picked up the book on the nightstand, opened it, and began to read, beginning with his favorite, his rich, deep voice lulling me into sleep.

"I have been one acquainted with the night..."

CHAPTER TWENTY-SIX

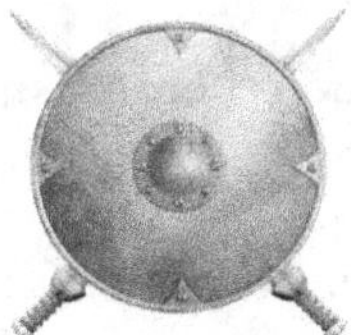

When I woke after the ordeal of the night before, I was stiff and sore and it hurt to do anything. A person never truly appreciates how much their back does for them until it's injured. I whimpered a bit as I pulled myself out of bed and across the hall into my bathroom. I took some ibuprofen from my medicine cabinet and popped two of the pills into my mouth, drinking straight from the bathroom sink's faucet to get them down. My face was a wreck of cried-off makeup, and I cringed inwardly that I'd looked so dreadful in front of Alaric and that he hadn't said anything.

Next, to remedy the horror-show clown face I sported, I dragged myself into a hot shower. Oh, that hurt at first, but soon the heat worked its magic and I was limber by just enough to try and tackle the rest of my day.

I went in to work, half-expecting the whole world to come down around my ears, thanks to Gunnar Volund, but was surprised when nothing of the sort happened. I quietly assumed my usual post at my workbench and opened my email. Nothing. I huffed a sigh and went to Jared's office, tapping on the door frame.

"Yes?" He looked up from the papers he'd been reviewing.

"Your Norse language expert is sorta killing me here," I complained, and sat down across from him.

"She was called away, is on a site in the middle of nowhere in Norway. No communications," he explained.

"How do you know?" I asked.

He looked sheepish. "I'm just as impatient as you are and called her office. One of her student assistants informed me."

"Blargh. I wish she'd finished before she went gallivanting off to Timbuktu."

He raised an eyebrow at me. So what if Timbuktu was in Africa not Norway? *Historical, geographical and scientific accuracy to the bitter end, I suppose.* I stuck out my tongue and Jared laughed at me.

"You know what I mean," I said.

"Yeah, I do," he replied, his laughter dying down into an affectionate grin. "How was dinner with Gunnar?" he asked, and when I sighed, his expression darkened.

I told him an abbreviated version of what happened, replacing Alaric with a random Good Samaritan. Jared looked apoplectic by the time I finished.

"Are you all right?" he cried.

"A little sore, a little rundown, but I'm okay. I think the big biker guy that came to the rescue scared him really good. All that black leather and he was even bigger than Volund, if you can believe that." I really, really, hoped that he did.

"You should take the rest of today off," he said judiciously. "Tomorrow, too, if you need it."

"Jared, really, I'm okay." I got up, though, admittedly, much more slowly than I would have liked. "I just really want to go back to work."

"All right." He frowned. "I'm still shocked a man like Volund would do such a thing." His brow wrinkled and he looked at me, concerned, then the light bulb went on; you could see it in his eyes.

"It's okay," I repeated kindly.

"Oh, Gracie, I'm so sorry," he said. "I should have listened to you about giving him your information." He was genuinely fretting now.

"It's okay," I repeated.

"I will make it up to you," he said.

"You don't have to Jared." I chewed my lip. "I wouldn't expect any more funds from him, though, no matter what else we find."

"I wouldn't take them anyways, it's the principle of the thing." He crossed his arms and scowled darkly. "In fact, I'm of a mind to return what he's already pledged."

"Don't do that!" I snapped but didn't mean to be so harsh.

"Why, when taking them might send the message that it was okay for him to do what he did?" he asked.

"There are a lot of people who depend on those donations and investments to stay employed and Volund is loaded beyond loaded. If he ponies up more cash, then you take it, but just keep him away from me."

I put my hand on the doorknob to his office and pushed my way through before he could argue with me. I hoped like hell that he wouldn't say anything to Volund, but knowing Jared, he would. I just hoped Volund wouldn't try anything, that Alaric had put the fear of God into him, or, would that be the Devil? I shook my head. The theological tangle was too much to wrap my brain around so early.

I went for the coffee, and my station, and buried myself in work for the rest of the day. It was the best thing for me.

CHAPTER TWENTY-SEVEN

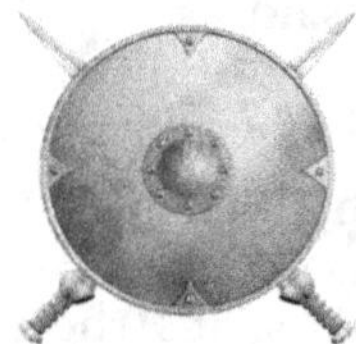

laric didn't come that night, nor did he come the next. I was terrified we'd been caught, pacing the apartment around and around worrying, stilling at every small sound to listen for the familiar rattle of scale or sigh of leather.

Nothing.

Empty.

It was how I was beginning to feel, hollowed-out and restless. I wasn't sleeping; I couldn't concentrate at work. It was awful. It was too soon, I wasn't ready to let him go. I would likely never be ready, but still. Was what he had done so bad? I mean, he'd done it to save me from... No, I would not think about that.

Not now, not ever.

It was the third night and I was pacing my bedroom, doorway to window to doorway to window...

A groan from behind me, I whirled and there he was, but something... something just wasn't right. He was clutching his side and looked to be in pain. I rushed to his side.

"Alaric! Alaric, what's wrong?" I asked.

"A flesh wound, Small One; nothing more." He grunted, and I helped him as best I could.

"Let me see." I guided him to the bed where he dropped heavily, making a strangled noise of pain. Without thinking, I reached for the bedside lamp.

"No! Gracelyn, don't!"

But it was too late. I had clicked on the lamp and turned. I cried out. Where Alaric had been was a creature that I could hardly describe to you as a man. He was skin and bones, lips blackened and shriveled, teeth jagged, yellow, and brown. His hair clung in wisps to his scalp, which for the most part, was bald. His skin was parchment-thin and jaundiced. It was so terrible: he looked like a walking corpse.

He had a hand up in front of his face, the nails thick and claw-like, jagged and stained brown-red. I bit back a sob when he lowered that hand; his cheeks were so sunken and he had no nose to speak of, just thin skin around twin holes in his face. He was covered in scars, every inch of him, some white with age, some deep purple, and others an angry pink or red. It made my heart twist and ache to see him this way. I looked into his eyes and they were the same, steady burning red they had always been.

"Gracelyn..." he said, a little helplessly, the same rich timbre of his voice emanating from the twisted mouth.

This creature was my Alaric, but how? I gathered my courage. I had been too-long distracted from my purpose already.

"Easy, I have to look," I said.

I gathered the material of his black shirt at the hem and did what I could to gently ease it over his head. He lay back and I cringed at the yellow staining the snowy white bandage beneath.

"I'll be right back. Don't you move," I ordered and got up.

I fetched every supply I could think of from the bathroom, a pot of hot water from the kitchen, and some clean washcloths from the linen cupboard. I returned to my room and knelt by the bed. I carefully clipped through the bandage with a pair of small scissors from the first aid kit I kept. He watched me, his alien features stoic, as closed-off as ever I had seen someone, and it made me cringe inside. Not his looks, though they were cringe-worthy, just that feeling that he was closed off from me.

"Explain," I murmured and was glad my voice didn't waver.

"We were out-flanked," he said. "Too many of them broke through our line. We engaged but..." I stopped him.

"Not about that," I said, gently. "I know you fight, I know you take wounds, but I also know you heal, you told me so. So, why is this different, and why do you look like... you do." I gathered my strength to finish the sentence, but the falter in it still hung between us in a pall of raw emotion.

"The wound was not made by a weapon."

He hissed as I peeled back the bandage and revealed three angry, pus-filled claw marks. The wounds had been crudely stitched and were weeping yellow fluid. I grimaced at the smell of infection.

"Pestilence demon, infection sets in the moment the skin is broken. Though we don't die, as we are already dead, we are forced to heal the wound slowly."

He leaned his head back against the pillows and closed his eyes, the bones of his orbital sockets standing out in sharp relief.

"This is gonna suck," I warned. "Like, huge."

I doused a cloth in hydrogen peroxide and swabbed the wounds. He fisted the covers and gritted his teeth. He sucked in huge wheezing breaths and I went on with it, my heart breaking at causing him any more pain.

"As to your other question, it is the direct light; you see me as I truly am now."

He let go of the covers and groaned.

"As you truly are?" I asked, confused.

"What you saw before, was me as I was... at the point when I passed off the mortal coil."

"So this is what a thousand years and more of fighting does to a person, huh?" I asked.

"Yes," was his only reply, his voice hard as granite and bitter as I'd ever heard it.

I finished my work in silence, and oh, did it take a while. Once the three deep cuts were cleaned they were still puffy around the edges and an angry red. I slathered them in an entire tube of Bacitracin and taped gauze over them piecemeal. The white gauze and tape stood out starkly against his yellowed skin and I couldn't help but stare.

"Gracelyn..." He sounded wounded, and I looked him in the eye.

There was such sorrow in his face. I ran gentle fingertips along his jaw and was surprised; his skin felt supple despite its awful appearance.

"Yes?" I asked.

"I never wanted you to see me this way." He waved a feeble hand over himself.

"Wounded?"

I gave him a wry twist of lips, and he closed his eyes and swallowed. This was really troubling him. It was troubling me too, but... this was Alaric. I closed my eyes, then opened them to find his on me and I smiled. I leaned down, and kissed his shriveled and blackened lips, and turned out the lamp.

I leaned back and he was back, as he ever was, gorgeous and whole.

"I love you," I told him. "You, Alaric, whatever form you take, however you look; it doesn't matter. I. Love. You."

He reached out so quickly and pulled me down against his chest, crushing my head to it, tucked below his chin. I made a sound of protest, concerned about his wounds, but his shaking stopped me. He shook, wracked with giant, silent sobs, and the tension eased out of me. I would let him have this. He needed it.

CHAPTER TWENTY-EIGHT

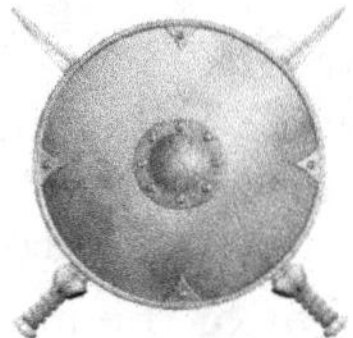

We lay quietly together, my head on the shoulder opposite the injury, side by side, our fingers entwined. Neither of us spoke for a long time, but one burning question refused to remain silent any longer.

"Why did you come, as hurt as you are?" I asked.

"I could not stay away." He kissed my temple.

"Why?"

"I did not wish for you to worry."

It was sweet and simple, but...

"Won't they noti..."

"Alrekr."

The voice that interrupted me was melodic, a tenor that was sweet and musical to the ear. We both sat up. A man in what appeared to be Roman Era armor, white tunic, bronze breastplate, complete with sandals, stood in the doorway to my room

"Alrekr," he repeated, and the set of Alaric's shoulders read nothing but defeat.

Sorrow constricted my heart and I sucked in a breath.

"Who are you?" I asked.

"I am Hasdiel."

He said it quietly, and his expression was almost sad, as if he were sorry he had to be here.

"He is the angel of benevolence," Alaric murmured.

I turned back to Hasdiel, a little wide eyed. He stepped a little further into the room and into the light of the moon through the window, the great swell of his wings behind his head coming into focus. They were drawn tightly against his back, so as not to knock into anything, and they looked distinctly uncomfortable cramped up against his body the way he had them. I couldn't tell what color they were from here exactly, but they weren't completely white, but rather white and dusted some other color, I think a golden or bronze, much like a barn owl's. His hair was close-cropped and brown, and his eyes an indistinct color due to the lighting, though I could tell they were light in color.

I wrapped both my arms protectively around the arm nearest me of Alaric's and swallowed hard. This was it... I had to let him go, but I wasn't about to without a fight.

"What's going to happen to him?" I demanded, and the angel looked a bit taken aback.

"Whatever our commander wills," he said, as if there were no other answer.

"Gracelyn, it is all right," Alaric tried to sooth me.

I shook my head violently.

"No, it's not!" I cried. "I'm not ready to let you go. I will never be ready to let you go. Nothing is ever going to be all right again!"

My lip trembled and my eyes welled with tears. *This was it. This was goodbye.* I would never see Alaric again and that was just... just...

Well, it was blatantly unacceptable!

"I will give you but a moment, brother," Hasdiel said, giving Alaric a short bow and me a look of deep sympathy. He vanished in a flash of light.

"Gracelyn, my love, my Small One."

Alaric gripped my face gently between his hands, then let me go, rising out of my bed, his hand pressed to the gauze taped over his wound. I scrambled to my feet after him.

"No, don't go," I begged. "Alaric, please, I need you."

He closed his eyes and bowed his head, as if praying.

"I must. I never should have come to you, but I did, and I will cherish every moment I have had with you."

He stepped back towards the corner of my room, the irregular puddle of darkness gaping on my floor.

"Alaric, please!" I hugged myself in my thin satin nightgown, his favorite, and shook, but not from cold.

"I love you, Gracelyn. Like I have loved no other before, like I will love no other from this time hence. I need to go."

He began to sink into the dark.

"I love you, too," I choked out.

This was really happening. He was really going, for the last time ever.

He kissed his fingertips and saluted as the darkness closed over his head, fiery-red eyes blazing in my direction as if to capture the sight of me forever before the darkness closed over him. I was devastated, my heart shattered into a million pieces. I was outraged at the unfairness of it all. I wanted to scream and kick and rage at the powers that be... I loved him with everything that I was, everything that I would be from now until the end of time.

Didn't that mean anything?

I looked at the slowly-receding pool of darkness and a determination took hold in my chest.

No.

No, this would not be the end of our story, it couldn't be the end of our story. I wouldn't let it! Even if I had to follow him, to Hell, or wherever he went during my waking hours.

I clutched the scale pendant from his armor in my hand, tightly, until it cut into my palm. Not knowing what I was getting into or what would happen, I took a deep, deep breath, and before I could lose even one iota of my resolve, I leapt, feet-first, into that puddle of darkness before it could close.

CHAPTER TWENTY-NINE

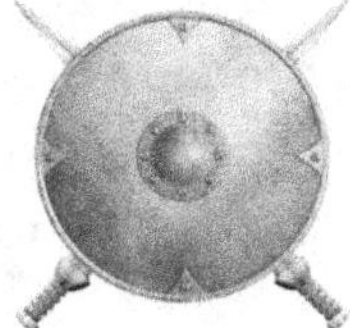

I didn't think, which was strange. I always thought about what I did before I did it, I never made impulsive decisions, never made a move without considering every angle first, but that's what I'd done this time.

I made a complete and utter leap of faith, feet first into the unknown.

And I fell.

My bare feet didn't connect with my bedroom carpet, as I'd half expected them to. No, I fell, and continued to fall through the suffocating black. I couldn't tell if it was so dark because my eyes were closed or not. I thought they were open.

I squeezed them shut and opened them again and wished that I hadn't.

The dark had given way to a great underground cavern. I was impossibly high and falling, while below me, a glittering sea undulated.

Wait, no, that wasn't right.

The sea moved in one direction until the darker half of the shore pushed back. The movement below was a push and pull, a back and forth of give-and-take, and the colors were all wrong. There was no blue, but rather, browns and blacks and grays, dotted with silver points of light.

Panic seized my chest as I fell and fell, realizing that there was nothing but that angry clash below to catch me. The wind plastering the thin satin of my gown to my body was hot and unforgiving, tearing the scream from my throat and whisking it away before I could really even hear the sound.

The roar was deafening, much more than wind; the grate and clang of steel reached my ears in a cacophony of sound that raked across my senses and along the inside of my skull like talons, and I continued to fall, helpless to anything but my plight, to be dashed upon whatever undulated below.

A screech.

I twisted in the air and screamed anew. Pinwheeling my arms, I tumbled midair plummeting head first as the winged creature came for me. It was brown, and naked, its leathery skin stretched over an elongated skeletal frame, impossibly long arms reaching, as its bat-like wings kept it aloft.

I screamed again as it caught me by the ankle, its talon-like fingers digging into the skin of my calf and shin, raking down my leg to the top of my foot. Tears stung my eyes, though from the pain or the biting wind, I don't know. I struggled in the thing's grip as it looked down at me, its mouth pulling into a rictus grin displaying razor-sharp pointed teeth.

A human shout dragged my attention away from the thing.

An angel winged nearby, and he'd spotted the thing with me in its clutches. With powerful strokes of his dove-gray wings, he drove through the hot, fetid air in our direction and I sent up a silent plea that he would make it in time. Terror rode paramount in my mind as something heavy landed on the back of the thing that had me.

It dipped quickly and screamed, the sharp, ichor-cloaked point of a blade protruding from its chest. It let go of me, and I screamed again, but it caught me up with its monkey-like rear foot. He had simply been freeing his hands, because with the change of angle when I looked up, I could clearly see between his legs, and yep, the winged demon-thing that had me was clearly a 'he' and not an 'it'.

My terrified mind prayed harder. I was helpless in this situation, as helpless as I could be. We were still plummeting toward the undulating mass below, although we were close enough in our descent that I could make out what it was I was really seeing.

Fighting.

As far I could see were men, angels, and demons, with sword, mace, maul, and whatever other weapon that could be brought to mind. Both sides locked in combat, each side pushing, the lines moving back and forth.

The creature that held me gave a final shriek, and my head snapped up. Whatever had landed on its back had finished it, and as the winged horror went into its final death throes... it dropped me.

CHAPTER THIRTY

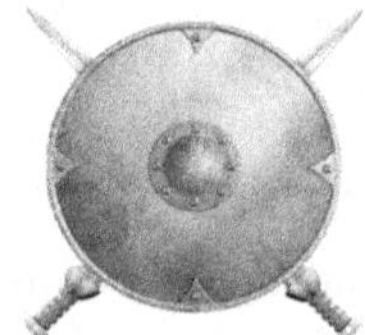

I screamed, for lack of anything more productive to do, but a shout below me came just as I swept past the angel with the dove-gray wings. He threw out his hands and I reached, caught hold and my shoulders jerked violently in their sockets; I cried out but held on for everything that I was worth.

The angel shouted something I didn't understand, I bit my lip and he tried again, the language pattern different than the first. He tried a third time, and a fourth, and then I caught on.

"English!" I screeched.

"Hold on!" he shouted, and beat his powerful wings, once, twice, a third time. We gained a little altitude. My hands were sweating and I could feel myself slipping.

"I'm slipping!" I shouted.

"Hold on just a little longer! Trust me!"

He then shouted in a foreign tongue that was musical to the ear, a lilting sound, and I redoubled my effort to hold fast.

"I'm going to let you go!" he shouted. "Trust me! You will be fine!"

"All right, tell me when!" I shouted.

"Now!" he said, and I let go and fell. I screamed and was jarred roughly as I was caught by another angel, powerfully built, with tawny golden wings. He had me behind my back and beneath my knees and I wrapped my arms around his massive shoulders to stabilize myself.

"What is your name?" he shouted above the din.

"Gracelyn, my name is Gracelyn!" I shouted back.

"I am Karael. You're safe now, Gracelyn." He winged us toward the back of one of the clashing tides.

Neat rows of tents stretched as far as my eye could see, to the cavern's back wall. These rows were broken by open areas dotted with camp fires. Larger tents were scattered here and there. It was a veritable city of canvas of every color and hue. We circled an avenue between tents and as we got lower and lower, shouts went through the camp.

"Thank you," I said as we neared the ground.

Karael smirked, his cool green eyes laughing. He had a generous mouth and long auburn hair that was pulled back into a tail at the nape of his neck, curling softly over his shoulder. He set down, alighting on his feet with surety. He straightened with me in his arms, holding me aloft as if I weighed nothing. I was grateful that my night-gown had fallen modestly back into place. While I had been upside-down, modesty had been the last thing on my mind, but now my cheeks burned with humiliation. The angel with the dove-gray wings set down next to us.

"Karael! How is she?" he asked.

"She is Gracelyn, and I'm fine." I hadn't meant for it to come out sounding so harsh at first, but I really disliked it when people talked about me like I wasn't there. A throwback to when my parents had died and it had suddenly become the thing to do between medical professionals and social workers.

I swallowed really hard and looked at the angel with the dove-gray wings.

"Thank you," I said to the gray-winged angel.

Karael was grinning. "I'd say she's doing remarkably well, Rizoel."

He winked at the angel with gray wings. I noticed now that his hair was salt-and-pepper in color, his eyes a liquid silver, though his face was still youthful in appearance. The whole image was quite striking.

"Uh, Karael?" I said.

"Yes, Gracelyn?" he purred.

Was he flirting?

"Could you put me down, please?" I asked.

He searched my face, the grin never leaving his.

"I could, yes," he said but made no move to do so.

He was definitely flirting. I swallowed hard. Our audience had grown and it was making me nervous. We were at the center of a ring of warriors. Angels, some of them; some of them like Alaric, looked like they were from the other side, trying to turn a new leaf. Some were human, like me... Men and women alike, armor and manner of dress all across the march of time.

"Please," I said, and tried not to let the trembling I felt into my voice, "put me down."

Everyone was talking at once, languages overlapping one another. I was the center of attention and all eyes were on me. I bit my lip. It wasn't the place I wanted to be and I had no idea how I was going to find Alaric in this vast, people-filled space.

"I quite like things the way they are at the moment," Karael was saying.

I began to squirm.

"Please put me down!" I was beginning to panic.

I shoved at his breast plate and he laughed.

"All right, all right, hold still!"

He set me carefully on my feet. I winced; the ground was sharp bits of gray shale. My calf spit fire as I took a few hurried-but-careful steps away from him, into the center of the growing ring of bodies.

"Is she human? Is she alive?" someone asked.

I wrung my long braid between my hands. Across from me, the crowd shuffled back and forth, making way for someone or something, and my breath caught in my throat. I had no idea what was about to happen to me, but people and angels were moving to either side, making way for whoever came forward. My heart leapt into my throat to push the pent-up breath out of the way in a gasp.

Two figures emerged from the crowd, the bodies around them parting like water. One was an angel and stood to the left of an imposing figure in black scale mail. He looked up, his eyes zeroed in on me, and my heart stopped in my chest. All conversation around us simply ceased and one piercing cry could be heard in the sudden quiet.

"Alaric!" I screeched and bolted for him.

He thrust his shield and helm to the angel next to him, who managed to take the round wood into his hands but dropped Alaric's helm with a muttered curse. I flung myself at him. He opened his arms and I crashed into him, wrapping my legs around his hips and my arms around his neck. He crushed me to him. I buried my face in the side of his neck. One of his large limbs curved around my back, the other my shoulders, his hand cradling the back of my head as I sobbed into his neck. An explosion of voices and chatter around us. His grip on me tightened, and he murmured into my ear four words.

"Hold on to me."

I thought to myself as his long strides carried us into the forest of tents, *Good luck getting me to ever let go again.*

CHAPTER THIRTY-ONE

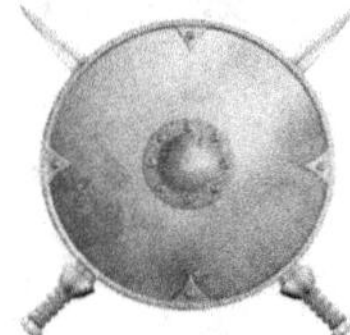

"Just hold on to me, Small One, we are almost there," he murmured, his long strides eating up the ground as we progressed further back into the rows of tents. He paused between two and scanned the area before darting across an open area. He ducked into the mouth of a tent and pulled the flaps closed behind us. Inside, the tent was nothing like it had appeared on the outside. It was quiet, well-lit by glass spheres giving off a soft white light. They sat upon the corner of a small writing desk, on top of the massive wood pillars on the four posts of the bed, and on either end of what appeared to be a workbench. Alaric took a seat on the side of the bed and, steady in his lap, I could finally ease up on the death-grip I had around his waist with my legs. My injured one screamed at me for relief.

"Is this your room?" I asked and he laughed lightly.

"No, Small One, it is a friend's. My tent will be the first place they look for us." He smoothed the loose tendrils of hair back from my tear-stained face. "How are you here?" he asked and peered into my eyes.

"I followed you," I said.

"You followed me?" A frown wrinkled his brow.

"I jumped into that weird pool of dark before it shrank away."

His hands cradled my face gently, his eyes widened in surprise.

"You jumped into a closing portal?" he asked.

"I guess so, if that was what that thing was."

I sniffed. He crushed me to him and wouldn't let me go, and I wouldn't have it any other way. A shuffling movement behind me had us both looking. The angel he'd thrust his helmet and shield at came through the tent's entryway. He spied us on his bed and quickly closed the flap before anyone could see from the outside. Immediately, the sounds from outside ceased.

"Oh, no. Not my tent, brother..." The angel gave Alaric a pointed look.

His wings were black, like a raven's, and his hair was equally dark, so dark that it held a blue sheen in the light. He raked a hand through the unruly locks and turned deep, soulful brown eyes on me.

"Is my tent being watched?" Alaric asked.

"You know it is," the angel replied.

"Hence why I am in yours, brother." Alaric smiled serenely.

"Enough of that now. How in the Savior's name did she get here?" He stabbed a finger in my direction.

I opened my mouth to speak, but then closed it. It was a good question. I turned to Alaric.

"She jumped a closing portal," he said calmly.

The angel blanched and crossed himself, which made me blink in surprise.

They do that too?

From both of their solemn faces, I gathered what I'd done had been very, very stupid, but right now, I didn't care. I was right where I wanted to be, in Alaric's arms... in...

Where was here?

"Where are we?" I asked quietly, disrupting whatever they were thinking about.

"Welcome to the first layer of Hell."

The angel grinned at me, but it held no mirth whatsoever.

"Thanks," I said, then, "I'm Gracelyn."

"Hofneil, but you can just call me Neil."

He gave a nod of his head, eyes flicking to Alaric.

"Nice to meet you, Neil," I murmured.

"You weren't lying," Neil said to Alaric and I smiled at the modern turn of phrase. Alaric cocked his head to the side quirking an eyebrow in question. "She's pretty in the picture, but she's a knockout in person."

He set aside Alaric's shield and helmet, stepping closer.

"Picture?" I asked.

Alaric stopped Neil from saying anything by speaking first.

"How long until we can move? She is hurt and I want to tend to her wound."

Neil frowned. "Hurt where?" he asked.

"I don't know yet. I smell the blood and it stained her gown when she ran to me."

I bit my lip and tried not to snap at the both of them.

"Guys, I'm right here," I reminded them coolly. I began to reluctantly untangle myself from Alaric but his arms tightened around me.

"Not yet," he said.

"Agreed, let's get her to your tent, you've got more stuff." Neil peeked out the front of his tent.

"Is the way clear?" Alaric asked.

"For now, c'mon, I'll scout the way."

He darted out and Alaric got to his feet. I clung to him like a spider monkey.

"Hold on love, it isn't far," his voice was soft and tender in my ear.

Thank you, God, for getting me back to him so quickly, I sent out into the ether, and wondered... Could God still hear my prayers from Hell?

I certainly hoped so.

CHAPTER THIRTY-TWO

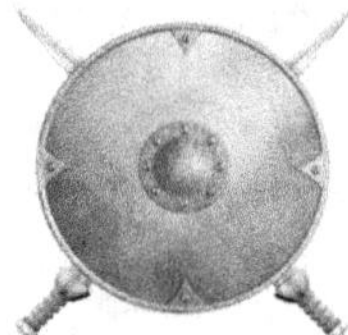

We wove our way between tents, Neil acting as our lookout. Eventually we came to one slightly larger than the rest. We were at the back of the tent and Neil bent, untying the bottom from one of the stakes holding it to the ground. He gave Alaric some hand signals and heaved the canvas up enough to duck under. He popped back out a moment later and lifted it enough for Alaric to duck underneath it with me in his arms.

The interior of the tent was black. Not black as in 'dark', but black as in 'everything in it, from the canvas walls, to the bedding, to the heavy, richly-carved furniture, all of it, was varying textures of black'. It was a little overwhelming at first, but so Alaric that I found myself smiling.

"What's so funny?" Neil asked.

"It's just so Alaric," I said, and was met with an answering grin.

"It is," he agreed.

The interior of the tent was lit like Neil's tent and it dawned on me that the direct light didn't change Alaric into the twisted creature I'd seen by the lamplight in my bedroom. At least, not down here.

Alaric marched to the bed and set me gently onto the voluminous bedding. I reluctantly let him go. Neil hissed when he saw my ankle. It was bleeding pretty badly and hurt something awful when I laid eyes on it.

What is it about being hurt that it doesn't really hurt all that much until you see the blood? This injury was like that. I hadn't noticed any pain except for the odd twinge, but now that I could see it, the claw marks gave a low angry throb and began to burn incessantly. I winced.

"What did this?" Alaric asked, his voice strained.

I described what the flying bat-demon-thing had looked like and he visibly relaxed. Neil handed him a basket full of stuff.

"Okay, I'm out," he was saying. "I don't know how much time you two have before you're found out, but I'd make the most of it. Word spreads through camp like wildfire, you probably don't have much time before they come." He looked pointedly at Alaric. "I'm sorry, but you know she has to go back," he said to him.

"I'm not going to have much to go back to, if I miss work without calling in." I said with a frown.

Neil laughed.

"Time in Hell moves differently than on your mortal coil," he said.

"What do you mean?" I asked.

"Everything is slower down here. An hour down here is about eight minutes up there." He shrugged.

I looked between the two of them stunned. I did the math in my head...

"So for every hour of my time, it was seven-and-a-half hours down here?" I asked.

Neil nodded and my heart constricted.

"So, even though I got to see you every twelve hours or so, you had to wait..." Again I did the math, "...almost four days to see me?"

Alaric nodded, but he wouldn't meet my eyes. I felt really awful all of a sudden. To think I'd whined if I didn't get to see him a night or two in a row, when for him, that had meant a week or more without seeing me. I closed my eyes.

"Make the most of the time you have," Neil told us and ducked out the back of the tent.

"Why didn't you tell me?" I asked.

"Would it have mattered?" he asked, rummaging through the basket.

"I suppose not," I said softly.

"He is right about the time we have being limited."

He was busy swabbing my cuts with some sort of salve, it stung a little, but not too bad.

"They'll come looking for us?" I asked.

"Yes, but they have searched in here already. They will not think to look here again, despite the two guards posted outside."

I gave the entryway to the tent a sharp look.

"They cannot hear us," he said, confirming my theory about the tents being some kind of soundproof. He was winding a bandage around my foot and leg.

"I couldn't let you go," I murmured, and he paused.

"I do not want you here. This is no place for you," he said, and I flinched. He captured my gaze with his own, and when he was sure he had my attention, said, "That does not mean I am not glad you are with me. I would have you by my side always."

"What were they going to do with you? With us?" I asked, looking around the inside of the tent.

There was a full-length mirror in an ornate black frame in one area, a small altar of sorts at its base. On the little altar was a framed photograph of me at the Scotland dig site that had once resided on a shelf in my living room. I hadn't even noticed it was missing. There were several other trivial items from my apartment on it. The empty bottle of mead, its dried and shriveled Valentine's rose looking a little forlorn, several of the bobby pins from my hair that he'd taken down after the disaster with Volund... The book of Frost's poetry I'd gifted him also resided there. I gripped the scale at my throat. He'd done the same thing in his own way. He just didn't wear his keepsakes.

He was watching me, the task of fixing me up done. I looked down at him where he knelt in front of me.

"I don't know," he said softly. "I was to return to the front lines while I awaited judgment. I believe your being here has drastically changed things, however."

He looked at me and we spent long moments in silence just looking at each other.

"I love you," was all I could think to say and was rewarded when he gently brought his lips to mine.

My fingers glided against his cheeks as our lips met. He flicked his tongue against my lower lip sweetly, and I opened for him. Our kiss was bittersweet, tinged with both love and sadness. He pulled back reluctantly and looked me over once more. He rose and unstrapped his pauldrons and greaves, shucking out of his scale. He pulled his shirt over his head and let it fall to the floor.

"What do you want to do, Gracelyn?" he asked me gently.

"I want you," I said. "If this is it, the last time we will have together, I want the memory of being with you this one last time."

He closed his eyes and bowed his head, fists clenching and unclenching the air. He stalked across the tent and stopped in front of me where I sat on the edge of his bed. He settled his hands on either side of my hips and brought us nose to nose. I stared into his burning red eyes from mere inches away.

"I cannot promise to be gentle," he murmured against my lips.

"I know," I said, butterflies in my stomach.

"I don't want to hurt you." His voice was barely above a whisper.

"I don't think you will."

"Gracelyn." He said my name with such longing and heat that my eyes slipped shut and I groaned.

"Please, Alaric," I said and opened my eyes. "Please," I repeated and he was on me.

His mouth crushed down over mine, brutally, his need crashing into me, overwhelming me and dragging me under so thoroughly I didn't want to ever come up for air.

My hands tangled into his straight, snow-white locks, pulling them back from his widow's peak and away from our frantic lips. Our tongues danced so sweetly, playing for keeps, his conquering my mouth, mine exploring his as much as I could. There was an awful, wet, tearing sound and the warm air of the tent slid against my exposed skin, still slightly cooler than it had been before. He kicked off his boots, all the while his mouth never leaving mine. I let my hands roam, down over the swell of his shoulders, across the planes of his chest, along his ribs, while he fumbled at the ties of his leathers. My hands slid over the hills and valleys of his abdominals, and with a growl, he snapped the thongs holding his pants up. I pushed them off his hips, his smooth skin so warm beneath my hands, and he pushed me back, one arm snaking around my lower back, the other bracing further up on the bed.

He lifted me with a snarl, breaking our kiss and slid me back completely onto his massive bed. He went to one knee on the edge and clambered up after me, placing the other knee firmly between my knees. He was achingly hard between my thighs and I reached between us and curled my hand firmly around him, stroking him, his foreskin pulling back to reveal a pearly drop of precum at his tip. He planted both hands on the bed and let me stroke him for several moments before stilling my hand with one of his own.

"Not yet," he breathed, and pushed me back.

He slipped a finger into my crevice and slicked my wetness up over my clit. I cried out when he circled it with a finger and his face radiated joy at the sound. He bent forward and captured my mouth again and I loved it. I loved him. I felt him reach between us and position himself at my opening and my hips rose off the bed in a silent plea. He groaned into my mouth and worked his way into me, swallowing my pleading whimpers. I arched into him, my hips thrusting forward to meet his, until he was fully seated inside of me.

He drove into me that much more and I cried out with the pleasure of it, which encouraged him, because he soon found a powerful rhythm that was just this side of punishing. God, did I love it, too. I grabbed his ass and urged him on harder, crying out his name. I trailed my hands up his ribs, relishing the ripple of muscle underneath. He thrust into me, hard and harder, and I wrapped my legs around his hips as my orgasm began to build. Our mouths clashed together as our bodies moved in synchronicity; I felt the pleasure begin to rise and clenched down on him, and when I sailed over the edge of the cliff, I was dimly aware of my nails scoring down his back as I screamed his name.

He thrust into me a final time and bowed his head as he shuddered his own release, placing a gentle kiss on my shoulder. He said something in a language I didn't know, but it sounded good, so I didn't ask. I just wrapped my legs tighter around his hips, even though they were trembling, and my arms around his shoulders, and pulled his warmth down on top of me. He lay atop me willingly, his arms taking the brunt of his weight to either side of my head. Joined at the sex as we were, he was still head and shoulders taller than me, so I placed a kiss on his chest, which was all I could reach and right in front of my face. I smiled against his sweat-dewed skin.

"I love you," he rumbled between breaths.

"I love you too," I whispered, and I suddenly realized that I would never be able to tell him often enough.

He shifted, slipping out of me and I shivered with delight. He moved off of me and to the side, and pulled me snug against him. I lay my head upon his shoulder and the swell of his chest as he cradled me. He pulled the turned-down blankets up over the both of us and I sighed in contentment. For now, I was happy. I didn't know how long it would last, but I would hold onto this for the rest of my days.

"I have longed for this, for you cannot know how long," he murmured. I knew what he meant. He'd always been so careful of me, with me, and now it was like he was completely unfettered.

"Me too," I whispered, and I had.

"I did not hurt you?" His voice was tinged with concern.

"Not in the slightest. You feel incredibly good." I wriggled a bit and smiled.

"Never have I felt anything as soft, warm, and pure as you, Gracelyn. I am honored that you would let me love you without restriction," and to that, I had nothing I could think of to say.

CHAPTER THIRTY-THREE

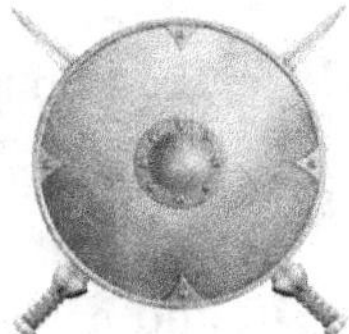

*V*oices.

I woke, still pressed to Alaric's side, my leg over his, a little too warm beneath all the blankets. My mouth was dry, and certain muscles, unused to such rigorous activity, were sore, but not unpleasantly so. My shoulders and back ached fiercely but I was sure that was from my fall. I tried to get my mind, still fuzzy from sleep, to focus on what was being said. I did not open my eyes. By the way Alaric's arms tightened around me, I was sure he knew I was conscious, but I wanted to hear.

"Wake her. You are to be taken before the Archen." The voice was soft and had that musical quality that all of the angels I'd met did.

"She is exhausted. A little longer, Ansiel, please?" Alaric said, and I was unused to the note of pleading in his voice.

"Would that I could give you more time, Alaric, not only for her sake, but for yours, but I cannot. You have been summoned." The angel sounded sincere, his voice tinged with pity.

I opened my eyes and looked across Alaric's broad chest.

"Ah, she is awake."

The angel, Ansiel, smiled at me, and I felt awash in love and peace. I smiled back sadly. He was graceful, in a long, light-gray robe that reminded me of the mist that sometimes rose from the Hudson in the early morning light. His wings were the first truly white wings I'd seen so far, as pure as freshly fallen snow. His hair was a deep blonde and his hazel eyes jewel-like, set in a very handsome face with very fine bone structure.

Alaric looked down at me and I looked up at him.

This was pretty much it for us.

We both knew it; we both felt it, and it was as if my heart were slowly turning to ash in my breast, sifting away, grain by grain, along with each bit of sand in the hourglass. I sat up and clutched the sheet to my chest.

"Oh, my."

Ansiel had the grace to look embarrassed, but I wasn't. There was no shame in what Alaric and I had done. None at all. The angel's gaze roamed the room and, of course, landed upon my torn nightgown on the floor. He stooped and picked it up, 'Tsk'ing under his breath.

"Really, Alaric," he said, but the admonishment was tinged with a bit of humor at my beloved's expense.

A flash of light, and the torn scraps of material were whole, and what's more, pure and clean in the angel's hands as he held it out. Alaric's long reach took it from him.

"A bit of privacy please?" Alaric asked and Ansiel left the tent.

I pulled the gown over my head slowly. Alaric rose and pulled fresh clothing from the trunk at the foot of the bed and dressed as well.

Neither of us said anything. What do you say when you know it's going to be goodbye, but everything in your soul is screaming that you don't want it to be?

He held out his hand to me and I took it. With one last meaningful look between us, and a reassuring, but hollow, squeeze of our hands, we bravely exited the tent, meeting Ansiel and a small phalanx of guards outside.

"Ah, very well, then," Ansiel said and turned to lead us, the guards ringing our little group.

Alaric swept me up into his arms and stood tall, looking forward. I let him carry me over the chipped and broken shale, pressing a kiss along the side of his neck, the only place I could reach, in thanks. My arms wound around his shoulders and he marched with our guards, as if I were nothing at all of a burden.

The route we took was lined with warriors to either side. Men and women, young and old, all curious. I was amazed though at how many took off helmets or caps as we passed or pressed a hand over their heart in salute. Not to Ansiel, or our guards, but to Alaric – and some, I even had the impression, were saluting me.

"What are they doing?" I asked.

"I have been their commander for millennia," he began in reply, "but I believe they are saluting you, for your bravery in coming here."

I blushed a deep crimson. "It wasn't bravery," I said. "It was that or lose you forever and I wasn't going to do that. Not if I could help it. It was love, if anything, that brought me here."

"We shall have to agree to disagree," Alaric said with a curve of his lips. He could smile all he wanted, I was still certain there hadn't been any bravery at all in doing what I'd done. I had been scared shitless the whole time.

"Child," Ansiel said, and I knew he was addressing me.

"Yes?"

"The definition of courage is to be terrified of doing something yet doing it anyway, is it not?" he asked.

Had he read my mind?

"I suppose," I answered.

"Then, by definition, you coming here, despite your reason and despite your fear, was a brave thing to do."

He didn't turn, so I couldn't see, but I could hear the smile in his voice. I couldn't help but smile myself.

"Well played, sir. Well played," I said and the grin from Alaric was something beautiful to behold.

We walked on, further and further, past row after row of tents, until the din of fighting had ebbed to a distant roar.

"Where exactly are we going?" I asked, apprehensive.

"To see the Archangels," Alaric said, and I gave him a long, slow blink.

"The Archangels," I repeated. "As in Michael, Gabriel, and the gang?" Disbelief shaded my tone.

"Yes, though I would be a bit more respectful, or at the very least, more tactful than that when in their presence." Ansiel's tone was a wee bit frosty. I shot a panicked look at Alaric.

"I'm sorry, I didn't mean any disrespect," I said hastily, adding, "I'm only human, you know." Seemed like he needed reminding.

Ansiel made a noncommittal and dismissive sound and my temper rose to the surface. I kept my cool but still, I had something I felt needed to be said.

"A year ago, I thought I just had a random case of the blues. Six months ago, I went to a doctor for meds, thinking I was depressed and it was a chemical imbalance in my brain. Two months ago, I thought I was going stark raving mad. If, at any of those points, you had popped up and asked me if I would fall in love with a man who'd been dead for over a thousand years or told me that I'd be meeting the Archangels in the first level of Hell, how do you think I would have responded?" I had an inexplicable need to defend myself here and was determined to do it.

Alaric, whose eyes had remained steadfastly fixed on a point out in front of us, was looking at me with an expression that was a mixture of pride and awe. Ansiel stopped, turned, and regarded me for a moment. Not unkindly, just like he'd never seen a specimen like me before. He looked up at Alaric, who was pretty much a giant, standing at least a head, if not a head and shoulders over all of us.

"Remarkable," he said. "I can see your attraction."

Ansiel then smiled serenely and turned back to the path only he and the guards seemed to know we were taking. We began to approach one of the larger tents that I had seen from the air. It resembled a big top, like when Cirque du Soliel set up their tent in Central Park. It was as if three round circus tents were sewn into one, each a different height, and varying widths, brought together as a whole. They weren't striped like circus tents, though. The canvas they were made from was a simple sun-bleached white.

Ansiel strode through the gaping maw of the tent, and Alaric didn't fall so much as a single step behind, despite my added weight. He wasn't even breathing hard, I realized, nor were his arms trembling. It really was like he could carry me all day without ever getting tired. Ansiel stopped and turned before we went through a set of curtains into whatever chamber lay beyond.

"You may put her down," Ansiel said and Alaric stiffened. My arms tightened around his neck. Ansiel sighed. "The floor is quite suited for her bare feet. No harm will come to her."

He made a motion with his hand, and Alaric and I exchanged looks. I honestly didn't think Ansiel got it. We didn't want to let each other go. I suddenly felt a little sad for the angel.

"It's okay," I whispered, even though it wasn't. Even though I was pretty sure that when this was through, I would never, ever be 'okay' again.

A muscle twitched in Alaric's jaw and he rested his forehead against mine for a long minute before sliding me gently along his body until my feet touched the floor, which was smooth and polished, and surprisingly warm. I captured his hand with my smaller one and held fast.

Ansiel nodded as if satisfied, and two of the guards pulled back the curtains.

CHAPTER THIRTY-FOUR

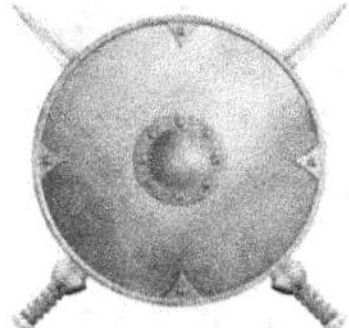

*A*laric and I both put up our free hands to shade our eyes from the blinding white light.

It took a moment for my eyes to adjust, and when they did, I was a little dismayed to see we were stepping into what appeared to be a courtroom-type atmosphere. There was a high bench on a raised dais, and seated behind it were three angels, with more empty seats to either side of them. I guess I was a little relieved we didn't warrant the full host of Archangels, but the three seated were intimidating as hell.

A chuckle swept the room and two of the three Arches' lips twitched as they tried to suppress smiles. The third, the most powerfully-built and seated between the two that had tried not to smile, remained stoic, as still as the surface of a pond on a windless summer day.

The rest of the courtroom was built much like a Roman senate or the Coliseum. Stone bleachers curved to either side of the dais, rising up and up and up to the very ceiling of the canvas. We moved up the aisle until we were basically at the bottom of the bowl of spectating angels. When we stopped, I could see Karael, the flirty bronze-winged angel; Rizoel, the dove-gray angel; and Neil, standing to the side. Neil looked grim, almost afraid, and I quailed, tucking myself closer to Alaric's side.

"Alrekr Hakon Frithjof." The Archangel who spoke was the one seated on the left. His hair was long and brown and pulled back from an angular face in a wild tangle, as if his first love was, and would always be, flying, and he didn't have time for such silly things as combing his hair. His eyes were honey-brown and warm, and his fingers long and tapered where they rested upon the bench in front of him. His armor was a highly-polished silver plate, and though it looked like it should be unwieldy, he wore it with grace and elegance. He smiled at me and I smiled in return, more than a little shyly. Alaric emitted a disgusted growl.

"That is my name no more." His voice was solid with conviction.

"I don't know, 'Peace-thief' seems to still fit, taking a look at your charge!" someone called from high up.

I narrowed my eyes and looked for the culprit. The Archangel who had spoken rapped his knuckles on the bench, but I had found my voice.

I looked in the direction that the insult had come from and said, loud enough to be clear, "Alaric is the only thing that brings me peace anymore."

I squeezed his hand and the gallery broke out in a sweeping murmur. The Archangel rapped his knuckles on the bench again and the sound seemed to be amplified. The Archangel in the center finally looked interested.

"If you do not wish to be known as Alrekr, then please, tell us, what is your name?" the angel on the left asked.

"I renounce the name I carried in life, for I am no longer he. For the purpose of this gathering, I humbly ask that you simply call me Alaric, for that is who I am now to my beloved Gracelyn, and who I wish to be until a time I be deemed worthy of final judgment." He made a fist with the hand that I wasn't holding and pressed it to his chest over his heart in a sort of salute.

The three Archangels exchanged looks, eyebrows up, mouth down, to a one-sided smile, and, from the scary blonde one in the middle, a one-sided lift of a shoulder.

"It is a paltry thing," the blonde one finally said, and his voice was rich and deep, almost like Alaric's but harsher somehow.

His golden hair was just above his shoulders and reminded me of a lion's mane. His features were thick and strong and extremely hand-some, with full lips and a nose that looked like it may have been broken a time or two. His armor was silver too, not tarnished, but not shiny like the first angel's in the row. I realized that it was because it was scuffed and dented, that the angel in the center was used to seeing combat. I realized with a small jolt that the center angel was the Archangel Michael. His eyes tracked away from Alaric and settled on me. Blue, like the sea before a storm.

"Very good, child," he said, and a small smile played upon his lips.

If he weren't so freaking imposing, I might actually like him, but as of right now, I was scared to death of what they were going to do to Alaric. It took me a second to realize I hadn't said anything aloud.

Crap, they really were reading my mind.

"Very well," the brunette Archangel said, and smirked at me,

"Alaric, beloved of Gracelyn, you are here before a Covenant of Three for the transgression of showing yourself to your charge, for knowingly endangering the balance, and for willfully doing so for months, despite taking an oath to never directly interfere. What say you?"

I sort of liked the Archangel for the way he said Alaric's name. 'Alaric, beloved of Gracelyn.' It was so true, and I appreciated that he recog-nized my love for him.

"Wait." The angel on the right finally spoke up.

He held up a hand to the other two, his eyes fixed on me. His hair was long, and the rich fiery red of a true ginger. It swept past his shoulders and down his back, the top half tied back out of his eyes. Unlike the other two, he did not wear plate, but rather a bronze colored scale mail. A bow leaned against the bench beside him, a quiver of arrows sitting within reach.

"I, for one, would like to hear their tale from the beginning."

A murmur of agreement swept through the gallery.

"Tell us, Alaric, how did this come to pass?" the ginger angel asked.

Alaric sighed and shifted uncomfortably. I squeezed his hand and searched his face for what he might be thinking, but came up empty; he was as shut down as I'd ever seen him, and it made my heart hurt just a little to see it.

"As you know, Raphael," he nodded to the brunette Arch, "you assigned Gracelyn to my charge as one of my trials."

Raphael, huh, so that's who that was.

I watched Raphael incline his head in acknowledgement of what Alaric was saying as he continued.

"She is a brilliant soul," Alaric said, looking at me, and I heard murmurs of agreement which quickly died with one rap from Michael's knuckles.

"By virtue of her shine, she had captured the attention of a demon, but not just any." He looked around at the gathering. "Shax," he said, and I heard a collective gasp.

If it was enough to make a crowd of angels gasp and three Archangels shift in their seats, apparently Shax was a seriously badass motherfucker. I heard a few laughs and frowned, my thoughts shifting more towards *Huh, so that's the name of the critter that was sifting around in my head.* The room went silent at that. Alaric went on.

"She was brilliant, a warrior in a true sense."

I realized he was talking about me.

"Shax was inside her mind, trying to make her feel guilt over her parents' death, but she fought him, without even knowing she fought. She refuted the insinuations Shax made for weeks, then months, until he finally had to accept defeat and change tactics. I admired her for that." Alaric paused for a moment then continued his narrative.

"In the beginning, I simply watched, made no interference, as she did not need my assistance. My own arrogance led me to believe that to be so. But Shax had changed his game, and I realized it too late, when Gracelyn stood nearly alone. He had convinced her friends that she was too boring, too drab, and too sad to spend any time with, and they went from her, save for one. By then it was approaching a mortal year since he'd begun to groom her for his own ends. He grew impatient. He began to circle her, drawing ever closer until finally he directly interacted."

"Interacted how?" someone called, scoffing.

"The roof," I guessed, and Alaric nodded.

"What did you say?" the ginger Archangel asked.

I swallowed hard and told them.

"I woke up standing on the edge of my roof. I thought I was going crazy, that I had sleepwalked or something. I almost went over the edge. I scraped my elbow throwing myself back. When I got back to my apartment, it was chained from the inside. I didn't know how I was going to get back in, but the chain dropped suddenly, I heard it, and my door was open. That was you wasn't it?" I asked. "You let me back in."

Alaric inclined his head.

"Go on." Michael's deep voice vibrated out into the throng.

"By then, Shax and I were firmly engaged over Gracelyn's wellbeing," Alaric continued. "When he backed down, I counted it as a small victory, but I should have seen his endgame with what he did next. He hurt her more blatantly this time, cut her wrist. He thought he was clever, putting her in situations where she only need take one final step or simply let the blood flow freely. She was too strong. Each time, she fought her way through his insidious possession, and both times she fought her way back from the brink. Gracelyn is so full of life, but what is more, she is brimming with a will to live."

"I took myself to the hospital," I said and showed them the scar on my wrist.

"Shax changed tactics once more. Using her only friend's jealousy against Gracelyn, turning her best friend's love to hate over a man who had no designs on Gracelyn at all. She directed my beloved to stop calling upon her, said that she never wanted to see her and the grief, it consumed Gracelyn. It was then that Shax and I had our final stand, and the night I could no longer resist my own desires to know this woman. I went to her."

He smiled sadly at me and I smiled back.

"If my heart were made of glass, that night it was like it had been pitched off its shelf, but instead of shattering completely on the floor, Alaric caught it, and it's been his ever since."

He took me in his arms and held me, kissing the top of my head. There was a lot of buzz, muttering and conversation. The three Archangels spoke with one another, finally turning back to us.

"How did she get here?" Raphael asked.

"I followed him," I said, head held high, "and I'd do it again in a heartbeat."

There was a whole lot of scoffing and laughter, and it took three mighty raps of Michael's knuckles to quiet the room.

"You would have us believe that you followed Alaric into Hell, willingly, of your own accord?" the ginger Archangel said, and then added disgustedly, "My name is Uriel, not 'Ginger'."

I couldn't help it, the thought just occurred to me: *Well, some of us aren't mind readers, so you'll have to forgive me.*

It was the first time Michael laughed, and the sound boomed out over all of us gathered and poured down like warm rain, reminding me of a storm, and I wondered briefly, and not for the first time, if there was any correlation between the Norse pantheon and the Christian one. God equals Odin and maybe Michael equals Thor? I was raised Catholic, and I believed wholeheartedly that there was only one true God, but so many worshiped him by another name or face or ideology I had to wonder.

I snapped out of my random theological thoughts to a lot of curious stares and a few looks of respect and blushed furiously. *I was born with a defective brain filter.* I was sure of it. More laughter.

"I can see why you are taken with her," Raphael remarked dryly. Someone cleared their throat, and Rizoel and Karael stepped forward.

"If we may?" Rizoel said.

"Speak," Uriel said.

"I caught her as she fell through the ceiling of the first. I don't know where she came from," Rizole said.

"I carried her to ground. We spoke briefly before Commander Fri–" He stopped himself and corrected, "Alaric, came through the crowd. She ran to him as if he were the only water in a desert. There was no way he brought her to this plane." He bowed and took a step back.

Neil came forward. "She jumped his closing portal. It's what she told me and she had no reason to lie about it." He gave me a small smile.

I wasn't sure about how I felt about being well-liked in Hell, but I would take it. I smiled back.

The three Archangels traded looks and facial expressions, and it was if they were speaking a silent language with them.

"Is this your final accounting, then?" Uriel asked, and Alaric hung his head.

"No, there is more, but I would ask that Gracelyn be excused from the remainder of this proceeding, and that it be recognized that she is an innocent, unaware of our oaths and covenants, and as such to be returned to the mortal plane free of judgment in these matters."

The three Archangels traded looks. Michael spoke, and with every word, he hollowed out my chest where my heart should be.

"It is done. You three," he indicated Neil, Karael, and Rizoel, "take her back to Alaric's quarters, I believe she will be most comfortable there. Ansiel, call for Ruman. After Alaric has had his say, I believe that he will be needed before we pronounce judgment."

He looked at me sympathetically, but my eyes were on Alaric.

"Please don't," I begged. "Please, don't send me away."

He held me at arm's length and cupped my face in his large hands.

"I would spare you any pain, any shame, and any more heartache than I have already caused you," he said, and when his eyes roamed my face it was as if he were committing it to memory.

My stomach dropped out, because that is exactly what he was doing. I choked on a sob, the tears coming hot, fast, and fierce. This was it.

I was losing him.

He kissed me, gentle, sweet, and weighted with regret... it tasted like goodbye.

No, no, no! This wasn't happening, this could not be happening!

"It is, child, and you must accept it." Raphael sounded sad.

Alaric smoothed his hands down my neck and gripped my shoulders lightly. My hand seized around the scale and I realized that I was about to never see the man I loved ever again and he had nothing of me, not a single thing to hold on to.

Lightning-quick, before anyone could pick up what I was thinking, I lunged for the guard nearest us and snatched his dagger from the sheath at his hip. There were screams and cries of outrage but the Archangels remained stoic.

"Silence!" Uriel boomed.

I took my long braid over my shoulder and cut it, raggedly sawing through the hair above the first hair tie that held it in its ponytail. My hair fell around my face in ragged chunks as the braid finally came free. I handed the sharp dagger back to the angel I'd snatched it from, and he took it, the hard set of his jaw signaling his displeasure. I turned to Alaric and pressed the braided length of hair into his hands.

"I love you," I said, brokenly.

"I love you."

He captured the back of my head with his hand and pulled me forward planting a final kiss on my forehead, his lips warm and silk against my skin and I sniffed as more tears fell.

"Take care of her, brother. See that she gets safely home." He was speaking over my head.

"I swear on my honor, my life, and in the Father's name, I will see her safe," Neil said.

"As do I." Karael.

"As do I." Rizoel.

Alaric closed his eyes and I watched twin tears slip free, trailing down his face. He handed me to Neil, who had to drag me bodily away. I couldn't help it. I wailed. The heartbreak I felt poured from my lips in an agonized peal of sound that reverberated throughout the silent chamber. I collapsed, dead weight in Neil's arms, and he almost went down with me. Karael lifted me, like a broken doll, into his arms. Alaric stood tall, back straight, and faced the three Archangels as I was taken out of the chamber, sobbing, hysterical, bitter, and as broken as I had ever been.

"It will be okay, Gracelyn," Karael said, and I could hear little doubt in his words. He honestly believed what he was saying.

"No, it won't." My voice cracked and was very small, but it was iron when I said, "I will never love again."

CHAPTER THIRTY-FIVE

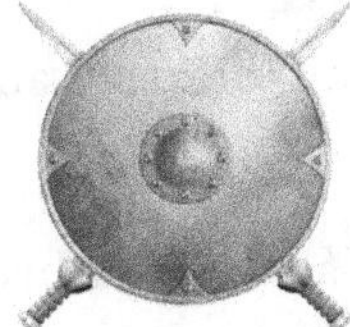

"Who is Ruman?" I demanded and the three angels looked at each other dubiously.

Neil raked a hand through his raven-dark hair and gripped the back of his neck, staring at the floor for several long moments, his other hand cocked on his hip.

"Ruman is the angel who takes account of evil men's deeds while in Hell."

Rizoel finally was the one to answer me, his voice soft. I was perched in the center of Alaric's bed, breathing in his smell, hugging one of his pillows to my chest. Tears welled in my eyes.

"What do they want him there for?" I asked.

"I don't know that we should be telling her any of this." Neil sounded frustrated. I looked at him sharply.

"Tell me," I said sharply.

"I promised him I would keep you safe, swore the strongest oath we have."

"Neil, I swear to–" I stopped myself. "I'm sitting in the center of the love of my life's bed while something potentially horrible is being decided. I feel angry, and helpless, and....and...and destroyed! There's an Alaric-sized hole in my heart and in case you haven't noticed he's pretty fucking big, so tell me what's happening to him!" I shrieked. I wasn't being very nice to them, and I should have felt bad about that, but I couldn't. I was just so overwhelmed by grief.

"He is likely to be judged," Karael said.

"Judged..." I repeated, thinking furiously, and trying to think in biblical terms.

"This," Rizoel gestured with a sweep of his hand, "all of this, is Purgatory. Souls are in limbo here," he supplied.

My eyes widened.

"She's got it," Karael said.

"I don't think I do," I said.

"You do." This from Neil.

"Spell it out for me anyways," I said and pinned him with my gaze.

"The time spent here can tip your scales in either direction. I don't know how much you know about Alaric, how much he told you..."

Alaric's words from Valentine's ghosted back to me. "I was an evil man when I lived, I was the foulest and most depraved soul in death, and a warrior of Hell for a little over five centuries of your time..." I said them aloud and Neil blinked in surprise.

"Yeah, that's a polite way of putting it," he said.

Karael laughed and Rizoel smiled.

"Okay I get it, he was the baddest of the bad m'fer's." I rolled my eyes. "But that isn't my Alaric, not anymore."

"Not for a long time," Rizoel affirmed, and smiled.

"So what's going to happen to him?" I asked.

"There is just no way to know, love," Karael said, and I finally knew how many times one person could break before they finally shattered, because I was in a million pieces all over Alaric's bedroom floor.

CHAPTER THIRTY-SIX

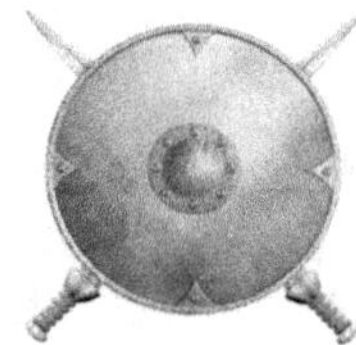

*V*oices.

It was déjà vu. I woke in Alaric's bed, surrounded by his smell, only this time he wasn't beside me.

Not so déjà vu after all.

"How is she?" I recognized the imperious voice as Raphael's

"Waiting for news, terrified for him." Rizoel sounded tired, and I felt bad.

"Do you know how to heal a broken heart?" Neil asked.

"No. Only time can heal that." Raphael sounded sad, so final, and I choked back a sob.

"I'm never going to see him again am I?" I asked, and four sets of eyes turned as one.

"I cannot say." Raphael looked sympathetic.

"Was he judged?" I asked.

"Yes."

"And?"

"And, it is time for you to go home."

He put a knee on the edge of the bed. His wings shone with a pearly iridescence up close and were so white as to be blinding. He held out a hand. I took it and let him help me up.

"I don't understand," I said.

"You were never meant to, child. This place was never meant for the living." He guided me to the mirror.

"You aren't going to take my memories or anything, are you?" I asked.

"No." He laughed, but it held no mirth.

"Good. I want to remember him; I need to." I wiped away tears.

"Be patient, Gracelyn. Good things come to those who wait. I know that your time on the mortal coil is fleeting, but wait. These are my parting words to you."

He reached out and touched the mirror and my bedroom appeared.

I looked at the three angels behind him.

"Thank you, all of you. I'm sorry if I was awful to you." I blushed with shame.

"We're going to miss him, too," Rizoel said and smiled.

I closed my eyes as more tears streamed.

"Go." Raphael smiled kindly and I tried to smile back, to be brave, but I couldn't.

I stepped through the mirror, and turned back, but all that was behind me was my open closet. I crumpled to my knees and sobbed.

I was alone. God help me, I was alone.

I prayed.

CHAPTER THIRTY-SEVEN

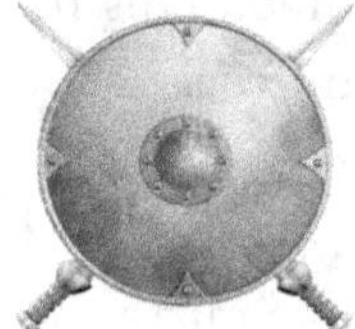

Four hours later the sun was coming up, but all I could do was stare at the clock, my fingers twisting in my chopped hair. I sat up and went to the kitchen, and picking up my phone, I did what I had never in my life done before.

I called off work.

I made up a story about going for an early-morning run and that I was attacked by a dog in the park, killing two birds with one stone. I would have to explain my leg somehow, might as well do it before anyone saw it. Jared told me to rest up and to take as much time as I needed, and the guilt and self-loathing for lying to him set in immediately upon hanging up. I dressed comfortably in jeans and a sweater and went out once it was late enough that a hair salon would be open. I walked until I found one that proclaimed walk-ins were welcome.

I sat numbly in the chair while a sweet, flamboyantly gay man 'tsk'ed over the state of my chopped-off hair and red-rimmed eyes. He assumed that I had gone through a horrible break-up, and I let him. He did a good job with my hair, evening the ragged butchery I'd visited upon it, giving me what he called a 'Victoria Beckham A-line', saying that I had the face for it.

It looked spectacular when he was finished, although it required more maintenance than I was used to. I'd have to use a flatiron to keep it up, my hair had too much of a natural wave to it otherwise. I bought one from the nice man and some hair products and left the salon. My head was so much lighter, and that made my heart just that much heavier.

God, I missed him.

CHAPTER THIRTY-EIGHT

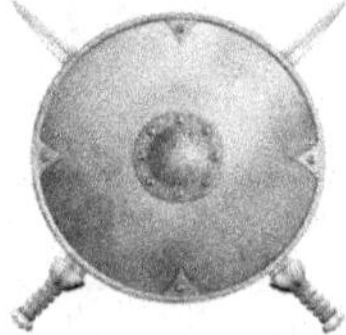

I went in to work the next day, I needed the distraction. Despair had taken a hold of me, and I didn't think demons had anything to do with it this time. Jared looked up from his desk and his eyes widened in shock.

"Your hair..." He blinked several times as if he couldn't believe it.

"I donated it to a good cause," I said and really it was a lie by omission. I had donated it to a good cause, it just wasn't what he was likely thinking. The man at the salon had told me I could bring in what I'd hacked off if it was over twelve inches long so, to make wigs for cancer patients. I guess it was a regular thing that some people did. I hadn't known.

"It looks good," Jared said, once he'd gotten over the initial shock. I smiled. He really was a good friend. My heart squeezed.

"How's the leg?" he asked and I propped my foot on the edge of his desk and pulled up my pant leg to show off the white bandage winding up my calf.

"Little shit got me good," I complained. He frowned.

"You go to the hospital?" he asked.

"Yeah," and it wasn't a lie, I had gone the day before, after the hair salon.

The doctor had given me a tetanus shot and looked at me skeptically when I'd said a dog had done it. He'd said that he had seen plenty of dog bites and scratches before and that "This was no dog." I'd stuck to my story, had gone against medical advice on taking the rabies shots and signed myself out as soon as I'd been fixed up. I took the prescription for antibiotics to ward off any infection, the memory of Alaric's wound still fresh.

I pasted on a brave smile for Jared and tried to breathe through the fresh stab of pain thinking of Alaric brought.

God. I. Missed. Him.

"Well, I have good news and bad news," Jared was saying, leaning back into his chair, hands clasped behind his head.

"Give me my dessert first," I said and flopped into one of the chairs across his desk.

"The verdict is in. We know what the runes say." He grinned. My eyebrows went up.

"Wait, so what's the bad news?" I asked.

"Gunnar Volund is in New York and coming in today. I was planning on calling a department meeting to announce the contents of the email. Thought it would be good for morale."

I chewed my lip.

"Sounds good. Lecture hall?" I asked.

"Yep, cleared it for a block of time at one. Figured I'd call it an early day and let everyone celebrate. It's big, Gracie."

He was grinning and I couldn't help it. My smile was genuine.

"I'm looking forward to it." I got up.

"See you there." He winked and I left his office, pondering what had him so excited.

The only thing I could come up with was that it was a name. What was Volund's ancestor's name? I stopped in my tracks. I realized I'd never asked. That I didn't know. Volund had only ever referred to him as 'my ancestor', had never given a name in my presence. He must have told Jared though. Jared was far too excited, otherwise.

I went to my bench and got to work on cleaning the boss from a shield. The boss is that large metal cap thing in the center of the round wooden shield that Vikings carried. It was traditionally where the shield was gripped, the hand being protected by the boss' metal bubble, and also making it a very effective method of using the shield as a blunt weapon by bashing one's opponent with it. The wood and leather comprising the rest of the shield had long since rotted away and the boss itself was severely misshapen by encrustations, but it was found in very close proximity to a bearded axe blade and my sword.

It has been long suggested that during combat, a Viking would use their primary weapon in their main hand and carry not only their shield, but also an extra back-up weapon with it, gripped along with their shield in their off hand. If the primary weapon were lost, then the secondary was available for use, all while maintaining a defense.

With the close proximity of these three items, and with the blade of the bearded axe so close to the boss, it was theorized that the three items belonged to the same person and as such when my work was completed, all three of these items would go on display along with carefully crafted replicas showing how they may have looked during the warrior's time.

We had big dreams of one day having an entire exhibit, complete with a Viking longship crafted exactly as they had been a thousand years ago. We wanted to make the exhibit one that could travel from city to city for years, a real phenomenon on the level of King Tutankhamun or the Titanic exhibits circling not only the U.S. but the globe, beginning and ending that trek in Norway.

I looked up at the clock and realized that it was almost one. I had a little under ten minutes to get to the lecture hall. Plenty of time. I cleaned up my area and put my tools away and hung my lab coat. I wouldn't need anything, so I stepped out and down the hall and used my badge to exit the restoration facility and enter the museum's office space. I took the elevator to the correct floor; my leg had protested the stairs a little too much this morning, and upon exiting it, ran smack dab into Gunnar Volund and Jared having a heated conversation. I stopped dead.

"Gracelyn." Jared looked startled, then a little guilty.

"Jared, Mr. Volund."

Volund's expression darkened, but then smoothed out. His eyes were fixed on the scale at the hollow of my throat. He nodded, his hands deep in his pockets.

"Ms. Adams. You are well?" he asked.

"Yes."

My heart ached. As much as I despised Volund, he'd been the only other person to see Alaric, and that made me want to make an effort.

"If I may, before you two have any more to say on the matter, I would like to say all is forgiven. Mr. Volund, I would like to enjoy this discovery and I would like you to enjoy it, too. I want today to be about the history, somebody's story. Not about an evening of too much wine and... and unfortunate decisions made."

I stuck out my hand. Volund stared at it a moment and finally engulfed it with one of his massive ones. We shook. Jared looked at me with no little admiration.

"Gracie, will you be all right if I...?" he let the question hang.

"Yes, go finish setting up. We'll be in in a minute," I said and took back my hand.

Jared nodded, concern etching his face, but he looked around at some of the milling museum-goers and decided Volund and I were in a public-enough space that I was safe. He disappeared into the lecture hall. I turned back to Volund.

"What was he?" Volund asked.

"He is what he is, Gunnar, and I don't think you'd believe me if I told you."

I sighed. He smiled.

"You called me Gunnar," he said.

"So I did." I was a little surprised at that myself.

"I am still the monster you think me." He cocked his head to the side.

"Gunnar, what you think you saw in the park was real, and the love of my life. He was probably a bigger monster in life than you could ever be, and he changed. Not for me, but for himself. If he can be redeemed, then you can, too. You just need to find it in yourself, and the right motivation." I turned from him and went into the lecture hall, my gaze lingering over my shoulder.

He stood behind me and watched me go, a curious look on his face, a mixture of confusion and deep thought. I left him to it. He would join the rest of us. I knew that he didn't want to miss this anymore than I did.

CHAPTER THIRTY-NINE

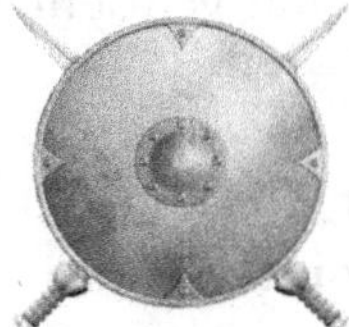

The lecture hall was vast and our department was pretty small. We all fit into the first five or six rows of seats in the center section, which, admittedly, was the biggest. Jared motioned to me from the front where he stood beside the museum's curator talking animatedly and motioned to a seat to the side at one end. I took it and looked up at the stage. My sword sat, seemingly suspended, in a clear acrylic case in front of the podium, a spotlight shining on it. A white screen sat to one side with a slide show presentation introducing the lecture Jared had planned.

Gunnar Volund crossed in front of me and slid into a seat three or four down from mine, in the center of the row somewhere. I paid him no mind. I was struggling not to think of Alaric, trying in vain to keep my mind occupied with something else, anything else. I resorted to praying for him, as a happy medium. The words swirled in my head over and over, until Jared took his place at the podium and the lights dimmed.

"Good afternoon..." he began. He spoke at length about our project and what we had accomplished so far, and I turned in my seat to realize that more of the lecture hall had filled up and that there was likely several philanthropists and potential investors in the audience. He was making a pretty grand show out of all of it, and I was proud of him. People seemed genuinely interested and engaged. At one point I had to stand and wave, a spotlight on me as he gave me props for discovering the runes obscured in the buildup of minerals and dirt that originally encrusted the hilt, and I did my best to smile and look proud, but quickly retook my seat.

Finally, he got to the meat of it.

"After much research, ladies and gentlemen, I am proud to announce that we have a name."

He let it sink in. There were murmurs and whispers, and he let them quiet until it was so silent you could hear a pin drop. The words that fell from his lips were like a nuclear bomb.

"Alrekr Hakon Frithjof."

Gunnar Volund jumped in his seat and made a triumphant noise, and I turned to look at him. He was grinning widely and looked ecstatic and, *Well, good for him.* I closed my eyes and pressed a hand over my heart and wanted desperately for the floor to swallow me up and take me away from the sharp burning pain that welled in my chest like acid, eating up the remains of my broken heart. I think in that moment I finally understood, even more so than when my parents died, about why people called God cruel, because I was cut to the quick and beyond.

Jared was speaking, but I didn't hear it. I sat numbly, in disbelief, and tried valiantly to rally myself. I plastered a grin on my face while all the while, I was screaming over and over inside my heart, inside my head. I rose and shook hands with people, trembling all the while. People laughed and commented and I just agreed, Yes, I was shaking because I was overwhelmed, Yes, this was an incredible breakthrough, Yes, I was shaking from just total excitement.

Never in my life did I want to die more than right then. To just crawl into bed and go to sleep and never wake up. I went on autopilot. I can't remember all that was said to me or what I said in return. Volund was elated and pledging millions, both in donations and investments; checkbooks were appearing like mushrooms after a rain; Jared looked over the moon; and that was what finally broke through. My friend, my boss; he was happy, and I was happy for him. I blinked several times, tears coming to my eyes as the grief I felt I was drowning in receded just enough so that I could breathe.

"There you go," was breathed in my ear and a small amount of comfort edged its way in. I turned, but of course, no one was there. But I felt him, as sure as if he was standing right next to me.

"Thank you, Rizoel," I breathed, recognizing the lyrical voice. I, of course, received no answer, but I did feel a little stronger.

A catered reception had been arranged in celebration, and those of us in the lecture hall retreated to the area set aside for us.

"This is good, yeah?" Volund sat down at my table, where I had my leg propped on a vacant chair. I looked at him and smiled tiredly.

"Yes, very."

"Then why do you look as if your world has been destroyed?" he asked and sipped from his drink.

"Because it has," I answered, then, "Meet me at Lupa, it's an Italian place on Thompson St. Eight o'clock. There are some things I need to tell you about Alrekr." I pronounced it correctly, which threw him. I could see it because his brow furrowed.

He nodded and I made my excuses, gathered my belongings from back in the lab, and went home. I was happy about our breakthrough, about our progress, and in some ways I was so glad that Alaric had been Gunnar's ancestor and that all of this tangled together as it did, all of us touching, despite the distance, despite the gap in time and despite all of us being worlds apart.

As I took the subway home, I had a moment of clarity. God really did work in mysterious ways, and as sure as I was of anything, I was caught up in some big plan. I just couldn't see the big picture. Raphael's words came back to me.

"Be patient, Gracelyn. Good things come to those who wait. I know that your time on the mortal coil is fleeting, but wait. These are my parting words to you."

Okay, fine. So I would wait, although hell if I knew what I was waiting for, and just because I would wait didn't mean I would let Alaric go from my heart or my mind. It also didn't mean I would sit on my ass and do nothing if I thought that Alaric and me, that we could do some good. At least our story might, anyway.

So I got ready for dinner and hailed a cab.

CHAPTER FORTY

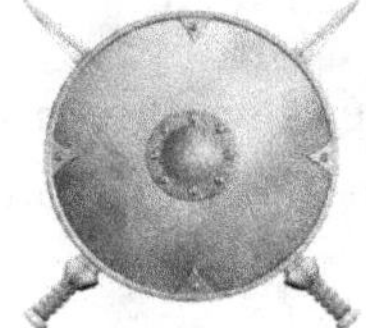

This was a role-reversal.

I sat quietly at a secluded table in the back and waited for Volund to arrive, which he did, security escort in tow.

"Lose the suit," I said, jutting my chin in the hulking bodyguard's direction. He frowned in suspicion, but finally nodded to the man, and he went to stand out front of the restaurant. Volund took his seat.

"You have questions, go ahead and ask 'em," I said.

"My ancestor's name, to hear it spoken aloud, it was as if you died. Never have I seen such raw pain on anyone's face before." He frowned.

"Is there a question in there?" I asked.

"Yes. Why?" He sat back, and the waiter came and poured us some wine and took our orders.

"I'm surprised you asked that, instead of about our little walk in the park," I said when we were alone again.

"I have many questions," he admitted. "That was just the first that came to mind."

"Fair enough."

I struggled with where to begin, finally settling on starting from the beginning.

"I was depressed," I said, and his eyebrows went up. "Just listen.

"I was depressed, and it was hard; my friends left me one by one, finally, in January I thought I had completely lost my shit."

He laughed, I glared, and he fell silent.

"I woke up on my roof, a step away from taking a fifteen-story swan-dive. I managed to get down and back to my apartment but the door was locked from the inside."

He looked at me skeptically.

"You want an explanation for the albino fire-eyed demon-warrior-thing in the park?" I asked, stumbling over the alien description of Alaric.

"Yes," he said shortly.

"Then take everything I'm saying at face value, as the truth, and I'll get to it," I said.

"Very well. Apologies."

He looked cowed. His curiosity must have been eating him alive. I pressed on.

"Where was I?"

"Your door was locked from the inside."

"Right, so one minute I'm in my bed, fast asleep, next I'm on my roof having an epic freak-out and now I'm out in the hallway at like three in the morning and my apartment door is locked from the inside. And then it wasn't." I took a sip of my wine.

"It wasn't," he repeated.

"Yep. I heard the lock let go, and the door swung open, and I went in."

I searched his face. He raised an eyebrow.

"Who was inside?" he asked.

"Nobody," I said.

"Nobody?"

"Nope. Little did I know, that was my first brush with Alaric."

I pressed on before he could say anything.

"I didn't know what to do, so I decided not to do anything. I pretended like what happened had never happened, and life went on. A few days later, I woke up at my kitchen sink with my wrist gushing blood down the drain."

I held up my wrist and showed him the thin white scar.

"Apparently, I cut it in my sleep with a kitchen knife. I wrapped it up, took myself to the hospital, and lied my ass off; said the knife slipped while I was cutting some vegetables for a late-night dinner. They called my best friend at the time, she was my emergency contact. It was also the final straw for her, when she showed up with the new guy she was seeing, and he couldn't stop talking about me for a few days after. She said she didn't want to be my friend anymore, and my whole world unraveled at the seams..."

We were silent for a few moments while I relived that particular hurt, which now paled in comparison with what I was living with. I swallowed hard and continued.

"That was the first night that he came to me."

I told him all of it, from how he appeared in my bedroom, to how he held me as I cried... Just, all of it. Volund remained quiet, listening, and then I dropped the bomb that had been dropped on me earlier in the day.

"Do you know what he said to me?" I asked, and Gunnar shook his head.

"'I am Alrekr Hakon Frithjof and I am here to protect you from yourself and the beings who wish you harm.'"

I let that sink in. Gunnar looked at me, his eyes a little wide, but I guess he wanted to hear the rest of the story, because he said nothing. So I told him.

"I couldn't pronounce it. His name. I tried several times, and he basically told me to stop trying and to call him Alaric, which was the modern pronunciation anyway. Said his name meant great king, high son, and peace thief." I rubbed my forehead.

"It does." Gunnar was looking at me speculatively.

"So, now I bet you are wondering how your Viking ancestor, who by your account was a marauding, raping, pillaging monster whose favorite way of accessorizing was to use the skulls of infants to decorate his belt, ended up looking after me on the third-worst night of my life on the eighth floor of a Manhattan apartment building." I sucked in a breath. That was a hell of a lot to say in one sentence.

"You could say that, yes," he said cautiously.

I searched his face for any sign of disbelief and found none. I sent up a tiny prayer of thanks that he was on board.

"So, apparently this is how things went down, from everything I can piece together."

I fell silent. Our food was being set down in front of us, we were told to enjoy, and Gunnar told the waiter that he'd be getting the biggest tip of his life if he didn't interrupt us again. I promised if we needed anything, we would signal. That seemed to make the waiter happy and he left us to our own devices.

"You were saying," Volund said before I could point out kindness went a long ways.

"Right. What I've been able to piece together so far is that Alrekr was everything you knew him to be. Scary, evil, you name it. Whatever, you know that side of the story better than I do. What you don't know is what happened after he died."

"He told you?" he asked.

"Yeah," I said quietly.

"Tell me..." he urged.

"Well, I guess it's pretty irrefutable that he died in the raid we're researching, but then, of course, he went to Hell." I ate a bite of tortellini. Gunnar had stars in his eyes. Not quite what I was going for so I laid it out on the line.

"He was conscripted into Hell's army. How much do you know about Catholicism or Christianity?" I asked.

He frowned at the abrupt change of topic, but he went with it.

"I was raised without religion, so admittedly, not much."

He looked uncomfortable when he spoke about his childhood. I filed that away for later and pressed on.

"You know what Purgatory is?" I asked.

"I have heard the word. I believe it is a state of between; it is also called limbo, yes?" he asked.

"Pretty darned close," I admitted, and took another bite, chewing slowly. I went on.

"Purgatory is the place that, we Roman Catholics believe, you go after you die when you've done wrong things in your life. You spend time there until you've made up for those wrong things, and then you go to Heaven. That is, if you repent. It's not a pleasant place, and as I was told, it's pretty much the first plane or circle of Hell."

I watched him; he was thoughtful as he chewed his food.

"I understand," he said finally, and it looked like he did, so I pressed on.

"Well, that's where Alrekr ended up. On Hell's side of things," I said.

"How do you mean?" he asked.

"Purgatory is a battlefield," I said. "Hell's army facing off against the Army of Heaven in a never-ending campaign, in this great, hot cavern…"

"You speak as if you have been there." He laughed.

"I have." At the dead seriousness of my tone, he stopped.

"How?" he asked skeptically.

"We'll get there," I promised. "So Alrekr died and went to Purgatory and ended up a grunt in Hell's army."

Gunnar nodded, and so I continued.

"He spent five hundred of our years doing the Devil's work, climbing the ranks and though he didn't tell me how high, I guess it was pretty high up there on their food chain and there's only one way you do that when you're battling alongside those creatures."

I shuddered remembering the winged horror that had gotten a hold of me.

"He was brutal." Gunnar smiled.

"And smart, and dispassionate, and cold as freaking ice," I said.

"So what happened?" he asked, and I closed my eyes; I was back in my apartment with Alaric before me, a single red rose in his hand.

"*I was an evil man when I lived, I was the foulest and most depraved soul in death and a warrior of Hell for a little over five centuries of your time. I could not tell you what it was, my beloved Small One, but one day the killing held no more joy for me. I grew tired, could not stand it anymore. I realized how wrong I had been for so very long.*"

"He got tired," I answered. Gunner's eyebrows rose in disbelief.

"That is it?" he scoffed "He got tired?"

I shrugged and threw down my napkin beside my plate.

"That's what he told me. He said the killing held no more joy for him and that he got tired, couldn't stand it anymore, and that it hit him how wrong he'd been for so long."

I crossed my arms, and it was more to hold myself in than defend myself against Volund's mocking glare. The memories of that night, our first 'I love you's, had me twisted all in knots. The grief was welling up, hot and fresh.

"He hurt you?" Gunnar asked softly.

"What does it matter to you?" I asked harshly. "You wanted to hurt me." I couldn't help but lash out. I immediately felt sorry. "I'm sorry," I said, before he could say anything. "I told you I forgave you for that. It's not fair of me to forgive you and then throw it back in your face a few hours later because I'm feeling shitty." I wiped at my eyes with my napkin.

"I deserved it," he said after a long silence. "Please go on."

"Right, so he got tired, and so he went to something he called The Host, which I'm pretty sure was the Archangels, or at least the good guys' side of things, and he threw himself on their mercy, and pretty much expected them to end him there." I took a drink of wine.

"They didn't," Gunnar stated.

"Um, obviously not, if it's five-hundred-and-thirty years later, and he was able to show up in that park."

I sighed and my shoulders slumped. I was being a catty bitch and I knew it.

"You are hurting and I wish to hear the rest of this tale, so before you begin apologizing again, please, just go on." He waved me off as I was just about to do just that – apologize.

"Okay, so Alaric went to the angels and said, 'Okay, here I am, I'm a dick and have been for a really long time, do whatever you want with me.' The angels, I guess, said 'Here's your weapons back, if you truly repent or whatever, you fight for us now.' They turned him around, gave him a pat on the back, and sent him out onto the front lines to kill demons and unrepentant sinners."

I scrubbed my hands over my face. This was taking a lot out of me.

"Do you wish to stop?" he asked and waved the waiter over to us.

"No, no, it's fine." The waiter refilled our glasses and took our empty plates. Gunnar ordered us dessert.

This was going to be one long-ass night.

CHAPTER FORTY-ONE

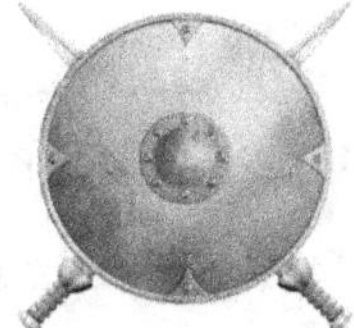

The waiter set down a decadent slice of chocolate torte swimming in a raspberry sauce in front of each of us. I couldn't help myself. It looked mouthwatering and I took a bite. The flavors exploded across my tongue, rich, and sweet, and thoroughly satisfying, and after a moment or two I felt better.

"You looked like you needed the sugar," he commented.

"What was my color off, or something?" I asked.

"Or something," he said, and waved his hand for me to continue.

"Right, so he switched sides and fought on the side of the angels for the last five hundred and thirty years. Now, let me be clear, I'm not one-hundred-percent on some of this, so you'll have to bear with some holes in the story, because I am telling you what I know. Everything." I stabbed my chocolate covered fork in his direction by way of emphasis.

"All right," he said.

"I'm not sure if the angels went to him or he went to them, I can't remember, but in any case, I was assigned to him," I said.

"Assigned, how?" he asked.

"That's what I asked. From what he told me, Hell was looking to turn the tide on Heaven, and cooked up a little scheme to pad their army. They started looking for strong or bright souls. Living people here on earth, to attach themselves to."

"To possess?" he asked.

"No, something a little more insidious than that."

I took another bite of cake and watched him try to work it out. He finally gave up with a shrug and looked to me to clue him in.

"They were tormenting us. Doing things to drive us crazy, trying to break us," I said.

He shook his head in confusion.

"Suicide is a sin. One of the Cardinal ones. Commit suicide, and you land your ass smack-dab on the front lines of Hell's army in purgatory."

I took another bite of cake.

"Tactically, it is genius," he said, but I could see the cracks in the form of a frown on his face.

"Morally, it's corrupt, and it's some seriously honor-less bullshit, but hey, it's Hell and these are demons we're talking about, so does it really surprise you?" I asked.

He scowled.

"I didn't think so," I said, and pressed on.

"You know I told him about you. He didn't like the sound of you from the start, didn't want me to go anywhere near you. Wanted me to cancel that dinner. I didn't though."

That was the point I think I broke through. Gunner's face held shock, and then, after long moments, dismay. I realized what I'd done and cursed myself for lack of tact. I'd just told him that the ancestor he had looked up to his entire life and wanted to emulate didn't like him. I could see that lost little boy inside the man in front of me cringe, and it really sucked. The silence stretched between us.

"Sorry," I said.

"Never apologize for speaking the truth," he said softly, then, "I am glad that you went."

"Why?" I asked.

"While I am sorry now for my behavior, if you had not come, if I had not done what I..." He clenched his jaw.

"It's okay. I get it. I'm glad you got to see him, too," I said. "Makes telling you all of this a lot easier. Not sure you would have believed me otherwise." I shrugged.

"That is also true," he conceded.

"Yep." A gulf of silence opened up between us again.

"So," he said finally, and I snapped my eyes up to his. "Why the sadness?"

I told him the rest. About how Alaric was in deep shit for revealing himself to me, about how he broke some serious oaths and covenants, and finally, about me, following him down to Hell. Gunnar was a good listener.

He took it all in and said finally, "I am sorry that happened to the both of you."

"Yeah. Me, too," I said.

"Does this mean you are now the charge of three angels?" he asked, and my eyebrows went up in surprise.

Well, hell. He'd caught that and I hadn't, but after my little moment in the lecture hall, I was pretty sure he was right. I mean, I'd heard Rizoel plain as day. They must be taking shifts or something.

"I think it does," I said.

"It does not matter. I do not think I would hurt you now, not after your kindness, not after all you have told me. I have much to think about," he said.

The restaurant was closing, our waiter shifting nervously off to the side, away from us. I smiled at him and gave the signal for the check, and he looked relieved. Gunnar looked over and was surprised that we were the only two left.

"Remember your promise. He was awesome and stayed away," I muttered under my breath as the waiter approached.

Gunner looked at me, pulled out his wallet and a wad of one hundred-dollar bills and gave them to the kid. The bill was maybe sixty bucks. Gunnar was more than as good as his word.

"No change," he said to the man and stood, pulling on his coat.

I stood and winced. Though it was healing, my leg was plainly unhappy. Gunnar frowned.

"I'd heard you were attacked by a dog from Mr. Worth."

"If a dog is the size of a man, with brown leathery wings and a mouth full of fangs, then, sure," I muttered out of the side of my mouth.

His eyes widened. "Something down there bit you?" he asked.

"Grabbed me, talons did it," I said.

"Please, allow me to drive you home." We were out front of the restaurant, the lights turning out behind us.

"I'd like that," I said, and he held the door to the back seat of his town car open for me himself and I slid in.

He climbed in after me and said,

"Thank you, Gracelyn."

I nodded and said, "Sure."

"I believe you will be happy again," he said.

"Not without him," I replied immediately. "Without him in it, life is kind of a pale imitation." I smiled and I knew it was sad.

Gunnar sighed.

"Peace between us?" he asked.

"Sounds good."

He put his hand over mine and it was a familiar gesture. It was what people had done when my parents had died. I had appreciated it then, and I appreciated it now, only this time, instead of praying that things would get better, like after my parents, I prayed they never would. If they did, I somehow thought that it would be a betrayal to Alaric's memory, and I would never ever betray him.

God help me. I was so horribly and terribly torn in two.

CHAPTER FORTY-TWO

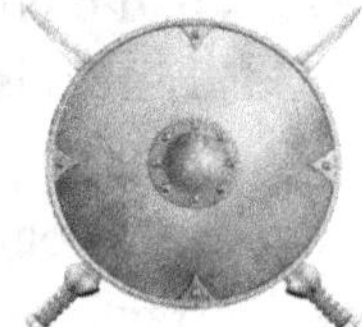

The ancient Greeks believed that we were all born with four arms, four legs and two heads, and then Zeus, for whatever reason, threw bolts of lightning down from the sky, splitting us all in two, and that we were all doomed to spend the rest of our days wandering the earth, seeking the other halves of ourselves.

I had always thought that was a silly tale to tell children about how our belly buttons are made. You know, to make them laugh. I had laughed. I wasn't laughing anymore, now that I knew the truth of it.

I stood on the roof of my building in my nightgown and robe and looked out over the night-lit city. The pain in my heart was overflowing. It had been a week. Just one week since Alaric had been taken from me, or I from him... I scoffed, the details didn't matter.

The simple truth was that he was gone and I couldn't sleep anymore.

The sun would go down, night would appear, and I suddenly became restless. It was affecting my work, but not too badly yet. I was debating asking Jared if I could start coming in at night, but I knew he needed me to meet with the suits, to explain what we did. I sighed and hugged myself, until the scrape of gravel behind me caused me to turn. The crushing weight on my chest eased marginally.

"Neil," I said, gladly.

"Hey, Gracelyn, you look like you can use a hug."

He opened his arms, and I went to him and hugged him tightly.

"I miss him so much," I sobbed into his leather breastplate.

He smoothed back my much shorter locks and smiled down at me.

"We know," he said

"What are you doing here?" I asked, pushing free of the embrace.

"Coming to check on you," he said.

"I'm surviving," I said and wiped my face.

"On the roof? At four in the morning?" he asked.

"I haven't been sleeping so well," I confessed.

"Alaric would have our balls in a basket if he saw you like this." He grimaced.

"I'm sorry," I said.

"Don't be. We all miss him." He shrugged.

"Won't you get in trouble?" I asked, waving my hands.

"You're a special case," he said. "You know about us. Alaric already let that cat out of the bag."

I laughed. "Look at you, with your modern colloquialisms"

"Hey, we aren't all Viking warriors with sticks up our asses." He smiled and I punched him in the arm.

"Don't talk about my man that way!" I cried, but I was smiling.

I knew that Hofneil and Alaric had been friends. Neil had helped us squeeze out just a little bit more time together. That proved all it needed to.

"Do you know what happened?" I asked, and he sobered.

"He was judged," he said carefully.

"And?" I asked chewing my lip.

"That's all I can say," he said, and didn't look happy about it. My shoulders slumped and I turned back to the city.

"I feel like I somehow screwed everything up for him." The guilt weighed on me.

"No. Don't think like that. His love for you, hey, your love for him, that's the stuff legends are made of." He laid his hands on my shoulders.

"Not all legends get a happy ending," I said.

"No, but yours isn't over just yet, babe. Not while you draw breath."

I turned to look at him. "Now, just what the hell is that supposed to mean..."

The words died on my lips. He was gone.

CHAPTER FORTY-THREE

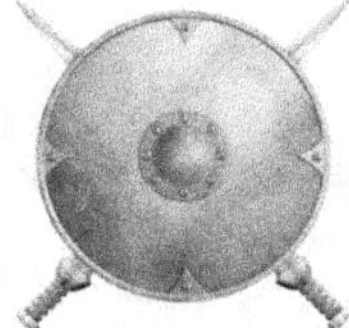

Two more weeks, and I still felt as raw as the night we'd been separated.

I wasn't sure how I kept going, how I hadn't just expired from a broken heart. I went to work, I came home. I'd forget to eat until food was put in front of me, usually by Jared or Gunnar. Well, okay, Gunnar didn't put food in front of me, he put me in front of food, but still, I was losing weight.

I was sleeping better since Neil had come to see me, although I wasn't sure if Neil had something to do with that, or if my runs did. Now that the weather was warmer and the daylight hours were longer, I'd taken to running every day after work, running extra-long on weekends. Turned out Gunnar was a runner, too, and sometimes he would join me.

We were actually becoming friends. We'd get into long theological debates that would last hours, and even though we could get so mad at each other, neither of us would stay that way.

Still, despite my extra-hard run that day, here I was on my roof again, staring up at the few stars I could see in the sky with all the light pollution. I sighed.

"God," I said, "I miss him."

"We know you do."

I smiled at the musical voice as Rizoel stepped up next to me. He put an arm around my shoulders and I leaned my head on one of his. He tucked me under his wing and I cried.

"It hurts," I said. "But I'm glad I don't feel any different. I miss him so much, Rizoel." I shook with silent sobs and he gave my shoulders a squeeze.

"Shhh," he soothed. "Come now, what would Alaric think of all of this?" he asked.

"He wouldn't want to see me cry," I said, and wiped my tears.

"He would want you to be happy. No?" he asked.

"Yeah."

We stood like that for a long time, mutely staring out into the rest of the city.

"Don't close yourself off to happiness, Gracelyn," he said.

"Okay," I whispered.

"He wouldn't want that." Rizoel spoke with a conviction that startled me.

"Okay," I said, a little stronger.

"It's coming," he said and pulled away. "Just be patient, and when it finds you, don't be afraid to let it in." He smiled sadly and fingered a lock of my hair.

"I miss that too," I laughed. "And I promise to watch out for it, and when it shows up I'll do my best to be happy."

"Just be patient a little longer," he said, and opened his wings with a snap, launching himself into the sky with a few strong beats.

Now, that was something to behold.

CHAPTER FORTY-FOUR

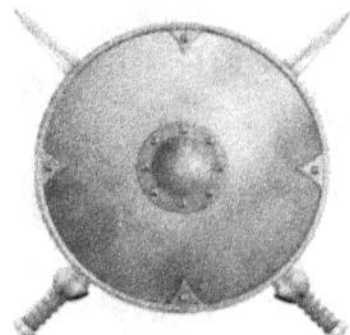

Another week passed since my visit from Rizoel, and I did my best to keep my eye out for happiness and let it in when I saw it. I was smiling more, sleeping a little better, but still. My heart felt like a weighted stone in my chest. Life just wasn't, nor wouldn't be, the same for me without Alaric in it, and if I said that that was okay, I would be a total freaking liar, because it so wasn't.

I was in my fifth week of life without the love of my life in it and having another sleepless night. I skipped the roof. I just wasn't in the mood for a potential drop-in from any celestial beings. I guess it was just my luck, as I wandered Central Park, that Karael was the pushiest of my three new protectors and didn't really give a shit what I wanted. He dropped from the sky and landed noiselessly in the grass beside me. I nearly came out of my skin.

"Jesus Christ, Karael!" I cried, and he rose from his crouch and laughed.

"I'll tell him you said so."

He held out his arms for a hug. I gave it to him, even though I was none too pleased at the moment.

"I'd rather you didn't," I said sourly, and sent up a little prayer of apology for my outburst. Karael smiled.

"How are you doing?" he asked me.

"I'm not," I retorted, and took up my stroll again.

He walked beside me.

"Talk to me, Gracelyn," he said gravely.

I looked over at him and blurted,

"Should you even be here?"

"Yes," he said.

"What if somebody sees you?" I asked, and he gave an unconcerned shrug. I narrowed my eyes in suspicion. "I don't look like I'm talking to myself, do I?" I asked, suddenly tired, and then frustrated that I hadn't been tired before, to have avoided all of this. Ugh, I was an emotional mess tonight, all over the map.

Karael laughed.

"No, you look like you're walking with a handsome man in a brown trench coat."

"I thought angels weren't supposed to be egotistical," I said, needling him on purpose.

He stopped me and turned me to face him.

"What's going on, Gracie?" he asked, and at the familiar shortening of my name I kind of wilted a little.

"I miss him," I said simply, and expected him to say that they did, too, but he didn't.

"I know. I hate to see you this way."

I looked up. His warm honey-colored eyes radiated warmth.

"Thanks," I said.

"You're welcome."

We continued walking; he held my hand.

"My patience is slipping," I confessed.

"I know," he said.

"That really why you're here?" I asked. "To give me a pep talk?"

"No. I thought I would just go for a walk in the park and wanted a pretty little human to hold my hand, I thought you fit the bill."

I grinned and shook my head. "You always such a flirt?" I asked.

He simply shrugged.

"You seem lonely lately. I thought I would keep you company." He swung my hand a little.

"I'm not lonely," I protested, facing him, and he drew up short, very little room between us.

He looked deep in my eyes and I held my breath without realizing it. He bent and placed his lips against mine. I put both of my hands against his chest and with everything I had, shoved him away.

"What the hell is your problem?" I cried.

He had a huge grin on his face.

"Had to see," he said.

"Karael, I belong to Alaric, whatever they did, wherever he is, Heaven or Hell or still in between, I. Belong. To. Him." I stabbed a finger into his chest to punctuate each word.

"That's our girl, Gracelyn." He smiled.

"What are you talking about?" I demanded.

"I can't say. I have a message from Raphael. 'Just be patient a little bit longer.' Remember what Rizoel said."

"Yeah, keep an eye out for some happiness," I said, miserably.

"And don't forget to let it in."

"I'm trying."

"You're doing well," he said, and smiled.

"Thanks, I guess."

"Hey. We love you too," he said, and then he was gone. I didn't even blink, just one second, he was there and the next, just blinked out of existence.

I sighed and looked up through the trees. *Ugh*.

CHAPTER FORTY-FIVE

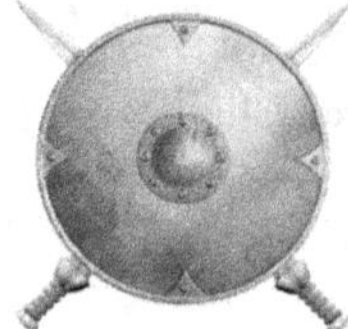

Six weeks, no Alaric, and I was seriously running on emotional fumes. I didn't even think my heart beat any more, it was so heavy.

I had gotten into the waiting town car and was being whisked to Gunnar's swanky hotel. I was supposed to be one of the guests of honor at some black-tie gala event along with Jared. It was being thrown by Gunnar, and apparently a metric ton of potential investors and potential donations were to be had. He'd reached out to a whole lot of rich folks in Sweden, Denmark, and Norway to come to New York and look at our discoveries, which had originated in their home-lands but were found upon a distant shore.

Sheer marketing genius.

He had managed to get this thing put together in just six weeks; the museum had been chaos when I'd left at closing in preparation, and I had to say, I was impressed by what was being done. He had spent the better part of an afternoon convincing me to allow his team of stylists to make me presentable.

I was trying to grow my hair out again, and it was in that awful in-between phase where little, if anything, could be done with it. It was ugly and hopeless, and though I was okay with looking like a tousled mess on a daily, not so much for this. With as much time, effort, and money as Gunnar had spent on doing this for the project, I had knuckled under on this request with very little arm-twisting.

I sort of wished I had resisted a little more when I got to his suite. He was on the phone speaking in his native tongue when Maximillian let me in the door. A veritable army of people standing to the side were talking in hushed tones. They all turned expectantly towards me when I stepped inside.

I gave a little wave to Gunnar, not wishing to interrupt his call, and he nodded to me, lowering the phone enough to say to the group of people, "That's her," before resuming his call.

That did it.

It was like a feeding frenzy. My purse was taken, just gone, before I even knew it had been whisked off my shoulder; someone was untying my shoes; and another was whisking away my hoodie. Gunnar winked at me and disappeared into the next room, the door shutting behind him with a soft click.

I was going to kill him.

The men and women wasted no time. I was waxed, plucked, and filed. Inside of two hours, I was sitting in the hairstylist's chair in front of a mirror. The man was fussing over my hair, mussing it and teasing it, one direction then another.

"I think we should go lighter." He clapped his hands, and my eyes widened.

"You're not dying my hair," I said.

"Don't worry, honey, you're going to look fabulous, you want to look fabulous, don't you?" he asked.

I opened my mouth, closed it, opened it again, and shut it again. Tears burned my eyes and my throat had grown thick with them. Alaric loved my hair, said it had reminded him of the grain fields of his homeland.

"Gunnar!" I screamed. He was in the room like a shot, took one look at my tear-stained face and went scary with the flip of a switch.

"Who has done this?" he asked.

Everyone took a step back from me like I was radioactive or something.

"He wants to dye my hair," I whimpered, and Gunnar's expression went from anger to confusion.

Everyone visibly relaxed.

"I do not..." he started, but I interrupted.

"Alaric loves my hair," I said, and his expression smoothed out from confused into the familiar lines of pity.

Everything just sort of snapped into place for me. It became real all of a sudden – I was never going to see Alaric again. He was gone, really gone.

I sat there, gasping like a landed fish and clutched at the scale from his armor. Gunnar came forward.

"Gracelyn?" he asked.

"Oh, my God," I said in horror.

"Gracelyn, no..."

"Oh my God!" The tears poured out faster.

I heard someone say, "Oh no, somebody please get this bitch a paper bag or something," but I was in the grip of a full-blown panic attack. My chest was tight and my heart hammered in a frenzied staccato. My breath sawed in and out of my lungs, I just couldn't breathe anymore.

Finally I managed to force out, "He's really gone, I'm never going to see him again."

I think it was the first time I had said the words aloud and actually believed them.

Gunnar knelt down in front of the chair and took my hands in his, rubbing the backs of them with his thumbs while I cried. He spoke soothingly to me in a language I didn't know. Occasionally he would say something to one of the people around us in English. A glass of water appeared and he pressed it between my shaking hands and helped me to drink. It slid down my throat, cool and refreshing. We stayed like that until I felt calmer.

"Better?" he asked.

"Yeah," I said, and sniffed. One of the female makeup artists smoothed my hair back from my face and wiped away my tears with a cool damp cloth.

"I will let them get you ready then," he said softly, then, scary Volund back in place, turned on a skinny man wearing too much makeup.

"You would call a woman in the throes of grief over her lost love a bitch?" he asked.

The man stuttered, holding up his hands as if to ward off a blow. Everyone shrank back.

"You are fired. Get out."

Gunnar's voice was low. The man just went for the door without a word. He turned on the stylist.

"No dye," he bit out, and the stylist raised both his hands, palm out, in surrender and nodded vigorously. Gunnar left the room. When the bedroom door clicked shut behind him, there was a collective sigh of relief.

"Okay, hon, let's get you fixed up." The makeup artist was kind and dabbed at my face a little more.

The hairstylist sighed and looked at me in the mirror over my head.

"I'm sorry, darlin'," he said. "Let's see what we can do. Forget fabulous, let's go glamorous." He smiled a little sadly, and I gave him a tremulous smile in return.

CHAPTER FORTY-SIX

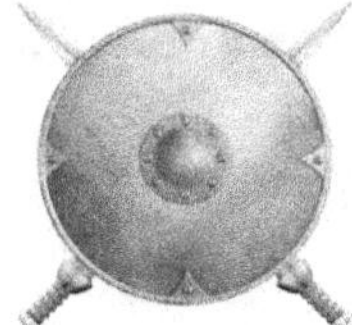

Hollowed-out and just plain numb was how I'd felt as they'd worked on the rest of me. Now, as I stood in front of the full-length mirror, I looked, well, flawless and sophisticated. My hair had been expertly fashioned into what appeared to be a French twist despite how short it was; the man was kind of a miracle-worker on that front. A line of white rhinestones rode where the hair tucked under, courtesy of some blinged-out hair pins.

The gown was a rich light-bronze color and spangled with glittering rhinestones along the one shoulder and across the chest down to the opposite side's ribs. More swept out from the hip along the asymmetrical hemline, which was short on one side and floor-length on the same side as the shoulder strap. It was a beautiful dress, and almost the same color as my hair, which was to say that if stars had fallen to earth on a wheat field, then I was wearing it. My feet were in a pair of bronze satin heels that matched the dress to perfection.

My makeup was subtle and made my eyes seem larger than they actually were, the blue standing out in startling relief. I turned around one more time and took it in. I looked like some whole other girl. Not

'Gracelyn Adams, historical artifact nerd', more like 'Gracelyn Adams, secret celebrity' or something.

Gunnar stepped into the room, adjusting the bow tie on his tux, and froze just inside the door way, his face splitting into a huge grin.

"Well, do I clean up nicely?" I asked.

"If you did not belong to my ancestor, heart, body, mind, and soul, I would pursue you all over again," he said quietly.

I blushed furiously.

"I'll take that as a 'Yes'," I said.

"You do that."

"You look lovely, Gracelyn," he murmured.

"Thank you." I cast my eyes to the floor and gripped the scale in my hand. No one was taking it. They could pry it from my cold dead hands, so Gunnar had compromised with me, and had called in a jeweler. It now hung on a thicker, shorter rose-gold chain which went around my wrist. It allowed me to hold the scale in my hand, so I was okay with that. He promised we'd put it back on a necklace after the event. He'd even had the jump ring replaced and soldered shut, to ensure the scale would never slip off.

"Shall we?" he asked, holding out his arm.

I slid my arm through his and hugged it. He patted my hand with a smile, and we left the suite and the hotel.

When we pulled up to wait in the line of cars letting people off in front of the museum, he was watching me. I was taken in by the wide red carpet gracing the museum steps. Flash bulbs were going off in the crowd like heat lightning through the clouds. It was a lot bigger, a lot more grandiose than I had realized, and I suddenly became nervous.

"Don't," he said.

"Don't what?" I asked.

"Don't do that, don't be nervous. The way you look tonight, you rival and eclipse them all." He crossed his arms, a sure sign he was not to be argued with. I smiled.

"This isn't my usual thing, Gunnar. I'm a scientist and historian, I don't... Oh, my God, is that Alexander Skarsgard?" I couldn't believe it.

Gunnar laughed.

"As I said, you will be fine."

We pulled up to the curb and the door opened. I was blinded by the dazzling lights as Gunnar got out of the limo and held out a hand for me. I took it gratefully, a little unsteady in heels higher than I was used to wearing and stood straight.

Questions were being shouted from every direction, and I was admittedly overwhelmed. A microphone was shoved into Gunnar's face.

"Mr. Volund! Who's your girlfriend?" Gunnar smiled his charming smile and laughed.

"This is Gracelyn Adams, she is not my girlfriend, but rather a colleague. She is responsible for many of the restoration and preservation efforts being undertaken on the artifacts inside." His voice was rich and deep and carried easily for the cameras.

"So you're not involved?" A microphone was thrust in front of my mouth.

"No," I said softly, and kept my mouth shut after that. I was going on the old adage that you never had to unsay anything that you didn't say in the first place. Gunnar patted my hand, his whole persona smiling, and moved us forward through the gossip-magazine vultures. I was glad for his size; it made things easier.

We ascended the steps to the top and were ushered through the front doors and up the grand marble staircase to the left. We stepped into one of the museum's upstairs spaces that had been cleared out for the event. Several of the artifact finds and masterfully-crafted replicas stood in well-lit cases and roped-off areas. There were tables scattered throughout the room, draped in cloths to make them look like Viking shields, silver domes at the center of each to replicate the shields boss, all polished to a high shine, reflecting the candlelight from the tea lights placed around them.

It should have looked cheesy or ridiculous, but everything was so finely-made it looked strong and elegant instead. The hanging light fixtures had been replaced with chandeliers of antler and bone, the lights emanating from them a replica of firelight, both in intensity and movement. The chairs around the tables looked like they had been covered in skins and furs, and the whole thing looked as if modern day and the tenth century had collided in one room with a spectacular result. Music played, and it was ancient, haunting and beautiful. People milled about in small groups talking and laughing, drinks in hand, looking at varying displays. I looked up at Gunnar, and my heart swelled with happiness, and I let it in.

"Thank you," I breathed.

He said, "Do not thank me, this is your child, Gracelyn. Your find, which you have spent the last four years lovingly restoring. Go enjoy it." He smiled and let go of my arm. I walked across the marble floors and went immediately to my beloved's sword in its case. A tableau stood to one side with photographs and explanations about its origins and the discoveries made surrounding it. There was even a picture of me, long braid hanging over my shoulder as I smiled at the camera, sitting at my workbench, the sword on its stand beside me, dirt and other detritus flaked off beneath it across my work surface.

You could see the scale at my throat in the picture, and the ease and happiness in the way I held myself, in my smile and my eyes. Alaric had been with me then. I let the happy memories wash over me but refused to let myself cry again. I didn't want to ruin my careful makeup.

"You're her, aren't you?" someone asked at my elbow.

"I'm sorry what?" I looked into the smile of a very tall, very thin man.

"The doctor in the picture." He pointed at where I smiled out at everyone.

I blushed, embarrassed.

"I don't have a Doctorate, just a Master's degree. Jared is the doctor in all of this."

"You made the discovery of the runes?" he asked.

"Ah yes, I did." I smiled.

"Who do you think this man was?" he asked, and I resisted the urge to chew my glossed lip.

"I don't know," I replied, which was as close to the truth as possible. I didn't know who Alrekr was, I knew Alaric. Who he had been in life was not who he had been in death, nor beyond. To me, he was simply the man I loved. "Excuse me." I murmured and walked in the opposite direction as if I had seen someone.

As I went in the direction of the stage and saw Jared, relief at having seen a familiar face washed over me. He was talking to a giant of a man who had his back to me. The wide black expanse of his tailored suit jacket was interrupted by a spill of white-blonde hair that ended at his mid back in a blunt pony tail. It was held back by a round pewter disc, a medallion of some kind with a sort of ancient crest stamped in the metal. I couldn't make it out from this distance.

"Ah, Gracelyn!" Jared exclaimed and stepped past the man, who turned.

Jared wore his rectangular Gucci glasses with the black-and-silver arms. The lenses were bolted together with a thin black wire as a nose piece. I liked them. He called them his 'special occasion' glasses, but I'd told him I wished that he wore them all the time. They looked right on his face. He looked sharp in his tux with his hair styled just so, and my smile became a grin. He stopped me at arm's length and took me in with a low whistle. A bubble of laughter escaped my throat.

"Oh, come on, you've seen me dressed up before." We hugged quickly.

"Not like this." He lowered his voice and said in my ear, "You have me thinking I might need to rekindle that crush." I smacked him on his arm playfully.

"Oh! I'm sorry, how terribly rude!" He turned to the gentleman he was speaking with and I looked up at him.

My heart dropped into my feet for a second, he looked so achingly familiar. His hair was swept back from a widow's peak and his nose was straight and perfect, top lip thinner above a lush bottom lip. His jaw was angular and strong and his eyes were the clear gray of a mountain spring and bored into mine with such an intensity... I almost vibrated with the need to touch him, to see if what I was seeing was real.

This was impossible, wasn't it?

"Gracelyn?"

I snapped back into reality and looked at Jared.

"I'm sorry?" I said, shaking my head a little to clear it.

"I said, I would like to introduce you to Mr. Alec Wermund. He is from Norway, and very interested in our discoveries. Mr. Wermund, this is Gracelyn Adams, my best restorationist and preservationist."

Alec Wermund held out his long-fingered, massive hand to me, and I took it to shake, but he raised my hand to his lips, bowing to place a gentle kiss on the back of my hand, and again a shock of familiarity shot through me. Several loud thumps registered and I jumped, the spell I was under broken. Jared frowned at me.

"Gracelyn, are you all right? You look as if you've seen a ghost," he said, but before I could answer, someone was at the podium speaking into the microphone.

"I would like to thank everyone for being here tonight, if you could all take your seats, we would like to begin, as dinner is served."

Everyone began to move through the tables, looking for their little name cards. I turned back to Jared and smiled, which smoothed the look of concern off his face. I nodded politely to Mr. Wermund, who had yet to say a word, murmured that I was pleased to meet him and moved off into the tables myself. Gunnar signaled me and I went over. Jared joined us a few moments later and looked at me curiously. We took our seats and dinner was served.

I surreptitiously scanned the tables for Mr. Wermund and found him easily, as he was head and shoulders taller than most everyone else. He was about four tables from me, thumb and forefinger absently stroking up and down the stem of his wine glass, his eyes fixed on me. I tore my gaze from him and joined the conversation at my table.

They served us mead and venison, expertly prepared, with salad greens and pan-roasted vegetables. Gunnar had spared no expense on giving these people a decent and somewhat authentic meal. Everything was served feast-style and people loved it, live music was played during the dinner, the performers dressed in period costume and playing instruments from the time. Finally the lights dimmed, speeches were made by Gunnar and Jared, and then it was my turn.

I rose from the table and went up to the podium. I was in a spotlight; I couldn't see the audience beyond the first row of tables. I took a deep breath as a hush settled over the room. I smiled and made eye contact with a few people, then opened my mouth.

"My name is Gracelyn Adams. When I was thirteen, I lost both my parents, Jonathan and Laynette, in a car accident. I was the only survivor. At their funeral, people gave their condolences, and said they would remember my mom and dad, and then I never saw or heard from any of them again. I went to live with my grandparents on my mother's side, and when I tried to talk about my mom or dad, I was silenced. It was as if my mother and father had ceased to exist the night they died. Just gone. No one to tell their story.

"No one to tell anyone about how my father, an engineer, instilled in me a love and passion for science and the stars that shaped me into one of the better scientists in my lab, despite the fact that I hold no degree in that particular field. Or how my mother, a devout Catholic, and a school teacher, instilled in me an unshakable faith that everyone is inherently good, and that everyone deserves a chance at redemption." I smiled at Gunnar and he smiled back.

"They were just gone. Lost to the annals of time. Which is why history is so important. Not just to educate future generations, or to understand our past mistakes, but to tell the stories of those that have gone before. People like King Tutankhamun, those lost on the Titanic, Anne Frank, and now, with this discovery, the story of Alrekr Hakon Frithjof. A Viking warrior, by all accounts an accomplished raider, but also a man."

I paused, this was a bit hard.

"A man like my father, who lived, and died, in his time. Though, I am sure had they lived at the same time, they would have had a difference of opinion."

There was a titter of laughter and I smiled.

"My point is, everyone deserves to have their story told. It is through history and the preservation of our past, through the deeds that leave a mark on this world, either good, bad, or indifferent, that we become immortal. So I ask you, all of you. Please help me. Please help me bring Alrekr's story into the light, help me drag his story, his men's stories, and the stories of their victims out of the mud a thousand and more years after they died, and give these men the immortality that all of us deserve. And in doing so, perhaps gain a little immortality yourselves. Thank you."

I stepped down through applause and went back to my seat. Jared was smiling and giving me a subtle thumbs-up, Gunnar was smiling, too. I just hoped I had been convincing, and not cheesy.

CHAPTER FORTY-SEVEN

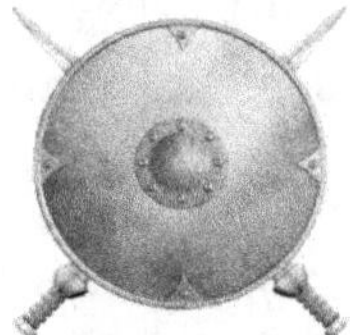

*P*eople were up, milling about, being social, drinking, writing checks which I was grateful for, but I just needed a breather, so I went out onto the terrace. It was cooler out here, a light wind blowing in from the Hudson. I closed my eyes and let it cool my exposed skin.

"There you are."

The voice was deep, and so achingly familiar I wanted to close my eyes and pretend it was him. I opened them when I heard the scuff of his dress shoe beside me. I looked up, craning my neck, and was more than half-disappointed at meeting cool gray eyes rather than burning red ones.

"You look just like him," I whispered.

"Like who?" he asked, his head cocked to the side, a small smile playing at the corner of his mouth.

"The only man I'll ever love." The honest admission was out of my mouth before I even realized I had spoken aloud.

"I see. I am honored." He inclined his head.

"Please don't mock me," I asked, my eyes closing. I turned back into the light breeze.

"I would not dream of it."

The tension in my shoulders eased a bit. We stood in silence for a long minute. Finally I spoke.

"I miss him," I said, and I didn't know why I was telling a complete stranger. Maybe it was that sense of familiarity or that he looked so much like him. I just couldn't stop myself.

"It's like there is this hole in my heart with him gone, and I know it's only been six weeks, but I still can't breathe, or sleep, I forget to eat. I don't know how much longer I can live like this. I know I was told to be patient, but patient for what?" I stopped. "I'm sorry, I must sound like a stark raving lunatic." I sniffed back some errant tears.

"No, you sound like a woman whose heart has broken." His voice was kind, gentle even.

"Sorry," I mumbled, then with a stronger voice asked him, "Were you coming out for some air or did you want to talk to me?"

"I wished to speak with you," he said and smiled.

"What about?" I asked, and his smile widened.

"Anything, anything at all. What would you like to talk about?" he asked and leaned a hip against the concrete balustrade.

I looked up at him and shivered; he looked so much like Alaric in the face and the timbre of his voice, but there were differences, too. I was at a loss.

"Um, what do you do?" I asked meekly.

"I am in international shipping." He smiled serenely. It sounded like a good question at the time, I mean he already knew what I did.

"Oh, what's that like?" I asked.

"Very dry and very boring." He cocked his head and I couldn't help it, I laughed.

Don't close yourself off to happiness, Gracelyn. He wouldn't want that. Happiness is coming, just be patient, and when it finds you, don't be afraid to let it in. Rizoel's words drifted back to me.

"I don't know, what I do is pretty dry and boring to some people," I said.

"No, what you do, you do out of passion. There is nothing dry or boring about that." He smiled, and it was wistful.

"So what would you do, if you weren't into international shipping?" I asked.

"So many things, I don't know where to begin."

"Fair enough."

We lapsed into a strangely comfortable silence.

It was growing chilly, but I didn't want to go in just yet and face the crowd and the mingling I was expected to do. I hugged myself and turned back to look out over the city. I often thought about what it might look like one hundred years or more from now. Wondered if my building would still stand, or if my museum would still be a museum or something else. Warmth enveloped my back and shoulders, and I startled back to the here and now.

"Forgive me, you looked cold."

He settled the tux jacket around my shoulders, drawing the lapels together at the front. I smiled and gave a murmured thanks. The sounds from the party grew louder and then diminished again as someone stepped out onto the terrace.

"Gracie." I turned and smiled at Jared.

"Hey, boss."

"Ah, Mr. Wermund, I see you found her, then."

Jared came forward. He was under the impression I had been through a pretty severe break-up. I hadn't done anything to correct him of the notion, I'd just gone with it, told him that he was gone. I was grateful he hadn't pried. I think he believed that he'd died, which, given the way I'd been and how things were, wasn't far from the truth. He drew even with us and looked me over.

"Alec and I were just talking."

I smiled and I knew it must have looked a bit tired. Jared gave me a one-armed hug and I leaned into it briefly before we broke apart.

"Ah, I see. I didn't mean to interrupt."

"Not at all, Mr. Worth." Alec inclined his head politely.

I sighed, I guessed my reprieve was over. I glanced back at the party, a little crestfallen.

"I suppose I'm needed back inside, then?" I asked.

"It would be nice." Jared gave me his winning smile.

"Starting to get to you, boss?" I asked and he laughed.

"That obvious?" he asked.

"Yeah, but only because I've worked with you for five years. I'll take over for a little while." I shrugged out of Alec Wermund's tux jacket and handed it back with a grateful little smile. "Thank you again," I said.

Our fingers brushed as I handed it over and that familiar little thrill went through me, causing my heart to jump.

Just because he looks like him doesn't mean... He can't be him.

I struggled with my inner thought process for a heartbeat; one touch and I felt like my brain was short-circuiting. I smiled again and went back to the party to deal with the suits. Jared had done more than his fair share, so no matter how I was feeling, emotional storm or not, I needed to pull myself up by the bootstraps and do my share.

I sighed as the heat and noise of the party reached out of the doorway and pulled me in. It was going to be a long night.

CHAPTER FORTY-EIGHT

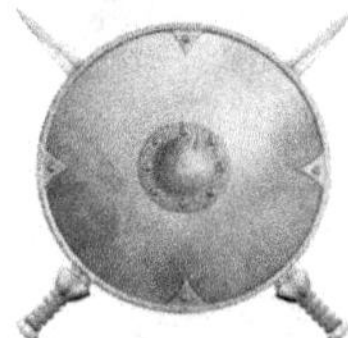

Midway through the tail-end of the evening, I ran into Gunnar, who had a stunning brunette attached to his arm. I had smiled wryly to myself, recognizing the predatory look in his eyes as she'd laughed at something someone had said. At one point he detached himself and came over.

I'd raised my hand with that same wry smile and said, "No need to worry about me or babysit me tonight, Gunnar. I'm a big girl. Have fun, I'll take a cab. Make sure to call me about some lunch next week."

He'd smiled his boyish grin that I wished I could see more often and had kissed the top of my head in a brotherly way. "You really are perfect in many ways," he'd said and wandered back over to the woman.

I couldn't help it, I kind of glowed with the praise. Over the weeks since our deep talk about Alaric, Gunnar's role in my life had been shifting and growing, much as his ancestor's had. He'd gone from nefarious predator out to conquer me, to sympathetic friend, and finally our relationship dynamic had settled into a protective-older-brother family feel, one that both of us were comfortable with.

It was in that moment, as he walked away smiling, that I realized how far and how quickly he'd come in controlling his temper. He had people around him, and they were happy. His employees were happier; even Maximillian smiled at me now. It was like Gunnar was on a more even keel, even though he still harbored some deep and ugly hurts where his childhood and immediate family were concerned.

I smiled as an older couple in their late sixties, maybe early seventies, approached. We chatted amicably, and before I knew it the event was almost empty, Gunnar and his prize for the evening had already departed, and people were filtering their way to the exits. Finally, there were just a few of us left. I waved at Jared, who was speaking with the museum's curator, and when I was sure no one was looking, eased out of my heels, found my clutch, and was padding barefoot down the marble stairs.

Let me tell you something, cold marble, after a night spent in heels inches taller than you were used to, while on your feet for hours, in a stuffy room... Well, that cold marble felt like heaven. I slipped out the front door to the museum and smiled in simple pleasure at the feel of the plush red carpet beneath my stocking-covered toes. Shivering a bit as the cold breeze whisked across my exposed heated skin, I stepped to the curb, shoes and purse clutched to my chest with one hand, and looked up the street for a cab.

All I could see was a very long line of black cars.

Good lord, was this seriously going to be the first night in the history of New York that a cab wasn't going to be at my beck and call? The breeze gusted, carrying with it the damp and musty river smell of the Hudson. I shivered, and was enveloped in the satin lining of a tux jacket, still warm from the body heat of the man it belonged to. I turned with a startled yip. Alec grinned down at me.

"I didn't mean to startle you," he said sheepishly.

"No, it's all right, my mind was elsewhere, I just didn't see you come up; that's all," I rushed out.

"I see. Still, my apologies." He pulled the tux jacket closed in front of me to keep me warm.

"Looks like cabs are in short supply." I bent to put on my heels; my feet were a bit swollen and protested loudly at being crammed back into the torture devices, but if I was going to have to walk home, which I could, I wanted shoes. Being essentially barefoot on New York City sidewalks... *Yuck. So not happening.*

"Would you be comfortable if I took you home?" Alec asked. I chewed my lip and considered it. It wasn't like he was coming up to my apartment.

I was torn. "Would you? It's really not far. I could walk."

He arched a brow. "In this city, at night, in that dress and heels... I think not."

A black town car pulled up to the curb and he opened the back door before the driver could jump out. He said something to the driver, who was tense in his seat, in what sounded like Norwegian. The driver nodded and Alec turned, asking me with his smiling eyes where to go.

I gave him my building's address and got in the car, sliding over to the driver's side. He climbed in beside me, translating my address and directions to his driver. We sat in silence in the comfortable hush of the town car as we waited to merge into traffic. Walking would likely have been faster, but my fatigued feet really did appreciate this much more.

The rustling of cloth against leather was what alerted me to his movement. I had been studiously staring out the window, avoiding looking at his painfully-familiar face. He snatched my ankles from near the floor boards and swung both of my feet into his lap. I gave a short, startled shriek, and tugged the hem of my dress down, both to maintain my modesty on the short side and in an automatic response of just not knowing what he was going to do.

He was smiling at me serenely as he took off one shoe, then the other.

Eyes wide, I blurted out, "What are you doing?" but he simply gave me a rakish grin and pressed the pad of his thumb deep into the arch of one foot and rubbed. I groaned, my eyes slipping shut in pleasure.

"How long have you lived in New York?" he asked me.

"A little over five years. I was brought on to oversee parts of this project by Jared, so really I went straight from Connecticut, where I was staying post-graduation, to the site in Scotland." I sighed as his long fingers danced over my instep, thumbs kneading the tortured flesh of the ridge beneath my toes.

"You went to school here." It was a statement, not a question, and I looked up at him.

"Yes. How did you know?" I didn't bother keeping the suspicion out of my voice. He chuckled, low and deep, and I could feel the vibration of it through the seat.

"It was in the short biographic paragraph beside your photograph."

I stared at him blankly.

"On the tableau beside the Viking sword," he said patiently.

"Oh!" I shook my head as if to clear it. "Forgive me, it's been a long day and an even longer night."

We were pulling up to my building and never could my words have been more honest. I was exhausted and just didn't feel like all my synapses were firing like they were supposed to. I sighed when he slipped my heels back on my feet, first one, then the other.

"Thank you," I murmured, reclaiming my legs.

"I would like to see you again."

His voice was soft and made me bite my lip between my teeth. Tears stung the backs of my eyes. A short war was waged between my heart and my head. My heart cried Yes, if only because he reminded me so much of Alaric, but my head, which was much quieter, said that would be an uncool thing to do to him. It really was.

I couldn't help it though. I agreed.

"Sure, I think I'd like that," I said, cautiously. The answering smile I received was worth it.

He slipped out of the car and held out his hand. I took it, wobbling a bit on the heels, and found my footing. I straightened and took a gentle step back, giving myself a bit of distance.

"I will be in touch," he said, his voice rough around the edges. I looked up at him and it was like he was drinking in my face, like he would never see me again. I went to slip off his jacket, but he was already back in the car.

"Your jacket," I protested, and he gave me that beautiful smile, that slow curvature of his mouth that damn near had me a puddle on the sidewalk.

"Keep it. I will get it from you later." He shut the door and with a purr of the engine the town car slipped into traffic and away from the curb. I frowned, I hadn't given him my number. With a sigh I punched the code into the front door and let myself into the lobby of my building.

When I entered my apartment, it was dark, and though not uncomfortable in temperature, it felt cold. I shut and locked the door behind me and set my clutch and keys on the entryway table. My breath escaped me in a shuddering sigh and I slipped the tuxedo coat from my shoulders.

I gripped the material in both hands and hesitantly brought it to my nose. I closed my eyes and breathed in Alec's smell. Crisp, and clean, the jacket smelled of just a hint of cologne. It was a rich smell that reminded me of the open ocean air on an icy winter day. I hung the jacket on the back of my door and felt foolish at my disappointment. I don't know why I let myself expect the acrid tang of burning metal to come from the jacket, but I had. I stepped into my bathroom, leaving the heels by the door and flicked on the light, blinking in the harsh glare.

I had to hand it to the makeup artist, I only looked slightly wilted around the edges after a good, what, nine hours in her handiwork? As I began to pull pins out of my hair, I hoped that Gunnar had paid her well.

I turned on the shower and carefully hung the dress, clutch and shoes in my closet before stripping out of the strapless bra, garter and hose. Stepping under the hot shower spray was a lesson in pure bliss. I soaped and rinsed my hair, and watched the last vestiges of my night circle down the drain even as thoughts of Alec and Alaric circled in my head.

"God, are you testing me?" I asked.

The steady fall of water was my only reply.

CHAPTER FORTY-NINE

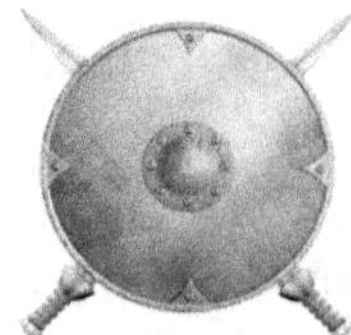

Sunday I spent off my feet, for which they were grateful. Gunnar called me that evening to see how I was. I told him fine, and that I had made it home just fine, too. He didn't ask how, and I didn't tell him. I wasn't sure why I wasn't ready to share about Alec, I just wasn't and I wasn't up for analyzing it, either. I diverted the conversation to the brunette he'd taken back to his hotel.

"She was a lovely distraction," he'd said. I rolled my eyes and asked if that was it. He said that it was mutual, and surprisingly, I believed him.

I ordered take-out for dinner, had it delivered, and went to bed early. I had a long day ahead of me the next day.

Monday, I kept glancing at the clock, waiting for it to tick down. I had roughly half an hour to go. The tread of heavy work boots behind me made me turn. I fought down a surge of joy that welled in my chest and then wondered two things. One, why was I fighting down being happy, and two, why was I so happy to see Alec? I barely knew the man, but it was like my body, or maybe my subconscious, recognized him or saw something in him that made sparks fizzle through me whenever I caught sight of him.

Much like every time I had seen Alaric.

My poor heart, mind, and body were at all sorts of odds with each other over this man I barely knew. I kept my smile in place, even though I knew it had wilted at the edges. That familiar fizzing radiated out to my limbs.

Alec came towards me, his cool gray eyes appraising. He looked delicious in jeans and an olive drab, form-fitting Henley. His hair was pulled back into a tight braid, giving him the appearance of short hair from the front. He stepped up to my work station and crossed his arms. Watching the play of muscle beneath his forearms where he'd rucked the sleeves of the shirt to his elbows was a treat, as was the way the soft-looking material clung to the lean, hard muscles in his biceps, shoulders and chest. I tried very hard not to blush.

"Hi," I said softly.

"Hello." His lips twisted into a wry grin and he said, "I told you I would be in touch."

I looked down, to the visitor's badge clipped to his brown leather belt and realized that everything he was wearing looked butter-soft with age and use. He was in comfortable clothes that he was used to working in. It made me smile and like him a little bit more.

"I wish I'd known you were coming. I would have brought your jacket," I murmured. I was staring at the floor and his well-used steel-toed work boots.

A touch of his finger beneath my chin made me raise my eyes to his. The appraising look in them was like a shock of ice water, with the familiarity of it.

"Do not go anywhere," he said, his accent a bit thicker than it had been a moment before with some unidentified emotion. He turned and headed in the direction of Jared's office, then turned at the last second to add, "Please."

I nodded mutely, and satisfied, he rapped at the door frame and disappeared inside, closing the door behind him. My skin tingled where he'd grazed over my jawline lightly with his thumb.

I turned back to my work and began wrapping it up for the day, quietly putting away tools and turning off my computer and lights. The boom of laughter, muffled by Jared's office door made me turn and look. The door opened and Alec stepped back out; the familiar sparkling sensation returned, and I resisted the urge to push it away.

Happiness is coming, just be patient, and when it finds you, don't be afraid to let it in.

I watched Alec stalk up to me and found myself going very, very still. I didn't feel threatened at all, in fact, I felt calmer than I had in weeks. Still, like a pond, the surface as smooth as glass. We stared at one another for a few heartbeats before he spoke.

"Do you have any plans this evening?" he asked.

"Um, yeah, actually I do," I said and picked up my little leather-bound journal. I had started writing poetry on the nights I couldn't sleep. It was a way to pass the time. I was actually going to brave a reading tonight. I did it from time to time. I'd run into Roxy only once, and I hadn't read that night. I'd just opted to listen.

"Forgive me, but I would like to accompany you, if that is okay." He stumbled over 'okay,' as if it were a new word for him. Come to think of it, I'd barely heard him use any slang type words at all since I'd met him, which, granted, was all of two nights ago.

I blinked. Had I said out loud what I was doing? I couldn't remember and I didn't want to ask. How embarrassing that I zoned out so bad while in his presence. I let out a shuddering breath.

"Sure," I said, and immediately wished I could take it back. It was a poetry reading, for God's sake!

I looked him over and tried not to let my hormones take off without me. If you could take masculinity and bottle it, the packaging would look like him. There he was, though, with Alaric's charming smile, and

I couldn't do it. I couldn't try and take it back. He plucked my spring jacket off the coat tree and held it for me to shrug into.

"So, where are we going?" he asked, and then I did smile. I hadn't said it out loud. Maybe this could be fun.

"Um, we're going to a coffee house around six blocks away," I said. I turned around and flipped what hair lay trapped by my collar out of it. He frowned slightly.

"I know, it's trashed." I blushed. It looked almost as bad as when I had first chopped it in Hell.

"What happened to it?" he asked, and I could see he was thinking about the pictures of me with it in its long braid.

I figured I might as well go with the tried and true. "I donated it to a good cause." That explanation had worked before.

He was frowning mildly and didn't look like he was buying it for a second, but he didn't say anything, simply gestured for me to lead the way. I grabbed my little leather-bound journal and left the workspace. We dropped off his visitor badge with security and I unclipped mine's reel from the waistband of my gray slacks and stuffed it into my purse.

We walked up the street, made the necessary turns, crossed the necessary streets, and before long, I was pulling the door open to Central Perk West. The rich smoky aroma of fresh roasted beans assaulted me and I instantly felt more awake. I wasn't sure you could become caffeinated from just the smell of coffee but it felt like I was. I looked up at Alec who was looking down at me curiously.

"Like coffee?" I asked.

"Black," he affirmed with a nod and I smiled. Simple. Why wasn't I surprised?

We waited in line at the counter and I ordered a large black for him and a Black Forest for me. It was one of the coffee shop's specialty drinks, which was to say it was coffee, chocolaty, cherry perfection. Sweet and rich, almost dessert-like, it was an indulgence I had been severely addicted to since I discovered it back when I came to hear Roxy read every Thursday.

When they had opened up a Monday night reading, I had been writing about a week and had decided to come listen; my second time I had read something. This was my fourth time coming.

"It's upstairs." I smiled and he asked me,

"What is?"

"It's a poetry reading." I blushed deeply and he broke out into a wide grin.

"You brought me to a poetry reading?"

"You don't have to stay if you don't want to," I said hastily.

"I did not say that," he gently chided as we took the bend in the stairs and went up the last flight into the smaller, attic-like space the reading was held in. We found a vacant table and I set down my coffee.

"I'll be right back," I murmured and went and signed my name. When I returned to my seat, Alec was sipping coffee.

"You are embarrassed, why?" he asked.

I looked everywhere but at him, staring at the dark plum walls, interrupted by the garish paintings of whatever artist was on display this month. They leaned toward brightly-colored graffiti-type images done in neon orange, pink, yellow, and green on canvases. I liked a few, but for the most part, killer clowns weren't my thing. The tables and chairs up here were a hodgepodge of antiques, water-stained and scarred with time. I sighed, realizing I couldn't escape his question forever, even as he sat patiently waiting for my answer.

"You don't look like a poetry type of guy."

The noise level up here was a bit loud; it was a good turnout and was about to start. A microphone stood in front of an old wooden box. I supposed it was supposed to harken back to the old soapbox. I caught Alec staring at me.

"I am sure that if you love poetry, that I will love it too." Surely he was just trying to be charming.

He covered my hand with his, where it rested on the table and again with that fizzing thrill through my veins. My eyes met his and there was something there, just beneath the surface, an intensity I...

"Ladies and gentlemen I want to thank you for coming tonight." Royce, the poetry group's founder, was at the microphone, giving his customary introductions.

Whatever I had thought I'd seen in Alec's eyes swirled away as he diverted his attention to Royce. I sipped my coffee and closed my eyes in pure flavor bliss. When I opened them, he was watching me, not Royce, a naked heat in his eyes. I flicked my tongue against my lips to make sure I hadn't left anything behind and the heat intensified.

My heart gave a spastic beat and I lost my breath.

God help me, in the dim light, with that look on his face, I could almost pretend it was him... I turned my eyes away from Alec, a storm of emotions blowing through me, and concentrated on the waif-like girl taking Royce's place on the soapbox. She was good, really good.

The next man was in his twenties, early, I'd wager. He shouted a lot of nonsensical things into the microphone and stomped his foot on the floor and went on like that until the barista came up to let Royce know that the other patrons downstairs were complaining. Royce never stopped a performance, but as the young man became more agitated, he stopped him and gently took him aside. He left, screaming that we were all a bunch of fascists, golden curls coming free from his pony tail and falling into his eyes. I doubted the boy even knew what a fascist was. I smiled, a bit bemused by the whole thing, and he spit in my direction. Alec got to his feet and the young man quailed, shooting down the stairs as if he were running from a fire. There was some nervous laughter. I looked up at Alec and he sat down with a lazy grin on his face and shrugged.

"Well, that was interesting," Royce stated dryly, and looked around the room.

"Sorry about that folks. Next up we have Vonfrost." There was a low collective murmur as a man stepped up to the microphone. He wore faded jeans and Chuck Taylor sneakers; a white dress shirt, unbuttoned at the collar and turned back to the elbow at the cuff, rode on his thin shoulders. He pushed round wire-rimmed spectacles up on his straight nose and glanced through a well-worn composition book, selecting a page and turning it back at its binding. He was very good, a crowd favorite, and everyone settled in to listen. I adored his poetry, but at times found him to be almost too somber. He cleared his throat and pushed his light brown hair out of his eyes.

"I've had too much to drink again..."

He wove an intricate poem about a man having had too much to drink, about his hopes and dreams of becoming better for his lover, so beautiful and asleep in their bed, then brought it crashing back to earth and into despair.

"...but I can't. I've killed you, I've had too much to drink again."

There was silence, then one person began to clap as his words sank in for the rest of us, then another, then it was all-out wild applause. I shuddered and Alec's hand tightened over my own on the scarred wooden table top. I blinked and looked down at them. I hadn't even realized he'd been holding it. I looked at him and he was looking at me very curiously, as if he wanted to see what I would do. I thought about it a moment, then slowly relaxed, leaving my hand where it was. It earned me a smile, which I returned.

We listened to several more performers, quietly finishing our coffees, and finally, with the last lingering taste of cherries on my tongue, my name was called. I breathed in deeply and let it out slowly.

"Gracelyn? Are you here?" Royce asked. "Ah, there she is folks."

I rose from our tiny table in the back near the wall and Alec let me go. I missed the reassuring warmth of his hand suddenly, this man I didn't know, as I got up to read a poem that essentially mourned the loss of

Alaric. I stepped up on the black soapbox and cleared my throat, suddenly afraid.

I'd just spoken to a room of over two hundred people two nights previously about the loss of my parents but suddenly, in a room of twenty or so, speaking about the loss of the love of my life seemed too personal, too raw.

"Um, hi, I'm, uh..." I cleared my throat. "I'm Gracelyn, and I've only been here a couple of times, only read once before." I swallowed, my mouth gone dry. I took a deep breath, centered myself, and, my voice stronger, I said, "Heaven, Hell, or somewhere in between, this is for Alaric. I... I love you."

A solid heavy silence fell over the room, I opened my little leather-bound journal to the marked page, and moving the little black ribbon aside, I began,

"Glister waters lap upon a serene shore.

She waits.

She hears a far-off scream

And all the rest is silence.

Silvery shadows move vulpine through the trees.

They take the poison from her lips

And breathe her insecurities.

She weeps.

Tears dropping into deepest night.

Calling for her lost prince."

My voice shook, my eyes brimmed with tears and spilled over. I sniffed.

"Um, thank you," I said and there were murmurs and a smattering of applause.

Royce got up, passing me as I stiffly went back to my seat, but Alec barred my way. He reached out and captured my hand, pulling me against his chest, and, God help me, I let him. One large hand pressed between my shoulder blades, holding me against his hard body, the other cupped the back of my head, fingers threading through my hair. I closed my eyes and listened to the steady rhythm of his heart. So familiar. He was warm and I let my arms wrap around his lean hips as he held me there.

"Thank you, Gracelyn that was really, wow, that was really powerful. Not sure exactly what it meant, but it meant something to you."

There was a smattering of nervous laughter. I didn't care, I knew my poetry wasn't great, didn't fit what was popular. I just hoped that wherever he was, Alaric had heard it.

Somehow, I was pretty sure he had.

CHAPTER FIFTY

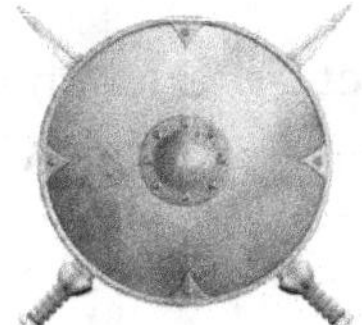

e listened to the rest of the people signed up to read. Alec had remained standing, pulling my back to his front. His long fingers laced with mine, his palms against the backs of my hands. He held me against himself, remaining silent, not letting my hands go, not even to applaud, as was polite. I took refuge against him, wrapped in his warmth, and let myself hope.

The last poem was read and people began mingling, complimenting and critiquing each other's work. That was usually when I would slip away, to go find some dinner or go home, whichever I felt like doing. This time, I just stayed where I was, wrapped in Alec, in a contemplative, almost meditative state. I was calm, the usual raging tempest of sadness, pain and loss quiet. That, more than anything, told me what I needed to know. The waif-like girl who had gone first drifted over to us.

"I'm sorry for your loss, your poem was really beautiful. Royce was kind of an ass taking a shot at you like that. I don't think he's comfortable when something actually makes him feel."

I smiled a little. "Thank you…"

"Kyrah," she supplied and smiled back. She pronounced it Kigh-ruh, and it was a beautiful and unique name. I told her so and she smiled even bigger.

She was very short, maybe five-foot-three, and built very small; she could easily be mistaken for a child. Her hair was the redder side of strawberry blonde and was back in a French twist, a fringe of bangs falling into her eyes, longer on the sides. She had intelligent green eyes and her smile lit her up from the inside out.

"Do you think we could meet for a lunch or a coffee some time?" she asked shyly. "I just moved here from the Midwest and could use a new friend. You seem nice."

Alec let my hands go, and I rummaged through my purse and pulled out one of my cards. I wrote my cell number on the back using the pen from my journal. I didn't even hesitate. I missed having a female friend. She smiled again.

"Call me tomorrow. Do you know where the Museum of History is?" I asked.

"The one with the upcoming Viking exhibit that's all over the news?" she asked. I smiled at myself – I needed to watch more TV, apparently. I looked at Alec and he was grinning, too.

"Uh, yeah, I guess my project has been on the news," I mumbled.

"You work on that?" Her green eyes widened. She looked at my card and really read it this time.

"Yeah."

"I will definitely call you," she said enthusiastically, bouncing in place.

"I look forward to it," I said. Someone called her name and she excused herself, disappearing into the small but crowded space.

I looked up at Alec.

"Hungry?" I asked and the predatory look he gave me made me shiver with desire. His arms tightened and butterflies took flight in my stomach.

"Famished," he said and that one word said so many things.

As we left the coffee house, we ran into a familiar face at the top of the stairs.

"Gracelyn," Roxanne said, and looked a little guilty.

"Roxanne." I looked her over. She hadn't changed a bit, which really was no surprise. I expected to feel hurt, or angry, something, but honestly I was surprised I felt nothing.

"How've you been?" she tried, and I realized that even though I felt no anger or sadness anymore, neither did I feel the need to give her another shot at hurting me again.

"Fine. I'm sorry, but we really must be going."

I went to brush past her and head down the stairs, but she caught my arm. I felt Alec's hand stiffen in mine and I craned my neck up and back to look at him. His eyes were not only the gray of a mountain spring, now they were just as cold. I looked back at Roxanne.

"Could you, maybe, call me, sometime?" she asked, and I felt a little thrill of anger.

"How could I possibly do that?" I asked. "I did what you asked and lost your number." She visibly cringed and I was surprised that I didn't feel one iota of guilt. I pulled my arm from her grasp and continued down the stairs.

Alec was smiling and I wondered when he was going to stop pretending, because I wasn't about to for a moment longer than I needed to.

CHAPTER FIFTY-ONE

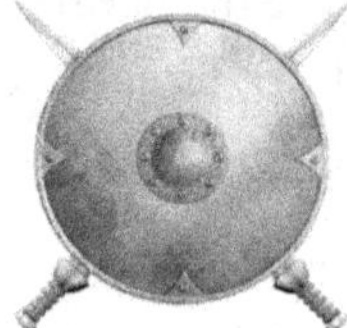

 unlocked my apartment door, the enticing smell of the Thai food we'd picked up on the way here causing my stomach to rumble. I pushed my way in the door and stood aside so Alec could come in. I turned on the lights and ushered him into my small kitchen. He set the bags down on the counter while I locked up. I quietly made us plates and poured us some white wine from the fridge. He leaned against the counter and watched me, an amused smirk on his face. Finally I stopped, handing him a glass of wine.

He'd gone very, very still.

I raised the glass to my lips, my gaze locked on his, and took a generous mouthful. The sharp click his glass made as he set it on the counter was all the confirmation I needed. I set my own glass on the stove, and he was on me, his mouth crushing down over mine. The sweet, crisp wine flooded from my mouth into his and he drank deeply of both it and me. His hands kneaded my ass, and I all but climbed his body to get closer to him. He broke the kiss and bent.

"Alaric," I gasped.

He lifted me and I twined my legs around his hips; our lips found each other again, and we kissed as if this were all some sort of beautiful dream and we would wake at any moment.

He carried me to the bedroom and we tumbled onto the bed. His body covered mine, hips grinding into me and I could feel how much he wanted to be there. His hands fumbled at my waist, pulling my peach-colored blouse from the waistband of my gray slacks so that his hands could delve beneath it, flattening in a caress along my ribs, over the lace cups of my bra. My hands were beneath the Henley, smoothing over the strong planes of his back.

I pulled the Henley off over his head and he brought his hands out from beneath my blouse to let me. He gripped the two sides of my blouse and pulled, buttons flying in every direction, and I didn't care. He flattened himself against me, skin against skin. He was so warm, so hard, and he was so mine. He kissed along my jaw and nipped the side of my neck. I cried out and he growled possessively. We stripped the rest of the way in frenzied, barely-controlled movements. He kissed every inch of me from head to toe and knelt between my thighs, looking down at me, drinking me in with his eyes as much as he had with his mouth.

"God, I love you, Gracelyn," he said, voice husky with need.

"Alaric," I whispered.

"Yes?" He looked slightly afraid.

"Is it really you?" I asked.

"Yes, my love, my heart."

He laid his ear between my breasts, over my heart, his eyes closed, listening. I pulled the elastic with its strange pewter crest from his hair, letting it spill over my ribs in a heated silken wash. I combed my fingers through it gently, my hands shaking as I kept it from his face.

"Would that I could tear my beating heart from my own breast and lay it in your hands, Gracelyn, I would... Oh, God, I would."

I tugged gently on his hair and he sat up, looking down on me with his new eyes, the overhead bathing him in bright white light.

"I like your heart right where it is," I said and dragged his mouth to mine.

He broke the kiss, both of us gasping and I wrapped my legs around his hips, pulling him closer.

"I love you, now, please, love me back," I whispered, and he placed himself at my entrance and pressed into me.

I arched from the bed and moaned his name. God, I loved the way he filled me. He seated himself completely, deep inside me, and slowly rolled his hips forward, rocking into me. He held himself off of me, arms straining, so he could look at me and I looked back. He withdrew and then rocked forward again. I cried out and his voice echoed mine. He made love to me. Slowly, deliberately. He would not be rushed, no matter how much I begged and pleaded with him. He brought me to the brink, slowly, tenderly, and I quivered beneath him, then he held me on the very brink for what felt like eternity.

"God, the angels, the Devil himself... legions of the demonic," he grunted, "none of them could keep me from you."

I gripped his shoulders and brought my hips up to meet his.

"Alaric," I gasped. There was no keeping the begging from my voice, as he lowered his body more fully against mine.

His gentle thrusts changed angle and he began to brush over that place inside me. I wrapped my legs tightly around his hips and devoured his mouth in the strongest, most passionate kiss I had ever given anyone in my life. I tightened around his thrusting cock as the sensations deepened. He changed his depth and angle just a little bit more and I cried out.

So close, I was so close.

"Please, Alaric, please..." I begged and he slipped a hand between us, placing the pad of his thumb against my clit. He brushed his thumb over the sensitive nub in a sensual circle and, my cup runneth over.

I came screaming his name, back bowing off the bed, nails biting into his shoulders. He made a triumphant noise and drove into me, hard and harder until he cried out, thrust one more time, and collapsed, folding me under him and against his chest, spilling himself inside me.

We lay for a long time on top of the covers, the dew of sweat gently cooling our skins. He placed a languid kiss over my thundering heart and looked up at me from between my breasts, easing out from inside my body and laying beside me, pulling me against his chest in that old familiar way.

Tears dampened the hair at my temples. I hadn't even realized I'd been crying.

"Tell me this is real," I said, my voice near breaking.

"My love, my heart, this is very real," he said and kissed my forehead and I wept tears of pure unadulterated joy. I sat up abruptly and straddled his hips, scooting down to lay my head on his chest, listening to the even tick of his heart, the blood rush through his veins.

"Tell me how," I said. "I want to understand. Neil, said you'd been Judged. How are you here?" I asked.

"Shhhhhh, there is time. I am not going anywhere." His hands smoothed over my skin.

"You're damn right you aren't going anywhere. I am never letting you out of my sight again!" I exclaimed. He laughed, an abrupt and oh, so-decadent sound.

"I want a bath. With you. Like before," he said.

"Explain first, or I won't let you up," I said stubbornly, then let out a short shriek as he got up anyways, holding me as if I weighed nearly nothing.

"That is so not fair!" I cried, clinging to him like a spider monkey. He laughed, that rich deep rumble like rolling thunder, and I wanted him inside of me all over again.

He carried us into the bathroom, set me down, and started the water. Picking up the lighter from the back of the toilet, I lit the candles in the bathroom and went and turned out the lights in the rest of the apartment. I returned to the bathroom and switched out the overhead light, and there he was, my Alaric. He had looked different under the electric lights; the softer candlelight hid some details but all that was missing was the red light to his eyes. He pulled me tight against him and kissed me fiercely. He groaned into my mouth and broke the kiss reluctantly.

He climbed into the bath and pulled me down after him. I settled against him and he let his hands roam, warm and wet, over every inch of me that he could reach. I relaxed against him and waited.

"I was Judged, and it was found the good I had done had outweighed the bad," he said, deep voice rumbling against my back. "I was to go to Heaven."

He fell silent.

"Then how are you here?" I asked when it became too much.

"I was asked by the Host if there was anything I had to say before my soul was to be taken, and I asked them why they would sentence me to Hell. That confused them; I would go to Heaven and so I told them... 'Gracelyn is my Heaven. To send me anywhere else, that would be Hell. Your Heaven, though pleasant, would still be a beautiful torment without her there to share it with me.' They were understandably puzzled by this." He chuckled.

I could barely breathe, so moved was I by his words.

"How are you here with me now?" I asked.

"Miracles happen every day." He kissed the top of my head.

"Alaric..." I breathed, frustration lacing my voice.

"The Archangels made it so," he said. "Do not ask me how, suffice to say it was very painful and it took weeks of your time... months of ours."

He held me close and I thought for a long while.

"You had been Judged before I ever left, hadn't you?" I asked, Raphael's words suddenly making a whole lot of sense.

"Yes," he said simply.

We stayed silent as the water grew tepid. Finally, he pulled the drain with his toes and stood us up, starting the shower. We kissed as the falling water gently steamed around us.

"When I left Hell, I asked if I would ever see you again. Raphael said he couldn't say..."

"We did not know if what was proposed would work," Alaric said, massaging shampoo into my hair.

"He told me to be patient right before I stepped through the mirror, told me to wait. It makes sense now."

"It was agreed by all of us, the Host, Neil, Karael, and Rizoel. You were inconsolable, we did not wish to make promises we might not have been able to keep. It was feared that if we told you anything, then if we failed, that you would break completely, and none of us wanted to see you fall to the dark." His expression was at once sorrowful and apologetic.

"You're really here," I murmured in awe.

"I am really here." He kissed me lightly.

"Forever and ever?" I asked.

"Until the day I die," he said gravely, adding, "And I intend to live a very long and happy life with my wife by my side."

"Are you asking me to marry you?" I asked.

"Yes," he said, simply.

"Alaric, I have been married to you in every way that counts for months," I whispered and he crushed me to him. "Anything else is just window dressing."

He laughed softly. "I know of what you speak," he said. "To become Alaric Wermund, I required quite the education." He smiled against my wet hair.

"What does 'Wermund' mean?" I asked suddenly.

"It means 'protector of man'," he said.

We ran the hot water tank out and got out of the shower. We reheated our food in the microwave and ate and talked until late. As we lay in bed together I made him promise he would be there in the morning. He swore to me he would be.

He was.

Thank you, God.

EPILOGUE

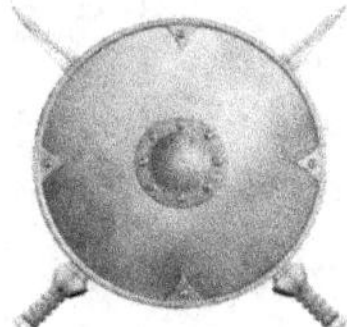

I called in to work the next morning, citing a myriad of personal things to do. Jared let me. Before I hung up, he said it was good to hear a smile back in my voice. I thanked him and promised explanations soon. It would take us a while to come up with a good story, but that wasn't my focus. Alaric and I didn't stay in bed as much as we'd wanted to.

We went to Gunnar's hotel.

I had to pour him a scotch at nine o'clock in the morning. It was pretty funny.

He got to ask Alaric everything he wanted to and then some. Alaric was patient, answering all of his questions one at a time, with me tucked against him. I listened to them talk for hours until my phone rang.

It was Kyrah.

I reluctantly left the boys to talk and met her for lunch as I'd promised. She was full of questions about the upcoming exhibit that I, sadly, didn't have all the answers to, so involved with my personal life I'd been. I promised to find out all the details and share. We talked about poetry and shopping and her schooling. She was smart, going to NYU on full scholarship.

She ended up being my maid of honor at our wedding. Alaric insisted, but I won on hyphenating my name. I went back to school and achieved my PhD. Dr. Adams-Wermund had a nice ring to it.

Alaric and I were inseparable; he went where I went and I went where he went. Never did we spend even twenty-four hours apart. He ran his business from wherever we were located.

The Viking exhibit took the world by storm. The story of Alrekr Hakon Frithjof became legendary in its own right, a lesson in greed, wrath, and the general folly of unchecked power. Alaric was proud of what I accomplished with Jared and the many others on the project. Documentaries were made by and for the History Channel, as well as a dramatic mini-series. Alaric was a bit horrified by the ugly brute of a man they used to portray him. He watched it with me, though, scoffing that he wasn't half so ugly. His vanity made me giggle.

We lived long and well, but alas, children weren't written in our stars. We never used protection or birth control of any kind. I simply didn't conceive. We didn't visit any doctors or scientists. We decided that it was God's will. If we got pregnant, then yay! If not, we had each other and that was enough for us.

We grew old together. We lived, we laughed, we loved, and when it was our time, we went together, passing within minutes of each other. Those we left behind said it was amazing, but when we passed into the light, and into the waiting arms of Hamneil, Rizoel, and Karael, the angels who were our friends, we could tell you it was because we would never be parted. Ever. Because soul mates are forever.

Through Heaven, Hell, and every place in between.

AUTHOR'S NOTES

Alaric and Gracelyn's story started almost twenty years ago when I had a dream. I was in high school, and, yeah. It was one of *those* kinds of dreams. When I started writing their story, I wasn't sure how I was going to go from the narrow focus and premise of what my dream had been to a full-length story. The pieces just sort of fell together in the right ways though, and after three weeks of writing almost daily, here you have it. I guess sometimes you just have to sit down and write it.

ALSO BY TIMBER PHILIPS

Hallowed Be Thy Light

Hunter's Choice

Love in Purgatory

ABOUT THE AUTHOR

Timber Philips hails from a land filled with beauty and steeped in magic; the Pacific Northwest. She swears you can see fairies and goblins, magic and promise around every tree and in every drop of water and she shares that magic whenever she can. She loves welcoming everyone to her worlds of romance rooted in fable and fantasy.

Stalker Information:
www.timberphilips.com

Facebook Group
https://www.facebook.com/groups/timberswolves

facebook.com/authortimberphilips

bookbub.com/authors/timber-philips

instagram.com/authortimberphilips

twitter.com/timberphilips